DANGEROUS PASSAGE

RESCUING JEWISH CHILDREN
IN WORLD WAR II

WILLIAM F. KELLY

authorHOUSE®

AuthorHouse™
1663 Liberty Drive
Bloomington, IN 47403
www.authorhouse.com
Phone: 1-800-839-8640

First published by AuthorHouse   7/26/2010

ISBN: 978-1-4520-3337-2 (e)
ISBN: 978-1-4520-3360-0 (sc)
ISBN: 978-1-4520-3359-4 (hc)

Library of Congress Control Number: 2010908964

Printed in the United States of America
Bloomington, Indiana

This book is printed on acid-free paper.

My love, appreciation, and gratitude to Polly
for her support, suggestions, and help.

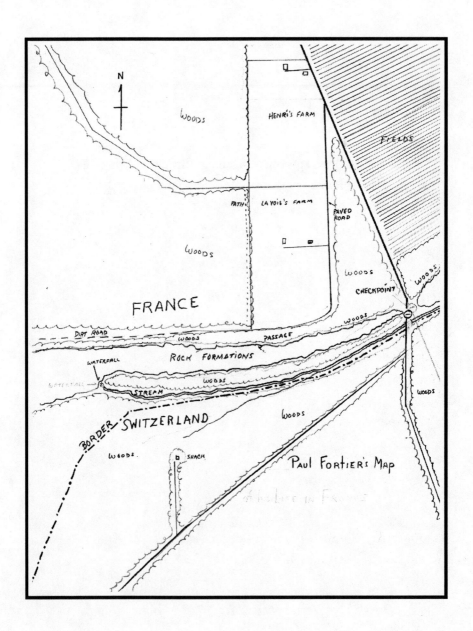

N

WOODS

HENRI'S FARM

FIELDS

PATH

LAVOIE'S FARM

PAVED
ROAD

WOODS

WOODS

CHECKPOINT

WOODS

WOODS

FRANCE

DIRT ROAD

WOODS

PASSAGE

ROCK FORMATIONS

WATERFALL

WOODS

WATERFALL

WOODS

STREAM

BORDER SWITZERLAND

WOODS

WOODS

WOODS

SHACK

Paul Fortier's Map

CHAPTER 1

The windshield wipers squeaked with each swipe. Paul knew he would have to endure the irritating noise to see the road. To keep the windows from fogging he kept a side window open.

Rick Benecase and Jack Clancy had left the car to buy a pack of cigarettes at the gas station. Paul wondered why it took two people so long to make a simple purchase. All of a sudden he heard a sharp noise and within seconds the two came running out, their black woolen watch caps with holes for eyes pulled down over their faces. Paul saw Rick tuck a gun into his coat pocket as he jumped into the front seat. Jack climbed in the back, clutching a wad of bills with his left hand.

"Drive, drive," shouted Rick even before he closed the door.

Paul put the car into first and pulled out of the service station onto Hillside Avenue.

"Move it, Fortier," said Jack as he pulled the cap off his head.

The 1934 Ford jerked as it moved from first to second gear and from second to third. It had a clutch that screamed to be replaced, even though the car was only five years old

"If we weren't in such a rush I would double clutch." Paul said as he shifted gears. "What happened in there?"

"Rick almost shot the attendant," said Jack.

"I didn't know the trigger was so sensitive. I didn't mean to shoot," Rick replied.

"Yeah, dat's gonna sound great ta da judge. 'I didn't mean ta shoot,'" mocked Jack.

As Paul drove, he heard the rest of the story from Jack. The two pulled their knitted hats over their faces as they entered the service station. They ordered the employee to give them the money in the register. He opened the drawer and when he didn't move fast enough, Rick got a bit nervous. The gun accidentally fired and just missed the attendant. While the frightened cashier backed into the corner with his arms over his head, Jack reached in and took all the bills. In the car Jack counted the money. It came to sixty-eight dollars.

"Did he see the car?" Paul asked.

"Probably, but I don't think he got a good look at the plates," was Rick's reply. "Anyway the car can't be traced to us."

Paul wasn't concerned about the plates. He knew the car was stolen and the police would soon be looking for a green '34 Ford.

"Where do you guys want to go?" asked Paul, hoping to get away from the two of them so he could ditch the car. He knew that the attendant would have already telephoned the police and there weren't many cars on the roads tonight.

"Drop us off at my parents' house so we'll have an alibi," ordered Rick. "We can sneak in the basement and they won't even know we were out. You get rid of the car. You can drop it off anywhere. Jack, give him his split of the money."

"Forget the money. Tell me where you got the car."

"Take twenty for the driving," Jack said as he leaned forward from the back seat and stuffed two ten dollar bills into Paul's shirt pocket. "We got da car in the parking lot at dah railroad station. It was parked near da freight platform. At least the evening wasn't a total waste," he joked as he handed Rick twenty-four dollars and kept twenty-four for himself.

Paul dropped off the two at Rick's house and continued on to the railroad station, taking streets through a residential section and staying off the main roads. He wanted to dispose of the car as soon as possible and was hoping he could park the car near where it was stolen. Possibly the owner wouldn't notice that it had been tampered with, at least for a while.

Paul drove the car past the railroad depot to make sure that no police cars were in the area. The station was dark and deserted. The last train for the evening would arrive in several hours, but Paul didn't know that. He suspected that the police could already be looking for a green Ford.

2

Paul wondered how he got involved in this stupid robbery. He had been asked to drive because he had the most experience and a driver's license. He had been driving cars and trucks since he was thirteen. Rick and Jack had both failed the road test even though they passed the written one. They couldn't drive worth a damn.

Paul thought the plans for the evening were to drive around, smoke, curse and maybe try to pick up some girls. But these guys had other plans they didn't discuss with him. Then it started to rain. He had not known that they had a gun and intended to rob a gas station.

There were only a few cars in the depot parking lot. He located a spot near the freight platform, as far from the station as he could get. He hoped that the owner might not even notice that it wasn't in the exact same spot when he came to claim his vehicle. Paul knew he was kidding himself.

He wiped off the steering wheel and door handles with his handkerchief, tucked the wires up under the steering column, locked the doors, slammed the driver's side door closed and started his walk back home.

The rain had let up, but he felt conspicuous being the only person walking the streets on a cold misty night. He walked quickly with the collar on his coat turned up and his watch cap pulled down.

During his walk home he had time to reflect on the mess he was making of his life. Being in a new town and making new friends was not easy. His parents, Leonard and Anna had moved the family to Albertson, a small bedroom community on Long Island, about twenty miles from New York City. It was not where he wanted to be. As a senior in high school he was supposed to be having the best year of his life. Yet he had no real friends and not even a girl friend. His anger toward his parents, since they decided to move from Vermont, was evident in his refusal to behave. He knew that his father had to move in order to make a living in these hard times, but it messed up his life. He was still trying to punish them for making him leave his Vermont friends, especially Celia.

It was the way Celia treated him that caused the most pain. He replayed the scene in his head a hundred times. It always made him angry, yet he played it again. He would always remember the words.

"After we get settled, I'll try to get a weekend free to come visit you."

"Where will you stay? My parents wouldn't want you to stay at our house."

"I'll sleep in the truck. Or I'll bring along a tent and sleep in the backyard. Don't worry. I'll find a way."

"Paul, when you leave here we will both be starting a new life. If you decide to come back for good, we'll talk about our relationship. But when you leave on Saturday, our relationship is over. You'll meet new girls and I'll meet new boys. That's the way it should be."

"We can go on being friends. I'll come back to see you once in a while."

"No, Paul. That's not going to happen. If you come back I won't be here."

"I'll write…"

"And I won't write back or I'll return the letters unopened. Paul. It's over."

They knew each other, touched each other and achieved some intimacy, even if they hadn't gone all the way. He promised her that he would remain true to her and would come back and visit her. She told him that he was wasting his time and she was not interested in a long distance friendship. It hurt his feelings and his pride. He didn't understand what was happening to him. All he knew was that he was unhappy and miserable and wanted to get even with somebody. He came to the realization that he was behaving so poorly because he felt unloved since Celia had rejected him. Recalling this event made him uncomfortable in the pit of his stomach.

Paul's big mistake was deciding to team up with Rick and Jack. They were considered tough guys at school and that was the impression he wanted to give. So he acted tough, and they accepted him into their little clique. He cursed around them, smoked cigarettes and acted like he didn't give a damn. Now he saw how stupid they were and how much trouble he could be in if that bullet had hit the attendant. He also wished he hadn't taken the money they gave him. It made him an accomplice and by law, as guilty as they were. They could all be jailed on charges of attempted murder and robbery.

Legal problems aside, Paul was truly sorry he got mixed up with those guys. He knew better and hoped that he could be forgiven and all of this would go away. He prayed on his way home, the first time in quite a while, even though he didn't realize he was praying. His thoughts included a promise not to have anything more to do with those two jerks. This wasn't how he wanted to live. These so called friends weren't friends at all. They almost ruined his life. What was he thinking? Paul was determined to make a few changes. Maybe he would start by being nice to his brothers and sister. He felt better after he made this resolution and realized that he was almost home.

"Where've you been?" asked his father. Leonard Fortier was usually a pleasant man but had recently adopted a more severe tone with the children. It was probably due to the effort to start a new business and a son who was surly, disrespectful and uncooperative. Paul knew that he was at least partly responsible for his father's change in attitude.

"We stopped off at the Double Dip for a banana split. Then it started to rain and we had to wait awhile," he lied.

"You should be home on a school night. Save the weekends for socializing," his father abruptly reminded him as he disappeared into the kitchen to get a bottle of Schaefer. His brothers, Harold and Edward and sister, Eleanor, didn't say a word but continued listening to the radio. Paul was glad none of them asked more questions. He grabbed his math book and made believe he was studying.

Paul worked in his father's shop on weekends and after school. He always showed an aptitude for working with his hands and took pride in his work. He loved shop classes at school and could do wonderful things with wood. He was good at math and was extremely agreeable when he wanted to be. He worked with his father in the summer as a carpenter's helper and loved building things. That was before his father bought the cabinet shop.

He now understood that showing his displeasure for the move by refusing to cooperate with his siblings was unfair to them. What did they do? They were forced to move whether they liked it or not. He found that they kept their distance from him rather than get in a fight. They didn't know this stranger who suddenly appeared in their midst and they didn't like this side of him.

Paul was rude and surly with his teachers, He acted up in class to disrupt the lesson and get attention. His classmates considered him a clown who was not using his talents. Tonight he finally realized this stupid behavior was messing up his life. He was determined to be more responsible, to improve his grades and make friends with a different group of students. That would be his new year's resolution.

Paul considered telling his father about what had happened. He finally decided to keep the incident to himself for now and to avoid contact with the two punks. He was hoping this one incident would pass and he could return to a normal school life. It might be wise to share the information with Harold, his older brother. He knew he could go to him if he needed advice. For now he would keep the incident to himself. This onetime stupid mistake was not going to happen again.

For a few more minutes he made believe that he was doing homework and then disappeared upstairs to the bedroom he shared with his two brothers. He took off his shirt and stood before the mirror. He stood five feet ten without shoes but looked taller because he was so thin. Underneath his tee shirt he could see muscles, the result of summers spent working in construction and winters on the ski slopes or shooting hoops. He liked what he saw as far as his appearance but hated the person he had become. He put on his pajamas and pretended to be asleep when his brothers came to bed.

CHAPTER 2

Five time zones away in France, near the border with Switzerland, several inches of snow covered the countryside near the small village of Faymont, as if on cue for the holidays. Annette was setting the table for dinner filled with remembrances of past holidays.

"Papa, I miss Mama, especially at Christmas."

"I do too, Child. The house is lonely without her."

"I'll try to decorate it like Mama used to, but she did so many things to make the season special."

"Do what you can, Annette. We can't replace Mama but can make the house a bit festive. This will be a difficult time without your mother."

Since her mother died six months ago, Annette missed her more than she could have imagined. She especially missed her during the holidays. Although she and her mother had disagreements, they were for the most part good friends. Each respected the opinion of the other and both were considerate. Her mother taught her how to cook, sew, knit and crochet and make the house comfortable. She also taught her to garden. At this time of the year, especially, she found ways to make their home warm and cozy. Annette could never replace her mother, and she missed her more than she cared to admit.

When her mother got sick, it was Annette who made the frequent trips up the stairs to the bedroom to bring meals and assist her with whatever she needed. When the doctor told Jacques the cancer had spread too far and that Marie would only live a few months, it was Annette who was able to keep it together and do what needed to be done. She did all of this in addition to school, tending the garden, feeding the chickens and assisting in the bakery. It had been a most difficult time for both father and daughter. The adversity matured Annette far beyond her seventeen years.

Annette looked very much like her mother as to facial resemblance but was much taller and svelte. She worked in the garden and the bakery. She rode her bike to school, the bakery after school and home when the bakery closed. This helped keep her fit. She had matured into an attractive young lady. Her mother wore her hair short while Annette's dark hair reached half way down her back. Her hair looked black but was really a dark brown as when seen exposed to sunlight. She sometimes did her hair in braids, with help from her mother, although she could do it herself. It would just take a little longer. Her classmates considered her a beauty, although she never thought of herself as pretty.

It was her dark eyes that were her most enduring feature. They were deep and sincere and she held you with her eyes. They were the eyes of a person comfortable with herself. Yet, when she was happy, they sparkled. Coupled with her grace when she walked and moved, and her complete lack of conceit, she was loved by all the villagers as well as her classmates.

She tried not to show she was depressed since her father seemed desperately lost without his wife. He continued to get up in the middle of the night to ride his bicycle to town to start making bread by four. He stayed busy all day until Annette came to relieve him after school. There was too much work for one person. It was too difficult to start to work at four in the morning and work until after three thirty in the afternoon every day except Sunday, without his wife to help him. Although he was learning to accept his loss, he still missed Marie very much. Jacques's heart was just not in his work. Previously, before Marie died, she would get Annette off to school, and then come to work about nine or ten in the morning after completing work around the house. Jacques could go home at noon and Marie would stay until Annette came to help her sell bread after school. Just having someone to share time at the shop and to help with the business was a big help.

Annette would arrive from St. Jeanne D'Arc School about three each afternoon and would sell bread until she closed the shop at six. When she came home there were the chickens to feed, the garden to tend, meals to be made and homework to be completed. Now that her mother was no longer with her she would shop almost daily to buy some item of food. She would run across the street to the butcher and get some meat, all the while watching the store for customers. They knew she would be right back if she wasn't behind the counter. Her bicycle basket could hold just so much, so it was wise to shop a little each day.

Christmas Eve was a humble meal of pasta and sauce as it was a day of fasting and abstinence from meat in keeping with Church tradition. Dinner was prepared for her father and his brother, Andre, from Chaumont, a village about two hours northwest by car. Her uncle arrived just as the sun was setting. Since he worked in the mayor's office and knew a lot about what was going on throughout France, Annette usually had lots of questions for him.

"Joyeux Noel, Uncle Andre. Welcome to Faymont."

"Joyeux Noel, ma petite. I'm so pleased you invited me to celebrate the holiday with you," he said as he deposited a bottle of wine on the kitchen table. He kissed Annette on both cheeks and hugged and kissed his brother as well.

"Welcome, Andre," said Jacques. "I'm glad you were able to come."

Her father was short and stocky while her uncle was tall and thin. Jacques was clean-shaven, with a ruddy complexion and gray hair while Andre had a mustache, goatee and black hair with just a touch of gray above his ears. They would not have been mistaken for brothers as far as appearance was concerned. Both were honest, sincere and plain spoken. Jacques was prone to lose his temper while Andre was always the diplomat. Yet they were brothers and close in affection.

"Uncle Andre, I hope you like ham with potatoes and string beans for our meal tomorrow?"

"Whatever you cook, Annette, will be wonderful. You're almost as good a cook as your mother and a lot better than your father."

"Andre, this will be the best meal you've had in two weeks. In any case it's better than what you cook at home," kidded Jacques.

The pasta was eaten with a bottle of local red wine. In spite of her sadness, she had decorated the house as festively as she was able and put a Christmas tree in the living room. She had decorated it entirely with blue lights in remembrance of her mother who liked all blue lights on the tree.

"So you think this Hitler guy is a madman, Andre?" asked Jacques, getting right to a question that was bothering him.

"I think he wants to take over the world. That's mad."

"He'll never take France. The French people would rise up. They would never allow the Germans to control them."

"I'm afraid you're wrong, Jacques. Hitler has taken over Czechoslovakia and Poland and has made treaties with Austria and Italy. He will attack France when he is ready. He may attack us after he has taken England."

"Are you sure that is true? Can no one stop him?"

"The French Army is sitting on the Rhein River waiting for him to attack. Besides being spread too thin, Germany will attack after we get tired of waiting. The Germans have built a powerful war machine."

"Hitler can't be as cruel as people make him out to be," offered Annette.

"Many people would disagree, Annette. What's more, he's killing his own people. He's killing people who are disabled or mentally defective, raving against homosexuals and has already started to kill anyone who is Jewish. He blames the Jews for all the troubles in Germany."

"He wouldn't kill children," Annette added, "just because they're Jewish?"

"I hate to tell you, but this bunch in Berlin are evil. They are taking children and women and putting them in work camps. If they can't work or get sick, they are exterminated."

Andre stayed the night and went to Mass on Christmas day with Jacques and Annette. It was after they finished the holiday meal that the subject again turned to war. Jacques found it difficult to believe that what Andre was saying could actually happen. Yet he had known Andre all his life and knew how sensible and levelheaded his brother was. He found his blood pressure rising just thinking of the possibility that France could be occupied by Germans.

"France will resist…I know it will," said Jacques. "We wouldn't just sit idly by and let Germany occupy our country."

"There is no one to help us," answered Andre, as he lit his pipe. "America is still neutral and Canada only just entered the war, prepared to help Great Britain. The Brits have their own problems with the bombings that go on almost every night and there is talk that Germany will invade England. Germany is free to take over France as well as Belgium, Holland and Luxembourg. We are alone and we will be occupied."

Annette found the conversation very disturbing and knew that her life was going to change if Andre was right. She had been thinking about their situation should France come under German occupation. Her father would need her. Now was the time to discuss the issue. She just had to wait for the right moment.

While her uncle was staying with them, she wanted to enlist his help in convincing her father that she should leave school to help in the bakery. She had only one more year of school and was near the top of her class. It was just that her father needed her now, even if he wouldn't admit it. She was only seventeen but believed that there were more important things to do with her life, just now. Going to school while her father was killing himself to support them, especially since he wasn't in the best of health, didn't make sense to her. She needed her father and didn't want him to end up in the hospital because he was working too hard. She knew she didn't have a chance winning an argument with her father unless she had some help from her uncle. After the meal was finished and the dishes cleared, she brought up the subject.

"Uncle Andre, do you think I should leave school for…"

Jacques stated his position even before Annette had finished her sentence.

"I want Annette to finish school. It has always been a dream of mine and I know her mother would have felt the same way, if she were alive. I can handle the bakery."

"Papa, the bakery is too much for one person to handle and we don't have enough profit to hire a full time helper. I won't stop learning. I'll just take time off from school until this crisis is past. Uncle Andre, do you have any thoughts?"

"Yes, Annette, I do. Do you want me to express them?" he asked, directing his attention to Jacques.

"Yes, Andre," replied Jacques. "You are always free to state your opinion. You know that."

"Then I will." After a fairly long pause and a deep draw on his pipe, he looked at his brother. "Jacques, you have no idea how your life will change once France is occupied. You will need your bakery and you need help to run it. These will be very rough times and survival will become your top priority. Many people will be arrested for speaking their mind and most of those won't be seen again."

"I can't believe all that you are saying," said Jacques. "Maybe you're exaggerating just a bit."

"Jacques, believe me when I tell you what is happening. I've spoken with many of those who have fled Germany. Hitler wants to exterminate all Jews in Europe and that means French Jews as well. Those who don't turn in Jews will be jailed, if Hitler's plans can be trusted and if we can believe what is going on in other occupied countries. Jacques, these are difficult times and you will need all the help you can get just to survive. Let Annette help you. And for God's sake, keep a civil head or you'll be carted off to a concentration camp. Learn to hold your tongue. That's my advice."

"I can't believe that it will be as bad as you say it will be. I know it is difficult on both of us now, with me getting up at three in the morning and Annette working until late at night. It would make it a bit easier. My health is not what it used to be. Annette, is that what you want?"

"Yes, Papa. I'll feel much better if I can help us get through these days. Annette put her arms around her father's neck and pulled his head toward her. We both miss Mama, but we have each other. Together we can weather the tough times ahead." These words were spoken with compassion and Jacques could not help but be moved by his daughter's sincerity and love.

The rest of the evening was much more pleasant and Annette was grateful for her uncle's help. She serenaded the two men with several Christmas songs and brightened the evening. She understood that she would not be happy to miss school but knew their lives would be a lot less hectic. Besides, she would be helping her father. She felt certain that she was doing the right thing. Annette told her father that she would come to the bakery at lunch time, freeing her Father three hours or more sooner than he was accustomed.

The conversation turned to more talk of Hitler and his theory of a master race. Andre told stories of the Jewish refugees that Chaumont was harboring. Most left their homes and businesses before they could be rounded up and sent to work camps where they would eventually be killed. It was becoming apparent why many wanted to leave Germany.

"Switzerland will remain neutral in all of this. They have in the past and it is their intention to remain neutral in the future. Even though you are only five kilometers from Switzerland," Andre continued, "we can expect no help from them. They will not provoke the Germans. The border will be sealed off, at least on the French side. Already German Jews are trying to leave Germany and are being turned back or shot by German soldiers as they approach the Swiss border. Once they cross the border, the Swiss will help them get to America or Canada or wherever they want to go. But they must first get over the border."

'They shouldn't have trouble crossing here. Will German soldiers kill anyone who wants to cross into Switzerland?" asked Annette.

"Yes, Annette. That is exactly what they intend to do. They will stop and arrest anyone who comes to the border and anyone who impedes their orders. This is a crazy group of people who control Germany these days. The Nazis are an evil group of thugs, intent on taking over the world and exterminating the Jews. They consider themselves superior to everyone else. They are arrogant and completely without compassion," Andre said forcefully.

"I find that difficult to believe," Jacques said. "This is France, you know."

"Jacques, please be careful. The authorities will know that you don't trust them, and they will not trust you. Your small farm is so close to the border that they'll be suspicious of anything that you do. By road it is five kilometers to the border but only about two kilometers or so if you travel through the woods and over the mountain behind the farm. Few people know their way through those woods and mountains, but you do. Let's just hope the Germans don't find the way through the mountain that we found as children."

"Remember when we played in those hills?"

"Yes, those were good times. Now I can almost guarantee that you will be watched and they will investigate any suspicious behavior. Be careful."

As the wine did its job, the two men began to get sleepy. Andre told Jacques once more that these were going to be dangerous times and Jacques needed to be wise. Andre emphasized that his life and that of his daughter depended on his ability to hold his tongue. They said goodnight and hugged goodbye as Jacques would be leaving the house before four in the morning and Andre would return home at dawn. Annette kissed them both goodnight and went to her room, aware that she was starting a new chapter in her life at the tender age of seventeen and a half.

CHAPTER 3

During the Christmas vacation Paul worked at the cabinet shop helping his father and Harold. Harold had worked with his father since their move to Long Island and did the accounting and bookkeeping as well as attaching the hardware to the cabinets. He liked doing this much better than working in a grocery store.

Over lunch, while they were eating chicken salad sandwiches, Paul made a simple observation. "There doesn't seem to be too much work."

"It will pick up by spring," said Leonard.

"Don't be too sure, Dad," said Harold. "Business has been slow since you've taken over the shop, if you ask me."

"Paul, when you finish lunch, I want you to deliver several cabinets," said his father in an effort to change the subject.

"Fine, Dad. Just give me the address."

"It's attached to the cabinets by the door. It's near the new subdivision just north of here."

Paul and Harold loaded the cabinets on the truck. He was pleased to have a few minutes away from the shop by himself. Driving north to a new subdivision just off Willis Avenue, he was surprised that the street wasn't where he expected it to be. New houses were being built where he thought the street was located. At a model home he stopped to ask directions. While waiting for a salesperson to get off the phone, he noticed the cabinets in the kitchen. The salesperson told him where he would find the street and Paul thanked him.

"Would you mind if I ask who made these cabinets?"

"Why are you asking?" the salesman responded with a question.

"Because they're made so poorly. We wouldn't let workmanship like that leave our shop," said Paul.

" What do you know about cabinets?"

"I know that these are poorly made. The wood is inferior. The hardware is cheap and the workmanship is sloppy."

"I guess you do know cabinets."

"This is a nice house and it's well built. It's a shame to install inferior cabinets," Paul continued. "Do you have any idea of the cost?"

"No, but Mr. Smyth will know. Talk with him. Mr. George Smyth is out to lunch now but should be back in a few minutes."

With permission from the salesman, Paul looked through the model home. It was nice in just about every way, except for the poor quality of the cabinets. It was modest but the range and refrigerator were first class. He also looked at the home next door. He saw the same attention to detail and good workmanship. The exception was the cabinets in the kitchen.

When Mr. Smyth returned from lunch, he invited Paul to sit down with him in the nook off the kitchen. He was a tall man, about six three, and very thin for such a tall frame. He was impeccably dressed in a dark wool suit and seemed to be full of confidence.

"Mr. Smyth. You're building a nice house with the exception of the kitchen cabinets."

"What do you know about cabinets?" asked Smyth.

"Let's go outside and I'll show you the type work that we do."

The two walked outside to where Paul parked the truck. Paul showed him the cabinets he was about to deliver, pointing out the hardware, the wood, the workmanship and the finish. Smyth seemed to be impressed.

"I'm buying these cabinets because of the price. They gave us the lowest bid."

"Do you remember what they are charging?"

"Not off hand, but we can look in the file cabinet for the invoice. I've only paid for the three model units so far."

Inside the model home Smyth took off his suit coat and started searching through the files. He quickly found the invoice. Paul could see that the price was unnecessarily high for such poor quality and knew that his father could easily beat that price.

"Suppose we can build cabinets like the one outside for the price that this guy is charging you. We would even store the cabinets until the day you need them and for another fifty dollars we will install them. Would you be interested?" asked Paul.

"You bet. But can you make a promise like that?"

"No. But my Dad owns the business and he would be happy to come by this afternoon to iron out any details and take an order. He's the only one who can sign a contract. Just how many homes are you planning to build?" inquired Paul.

He almost choked when Smyth said he was building fifty in the first phase. He also explained that the kitchens were all the same size and configuration, except that some were being built on the right side of the house and some on the left side. The only other difference would be the finish. Paul told him that they would be finished to his specifications.

"You said that you only ordered the three units?" asked Paul.

"Right. I haven't gotten around to giving the cabinetmaker a new order. It's on my 'to do' list."

"If you give us the contract, we'll remove the three units and replace them with our cabinets at no cost to you."

. Paul knew that he wasn't going too far with his proposal, and that his father would be pleased with this arrangement and would back him all the way on his recommendation. In fact he knew it would please his father that he wanted to do what was right by George Smyth. His father wouldn't allow inferior cabinets to be seen in the model homes. It would have been a poor reflection on "Quality Cabinets."

"We can't have people thinking that we made these inferior cabinets," was Paul's remark.

"That would be swell. When can your Dad come by?"

"He'll be here this afternoon, just as soon as I deliver the cabinets in the truck."

"Great. See you then. I'm looking forward to meeting your father," said a smiling George Smyth.

After he dropped off the cabinet he hurried back to the shop. His father was sanding a cabinet door and didn't hear his son come in. Paul went over to the electric cord and pulled the plug out of its socket, causing his father to look up, annoyed.

"What's going on? Can't you see that I was working?" his father barked.

"Dad, we just made a big sale. If you approve we can have a big contract with a Mr. George Smyth of J & R Construction. He builds homes and wants cabinets for fifty of them. You can sign a contract with him this afternoon," said Paul.

Leonard Fortier was surprised and pleased with his son's salesmanship.

Paul explained to his father all that had been discussed with Smyth and what the price was that he was paying. He also told him that he offered to install them for fifty dollars.

"Great, Son. That would give us a nice profit. When we hire a helper or two we'll make sure they learn how to install the cabinets correctly. Harold can supervise the installation until they learn how," said his father as he put his arm around his son. That simple gesture meant much to Paul.

The meeting with George Smyth went as planned. He was pleased that he would be getting superior cabinets for the same price as he was presently paying. He liked that he could choose both style and finish and get them installed. Leonard Fortier knew that making first class cabinets was the only kind of work he wanted to do and was pleased to build, finish and install the cabinets the way they should be installed. They had no trouble agreeing to a payment schedule and Smyth was pleased that Quality Cabinets would warehouse them until they were needed. Smyth gave Leonard a check and the two men shook hands. Then Smyth stepped forward and shook Paul's hand.

"You have a fine son there, Leonard. He saw that we were installing inferior cabinets and that you could do better. We look forward to a long and prosperous relationship."

"You'll be able to count on us. We won't let you down," replied Leonard.

On the way home in the truck, Leonard told his son how proud and pleased he was. They didn't talk much, but Paul was proud of what he had done to help his father. It felt good.

When they got to the shop and told Harold about the contract, Harold could hardly believe what he was hearing. "This was what we needed. We need someone to go out and get the business. There's plenty there. All we have to do is ask."

"I liked getting that sale. It was fun," said Paul.

"Well, little brother, you've earned your keep today. Now I won't have to find another job because work was too slow," said Harold. He was genuinely pleased that Paul had found all that work and they were able to land such a big contract with a promise of more to come. Harold walked over to his brother and gave him a handshake and a hug.

CHAPTER 4

P aul returned to school several days after the New Year, pleased with the sale of so many cabinets for the family business. He had gone to church with his family on Christmas Day and had resolved to avoid Rick and Jack. He no longer smoked, although previously he only did it when he was around his buddies. His family never saw him smoke. These serious and sincere resolutions gave him a new respect for himself.

Resumption of school was welcomed and Paul was determined to get serious about his grades. He was deep in thought when Jack tapped him on the shoulder.

"Hey, Fortier, did ya see the newspaper article?"

He handed Paul the paper folded so that only the article about the robbery showed. While Paul was reading the story, Jack said, "Dat article said that d'attendant was deliberately shot at. He's full of shit. I think he's trying to make himself sound like a hero or some'em."

'Did Rick deliberately shoot at him?' Paul asked.

"Nah. Rick didn't mean to shoot da gun. He was just nervous. The guy was lucky it didn't hit him."

"We were lucky it didn't hit him. Otherwise you'd be wanted for murder or attempted murder," said Paul.

Several days after that encounter, Rick and Jack were waiting for Paul as he came out of school on his way to the bus. They stood there with their hands in their pockets, without a book in sight and a smug look on their faces.

"We've got a job for you on Friday night," Rick said.

"I don't want to hear about it," said Paul as he turned away from them.

Rick grabbed his elbow and turned Paul to face him. "Ya better want to hear because you're on for Friday night. Be on the corner of William Street and Willis Avenue in front of the grocery store. Seven, sharp. We'll pick you up there."

"You're going to have to find someone else to drive as I'm busy on Friday. I'm finished hanging around with you guys."

"You'll be there. Tell him, Jack." With that remark, Rick walked away.

"If you're not dere, Rick is gonna say that you were the one with the itchy finger and that you and a friend robbed the gas station. You shot at the attendant. His parents will swear that we were at his house all evening."

Then he changed his tone and spoke in a low voice. "He's counting on you driving the car on Friday. He's got something big lined up."

"Tell Rick he can go to hell. I'm not gonna be there."

"You tawk big. You'll be there," said Jack.

Paul spat on the ground in front of Jack as he turned to walk away to the bus. Jack gave Paul his middle finger but Paul didn't see it. He heard Jack's parting remark, "You'll be there, if ya know what's good for ya."

All that evening Paul was disturbed with this sudden turn of events. He knew it had been a mistake to get mixed up with guys like these. He was surprised how difficult it was getting away from them. He had just wanted to be considered one of the tough guys. Now he understood that they were also the dumbest. Paul felt like he needed time to think. All he knew now was that he wanted to get away from these two jerks as soon as possible and as far as possible. Maybe now would be his opportunity to join the service.

The conversation at the dinner table that night played right into Paul's hand. No one in the Fortier household could understand why the United States hadn't declared war on Germany. The Canadians already did in September. America was needed. Even though they lived in the United States for seven years, they were still Canadian citizens. Paul was secretly trying to find a way to tell his parents that he wanted to quit school and join the armed forces.

Paul could get away from Rick and Jack and he would be doing something he was going to do next year, anyway. But he was still a Canadian citizen and Canada had already declared war on Germany. In March he would be eighteen and he could probably get into combat quicker if he went to Canada. He wouldn't even admit it to himself but he had already made up his mind as to what he wanted to do.

"Maybe I'll join the Royal Canadian Air Force," Paul volunteered. There was a long moment of silence. No one said anything. Finally someone had to speak and it was his father.

"Son, would you go to Canada?"

"Probably. I could stay with Aunt Harriet and Uncle Charles and join when I become eighteen in March. If I went now I could get the preliminary paper work out of the way and be ready when I turn eighteen. If I had a Canadian address there would be no doubt that I was a Canadian. I wouldn't have to prove it. I'm ready to go, now."

A fairly lively conversation took place with everyone wanting to talk at the same time. It became obvious that Paul had given his decision some thought. His mother and father wanted him to stay but the rest of the family was hoping he would go to Canada, although no one said so. They were all annoyed with his behavior and considered him to be a pain in the ass, even if he had been pleasant the last few weeks. The sooner he would leave, the better for all of them, remained the unspoken consensus. In their own self-interest they agreed that he was probably making a wise decision to join the Royal Canadian Air Force. He explained that he would be going sooner or later and sooner was better than being drafted.

The subject of school was brought up and Paul was ready. "I'm not doing well in school this year. I really got off to a bad start. It was my fault but I probably will fail this year. I just didn't like moving from Vermont and I was angry and took it out on you. My heart just isn't in school.

"You want to quit high school?" asked his father.

"Yes, Dad, but only until after the war. I know I'll be going in the service and I want to be a soldier or an airman. If I join now, I'll have more say regarding what I might do while in the service. I want to join the Royal Canadian Air Force and I'm sure they'll take me when I'm eighteen. No one knows when America will join the war."

"Well, Son. We'll be proud of you if you join the service. I think you're right that every capable young man will be in uniform soon. It's your decision and we'll support you."

"I'll call Aunt Harriet," said Anna, "and see if they're in a position to take you in."

"Thanks, Mom. Tell her I'm ready to leave tomorrow."

"You don't have to leave immediately but I'll tell her to be expecting you soon," said his mother.

"Mom, I want to go as soon as possible. They may not take me until I'm eighteen but I can at least go to the recruiting station and get all the paperwork taken care of. I can join then, as soon as I'm eighteen. I may have to be a citizen of Canada and living there would prove that I am. That makes sense doesn't it?"

Heads were nodding as his mother said that she would call Aunt Harriet first thing in the morning.

"Call her now, Mom. I want to go this week. Please."

"OK. I'll see what she has to say."

The dog needed to be walked and Paul took that opportunity to ask Harold to walk with him. Harold knew that something was bothering his brother. He wasn't telling everything and Harold was anxious to find out what it was.

It was misting outside as the two walked the dog in the almost freezing weather. The chance of snow was predicted. Paul finally got around to asking Harold to keep a secret.

"I can tell something is bothering you, boy. I wasn't buying all that patriotic stuff. What are you not telling? You can trust me to keep your secret."

Paul told Harold about the incident at the gas station and how Rick and Jack wanted him to drive again this weekend. Paul said that he didn't trust them. He also told Harold that they were really stupid. If he stayed in school he would probably be implicated in the holdup, since they couldn't keep their mouths shut.

"Harold, they had black watch caps with holes for their eyes and Rick is the one with the gun. He accidentally pulled the trigger and almost hit the attendant."

"Tell me where they live and I'll see what I can do."

"You'll have to do it fast because they are planning another holdup on Friday night. Rick Benecasa lives on William Street; the fourth house from Sperl's Grocery. Jack Clancy lives on Center Street where it meets Park Avenue.

"Paul, you're being smart going to live with Aunt Harriet and Uncle Charles. Leave as soon as possible and I'll talk with Rick's and Jack's folks. I'll get them to prevent Rick and Jack from doing something stupid on Friday night."

Paul thanked Harold and wanted him to know that he was pleased that someone could defend him, if necessary. Paul knew that Harold would never have to go into the service because he had very bad eyesight. The glasses he wore attested to that. He was glad that he had told his big brother. The two walked around the block and were experiencing the first snowflakes when they arrived back at the house.

"Aunt Harriet and Uncle Charles would love to have you stay with them," said Anna. "Paul, they have a room that is just waiting for someone. Aunt Harriet said to come as soon as possible. They'll pick you up at the Quebec railroad station."

Money arrangements were made and on Thursday of that week his father and Harold took Paul to the East Williston Station. The steam engine arrived from Roslyn on time and Paul took the Long Island Railroad to Pennsylvania Station in Manhattan. There he transferred to the train to Montreal. Rail Canada took him the rest of the way. He arrived in Quebec just before ten that evening. Aunt Harriet and Uncle Charles met him at the station and welcomed him into their home.

CHAPTER 5

Thursday evening, just before six, Harold approached the Benecasa home and rapped on the side door. Mrs. Benecasa told him that her husband was expected home shortly. Harold thanked her and walked to the street corner where he could see anyone approaching the house. It was drizzling and Harold pulled his collar up to keep the moisture out. He had been waiting about ten minutes when he saw a man dressed in a dark gray business suit, black overcoat and fedora approaching from the direction of the grocery store. The man was fairly tall and walked with a certain grace and confidence. He started walking toward the stranger anticipating that they would meet near the Benecasa house. When the man turned in toward the house, Harold spoke to him.

"Are you Mr. Benecasa?"

"Yes, what can I do for you?"

"Sir, I have some information about your son that you'll want to hear."

Benecasa stopped and said, "Yes, what is it?"

"Your son and Jack Clancy robbed the gas station on Hillside Avenue and almost killed the attendant. It was your son who fired the gun, although I understand that it was unintentional. They intend to rob again tomorrow night. I don't know where but the last time they hotwired a car and got my brother to drive it. He refuses to help them again and they are threatening him. They say they will tell the police that he robbed the service station and was the person who fired the gun."

"Wasn't that robbery just before Christmas?" asked Benecasa.

"Yes, my brother dropped them off at your house. They went in the back

25

door to the basement and you thought they were at home all evening. They weren't. Rick thinks he can use you as his alibi. Just take a look at Rick's watch cap. It has two holes cut out for eyes. They pull the hat down over their face so they won't be recognized. And Rick has a gun, a .38 caliber, somewhere."

"May I ask who you are, in case I need to confront my son?"

"I'm Harold Fortier. My brother, Paul, left today for Canada to join the Royal Canadian Air Force, thanks to your son and Jack Clancy. He would rather quit school, go to Canada and join the military than have anything further to do with Rick and Jack."

"Harold, I thank you for telling me about this. I'm sorry that your brother thought it necessary to quit school and go to Canada. I will take care of my son. If you wish, I'll call Jack's parents. We know them well. You have probably saved these two stupid boys from some time in prison and possibly from harming someone. I think they came close enough to ruining several lives."

"I'd like it if you could call Jack's parents. It was difficult getting away from the house and waiting to meet you. Besides, coming from you it will have more authority. If I can be of further help you can reach me at my father's cabinet shop, Quality Cabinets. My name is Harold Fortier. My father doesn't know about Paul driving the car and I would rather not tell him for the time being. I promised my brother. I hope you understand. I'll consider the matter closed unless you need more information."

"You can be assured that the matter will be taken care of. We usually don't learn about things like this until it's too late. I'll put an end to this stupidity. You have my word. Thank you."

"Would it be possible to tell me that everything had been taken care of? I can be reached at the cabinet shop. That would give some satisfaction to my brother."

"I will call you as soon as I settle this. Give me a day or two."

Benecasa shook Harold's hand with sincerity. He then turned and walked toward the side door of his house.

CHAPTER 6

Aunt Harriet and Uncle Charles lived in the small village of Saint Foi, a suburb of Quebec. They had a twenty-five-year-old son who was now working in Ontario for a bank. His former room was available. They showed Paul the room and suggested that since it was so late it might be best to get some sleep and they could talk in the morning. Paul agreed.

The room that Paul would occupy was modest, neat and clean, with a small closet behind the door and a completely empty dresser opposite the bed. The bed occupied the wall next to the window and an end table was located in the corner. A straight back chair was in front of a small desk. The room had a radio on the dresser and a framed photograph of a heeling sailboat hanging on the wall above the dresser. The window faced the west. Paul knew that the room would be filled with late afternoon sunlight and he would see some nice sunsets. He knew it offered a nice view of the street below, if his memory served him correctly from previous visits to his cousin. The room exuded warm yellow and brown colors that reminded Paul of autumn.

The next morning Paul woke early and joined his aunt and uncle for breakfast. While he was eating his cereal, his uncle asked about his plans.

"I thought that maybe you could use some help at the garage? It might help pay for my room and board," offered Paul.

"I could use the help. There are always the pumps to attend and small jobs to do. Why don't you enjoy the next few days and come in with me on Monday?"

"That would be swell. Where can I get a bus into Quebec?"

"Momma, tell Paul where he can catch a bus and show him the bus schedule. I need to get down to the shop. Enjoy Quebec. It's full of history," he said as he zipped up his coat and closed the door.

The old city of Quebec was filled with history, forts and quaint restaurants and hotels. Paul had been to Quebec before but never inside the old walls of this historic city and never as a tourist. Now he visited the first settlement of the town right on the river and walked the walls above the city. He met a young lady by the name of Barbara. She lived in New York City and was taking a year out of college to travel. They had a nice meal together in a quaint restaurant and enjoyed each other's company. They went Dutch treat and visited several museums.

Paul visited the city by bus the second day and spent time in the upper city. He walked a good portion of the wall that was built for protection. On Sunday he went to an early Mass with his aunt and uncle. He was raised Catholic and never missed Mass on Sunday until this past year when he was acting so rebellious. Paul announced to his parents that he wasn't going to church on Sunday. After several weeks of cajoling and arguing, his parents decided that the anger and fighting weren't worth the trouble. Now that he had decided to make a dramatic change in his life and to start acting more mature than he had been, church didn't make him uncomfortable. He enjoyed his visit to Quebec and looked forward to work with his uncle on Monday.

At the gararge Charles said, "Let me introduce you to the two best mechanics in Quebec. The big fellow is John." Paul shook his hand and observed that he was tall.

"How tall are you?" Paul asked.

"Six foot eight with shoes on."

"And William." He was the same size as Paul. The two also shook hands. "Right now," Charles continued, "they take turns dispensing gas and checking the oil. If you could do that they could spend more time repairing the cars. Fewer interruptions will help us get to some of those cars out back. I'm way behind on repair and if we don't get them out, we'll lose some customers."

"I'll try to handle everything out front so they can get more cars fixed," said Paul

"Great. Let's see how that works."

Charles was good with the customers and frequently asked his mechanics to listen to the customer explain the problem. While the problem was often diagnosed by the time the customer had finished telling him what was happening, he kept his opinions to himself until he was certain what needed to be done. He personally checked each automobile. He assured the customer that he would get to the car as soon as possible and would call him when the car was fixed. A test drive, after he fixed the car, assured the customer that the car was repaired properly. Charles believed in giving service and knew his customers appreciated his effort.

Paul was mechanically inclined and had no trouble pumping gas and checking oil, air and water. By the end of the first day he had sold six gallons of antifreeze. Charles was pleased.

At lunchtime Paul sat down with William and John and pulled out his sandwich. He had bought a quart bottle of milk earlier at the nearby grocery.

"Between waiting on customers," Paul began, "I have some time and don't like just standing around. If you have some work that I can help with, I want you to ask. It will make my day go faster."

"I have eight spark plugs," said John "that need cleaning. Maybe you could sand blast those. That would really help."

"And I have four pistons that need cleaning in the gasoline wash over there. I would appreciate it if you could wash them," said William.

"Sure. No trouble." The first day passed very quickly.

Paul noticed that when a car was finished being serviced, the two mechanics would have to wash their hands and put down a cloth so as not to get the car dirty. Paul suggested that he remove the car off the lift and bring in a new car. This saved a considerable amount of time and allowed the mechanics to get right on the next car. It saved them the nuisance of cleaning their hands and avoiding getting grease or oil on the upholstery. Then Paul would drive the car to the back lot and bring in a new car. Since there were three bays, the men could work in two while Paul brought in the third car.

The week went by, and Paul liked the idea that he was speaking equally in English and French. On Long Island he only spoke French at home and then, only occasionally. He was bilingual but recently his French was getting rusty. This provided him with the opportunity to use the language and to become fluent once again.

"Paul, work is over at noon for you today. We usually all quit at noon but we made a few promises and we are trying to keep them."

"That's fine, but I don't mind staying later, Uncle Charles."

"We don't really need you but I'll let you walk home, if you don't mind."

Harriet and Charles lived several kilometers from the garage and it was a pleasant walk to their home. Before Paul left the office, Charles paid him for the week.

"You don't have to pay me. Just staying with you is payment enough."

"You helped us do a lot of business this week and we fixed more cars than we ever did before in a week. You really helped us be productive."

"Good. I'm glad I was useful."

"When you go in the service, I'm going to look for a good helper to handle all the jobs that you did this week. Here's your pay," he said as he handed Paul cash.

"Thanks. See you back at the house."

January came quickly and Paul told Charles his plans. When the month ended he asked for a morning off early in February to go to the Royal Canadian Air Force recruiting office and make inquiries. Charles drove him there and showed him where the bus stop was located to return to the shop. The recruiters treated him with respect and told him that they could get the paper work out of the way and do some of the preliminary aspects of recruitment before his birthday. But they wouldn't let him join before March 21, 1940, his eighteenth birthday. He knew that would be the case but he was anxious to see action as soon as possible. They also told him that they needed airmen.

The work kept Paul busy and soon February turned to March. When the 21st came, a Thursday, Paul was at the recruiting office at eight in the morning and officially signed up. He was told that a new class was starting on Monday and he was to report to the recruiting office at eight o'clock. The officer referred to the time as eight hundred hours. Once they got to the camp the authorities would determine what aspect of air force training he would specialize in. Pilot training was out as Paul needed more schooling, but maybe bombardier or radio operator would be available. He would just have to hope that they knew what was best for him. Still, it was Paul's wish that he would like to be a radioman or a bombardier.

CHAPTER 7

Annette LaVoie liked her new schedule. She got up early, gathered the eggs, fed the chickens and started on the job of taking care of the house. There would always be dishes to do and a variety of chores. She appreciated that her father never left the house without making his own bed. During the winter months there was no garden to tend, giving her the feeling that she had lots of time.

Many years before, her father arranged with a neighbor, Henri Arsenault, to allow him to farm the land and use the barn for the storage of hay and equipment. In return, he paid a percentage of what he made off the land. He also brought a pail of milk each week for the LaVoie family. Once a year, usually in late fall, he would come over with his receipts and explain to Jacques how much he spent, what he received and how much he owned Jacques for the use of his land. He was so honest that he would rather cheat himself than his neighbor. This arrangement worked so well for both men that it never occurred to either of them to change it.

Annette saw Henri coming down the road with a milk pail for her and Jacques. She went outside to meet him.

"Good Morning, Henri."

"Good Morning, Annette. I brought some milk."

"Thank you, Henri. We still have a bit left from last week."

"Tell me if you need more. You shouldn't run out."

Henri handed the pail down to Annette and she went inside to pour the little milk she had left into a glass and returned the old pail to Henri.

"Say hello to Lucie."

"I will. Au Revoir."

"Au Revoir."

Henri's wife, Lucie, was not in good health. He worked his farm, took care of his wife and stayed to himself. They didn't socialize, didn't go to church, never had people visit them and were almost recluses. Henri always wore the same old pair of work pants, a work shirt, hat and boots. He worked hard and his body showed the wear and tear of all the effort. It would have been a mistake, however, to judge the man according to his appearance.

The same could be said of Lucie. She wore a dress covered with an apron for an entire week and would then change both dress and apron to a second outfit. The following week it was back to outfit number one. She wore work shoes as did Henri. Both were quiet but respectful to each other when they did speak. It was as if there was no need to say anything and both were comfortable just being in the presence of the other.

Henri and Lucie stayed to themselves and were hard to get to know. Yet they were honest and could be depended upon in a crisis. When Annette's mother was dying of cancer it was Lucie who never missed a day to help care for Marie. They were there when they were needed.

They had lost their only son several months before in a construction accident in Lyon and couldn't bring themselves to get rid of his things, even though they knew he would not return. Henri and Lucie still hadn't recovered emotionally from the loss. Jacques considered them to be a bit strange but good neighbors and he wouldn't have been happier if anyone else lived on the adjoining farm. They minded their own business, worked hard and were absolutely dependable.

With the money from Henri and the profit from the bakery, he and Annette were able to live comfortably. There was some money in the bank, and with eggs from the chickens, and bread from the bakery they knew they could get by when others might be hurting. The garden provided a welcome array of vegetables during the summer months, and Annette was able to store some vegetables over the winter. These included squash, potatoes, string beans, beets and carrots. They also had pear and apple trees close to the house. Henri sprayed the trees in the spring and they provided plenty of fresh fruit from late summer until Christmas for Henri as well as Jacques and Annette. The weather in this part of France was conducive to having a garden.

About a half hour before noon Annette made lunch and drove her bicycle to the bakery. She placed the bicycle behind the shop by the back door next to the flower pot and joined her father inside.

"How has the day been, Papa?" she asked as she tied on her apron.

"We were busy early this morning but it has been quiet this last hour."

"I'll get the bread out on the shelves. Do we need wheat flour?" asked Annette.

"We have enough for this week. Order some when the supplier comes by this afternoon."

"I'll take a break and have something to eat," Jacques said as he pulled out the chair from the table.

"I might have a chance today to make some pastry and buns. They always sell well," said Annette.

"Good. We could use the extra cash," he remarked even though he knew that the cash was not really needed. He just wanted his daughter to feel like she was needed.

Annette liked working in the bakery for it gave her the opportunity to talk with everyone in town. She was often one of the first to know all the news. Her pleasant personality made communication with her easy even if she didn't always have the kind of bread someone wanted. She was usually able to make a suggestion that satisfied them. She was a born diplomat. When she was a very young girl her mother would bring her to the shop while she worked. The townspeople considered her as they would their own child and they loved her. As she matured she became prettier and more pleasant and was loved and respected by all the villagers. She learned to wait on the customers and made few mistakes with the francs. Her classmates liked her, as Annette was always willing to help them with an arithmetic problem or a point of grammar.

The smell of fresh baked bread was in her blood. She could not remember when she didn't enjoy the smells of the bakery. When she arrived at noon the bakery was still filled with that smell and warmth and happy memories of her childhood were always evoked. She knew that the warm smell brought back memories of her mother for both her father and herself.

The making of bread would always do that. The tinkle of the doorbell woke her from her thoughts.

Each day it seemed the subject of the pending German invasion of France was discussed. Many believed it wouldn't happen, but the majority were more convinced that it was only days or weeks away. Several times a customer made the comment that if the Germans occupied France they could declare the currency useless and French francs would be immediately devalued. They spoke of buying silver or gold and burying it on their property. She decided one day that maybe she would talk with her father and ask him to take some of the money in the bank and turn it into gold or silver. It would retain its value even if the Germans took over the banks and used German currency for exchange.

That afternoon she was sweeping the floor when a long time customer came in for some bread. Annette liked the lady but knew she had a reputation for being outspoken.

"Annette, you won't believe what I heard on the radio late last night," she began and didn't wait for a response. "It was the BBC. A man was saying that they were taking Jews to camps and gassing them and burning their bodies."

"It hard to believe. How could anyone do such a terrible thing?"

"But that is what they are doing. That was not the first time that I heard about the Nazis killing innocent people. They say that Hitler says that the Jews are the cause of all the problems in Europe and they need to be annihilated. He says that sick, deformed and retarded people should also be destroyed."

"I hear those rumors from others also, Marlene, but still find it hard to believe. Maybe I just don't want to believe that it's going on. Tell me if you hear any more."

"I will, but only if we are alone in the store. I have no idea how people will behave if the Germans occupy our country. I wonder if we will turn against each other."

"I don't think we will. Still it might be wise be keep some of these rumors to ourselves."

CHAPTER 8

With tears in his eyes Paul said goodbye to his Aunt Harriet. His Uncle Charles drove him to the recruiting office where a large bus was waiting. They hugged goodbye and Charles told Paul that he would miss him at the garage but most of all he would miss him at home. He told him that he was welcome any time. The room would remain available for him to use. Paul pushed back his emotions as he shook his uncle's hand and headed for the bus.

Basic training was tough for some of the recruits but not for Paul. He was in great shape from working in construction and basketball in the winter and swimming during the summer. He let it be known that he was hoping for an assignment as a bombardier or a radio operator. He excelled in target practice and as a result was given special training with machine guns. The time passed quickly and soon Paul was packing for a ten day furlough.

Time with his family was pleasant. Even his brothers and sister were happy to see him. Edward and Eleanor asked most of the questions.

"Will you be a radio operator, Paul?" asked Eleanor.

"I would like that but they want me to be a gunner. They told me that because I have exceptional eye-hand coordination they pity the Messerschmitt that comes in range of my guns. I sure hope they're right."

"Will you be staying in Canada?" asked Edward.

I heard the RAF needs gunners to complete their bombing crews. I suspect that a group of us will be sent to England as soon as we report back to the base. We will probably see action sooner if that rumor is true."

Before leaving the table Paul had a short speech that he rehearsed and he asked everyone to stay and listen.

"First of all I want to ask you to forgive me for being such an ass." They started to object that he wasn't that bad but he shook his head to their objections. "Look, I was angry because we left Vermont. And then the way Celia dumped me really hurt my feelings and I took it out on you guys. I hope you will forgive me and I promise not to be so immature in the future. Mom, Dad, before this war is over I'll make you proud of me."

"Paul, we're already proud of you," said his Dad. "Just do your job and this war will be over soon."

The next day Paul had the opportunity to sit down with Harold and ask about the situation with Rick and Jack.

"How did the situation work out with Rick's and Jack's parents?"

"Mr. Benecasa appreciated that we told him about what Rick and Jack were planning to do," said Harold "He said that he would speak with Jack's parents and take care of the situation."

"Do you think he did?"

"Yes. He called me several days later and told me that he was sorry that this had happened. He also wanted you to know that he was sorry that you felt you had to join the service to avoid these two."

"So you believe it is all settled and they are out of the business of robbing people."

"I think so. Mr. Benecase is a take charge person and I believe he can control his son. You did those two a great service, although they probably don't know it. They might be sitting in jail right now if it hadn't been for you."

"Thanks, Harold. That makes me feel a lot better."

Paul was most thankful that this mistake in his life was behind him.

The days at home passed quickly. Paul heard the news that Germany invaded France, Belgium, Holland and Luxemburg. It made him angry what Germany was doing. He couldn't understand why the United States continued to remain neutral. Late on Mother's day, May 13, Paul flew back to Montreal. From there he took a train to Quebec. He spent his last day on leave with his aunt and uncle. His uncle drove him to the recruiting office where a bus took him to the airport He soon boarded with four others for their flight to England. The sun was just setting in the west outlining the silver wings as the plane banked above the clouds and headed to his new home, a base in Great Britain. Paul soon fell asleep.

CHAPTER 9

As the weeks passed more and more people spoke to Jacques and Annette about what they were hearing. Everyone felt the BBC could be trusted but not everyone understood English well enough to understand what he or she heard. Some had to rely on others for their information.

Somehow the news about the behavior of Germany leaked to the people. Because no one knew how people would react if the country was under German occupation, most villagers were careful with whom they shared information. People would tell Annette things if they were the only person in the shop, but if several people were there they would be more cautious.

At work, Annette listened to the radio for music but got some news once each hour. At home she also listened to music, but she and her father tried to listen to the BBC each night while they ate and she did the dishes in the kitchen. She heard that almost every night German planes were bombing London. The news would upset her but she had to listen. Both she and her father needed to be informed. After the broadcast, Jacques would usually have a glass of wine and go to bed between eight and nine o'clock.

She heard that Finland signed a treaty with the Soviets in March. A few days later it was reported the Germans dropped bombs on the British submarine base called Scarpa Flow. Then in April the radio announced that Germany invaded Denmark and Norway. Could France be next?

With the busy schedule that they both had they hardly noticed that winter turned to spring. When they did notice, Annette looked for Henri to begin to plow their fields. One spring like day she saw him plowing the field near the barn. She put on a jacket and waited for him near the driveway.

"Hello, Henry."

"Hello, Annette."

"If you have time could you plow up my vegetable garden?"

"Yes, I'll do it this morning. How are you doing?"

"Fine. And Lucie?"

"She's fine. I'll get to the garden soon."

Henri tipped his hat and started plowing another straight line of furrows. Annette realized that Henri said only what had to be said and that this exchange might be considered a long conversation. What he lacked in social graces, he more than made up in compassion and understanding.

True to his word, Henri dug up the area reserved for a vegetable garden, going over the soil several times to break it up as finely as possible. Annette waved at the farmer to tell him how pleased she was. He removed his hat as his way of saying that she was welcome. Before she left for work she had raked a small portion so that she would soon be able to plant lettuce and spinach seeds. She had already started tomato and pepper seeds in pots by the kitchen window.

One day in the spring when she had come home from the bakery, her father told her that he and an old friend had been to Bern, to transfer their savings out of France to a Swiss bank account. He said that he did it because Annette had suggested that French currency might be devalued. He said that putting money in a Swiss account was safer than changing it to gold or silver. He showed her the name of the bank and the numbers that would allow either of them to access the account once she signed the card and mailed it back to the bank. He even had the password written on a card.

"We'll never remember everything, Papa. Can we hide the information?"

"We'll have to. Where would you suggest?"

I'll find a good place to hide the information so that only you and I will know where it is. You'll see. I'll find some good hiding places."

"I'm sure you will, Annette."

The following evening after supper Annette told her father where she hid the information. "I put the bank's name inside that loose saw handle in the cellar. I put the numbers on a piece of paper and put it in the bottom of the coffee jar in the kitchen and put coffee in the jar. I hid the password under a dresser leg in my room. Even if they find them they won't know what they mean."

"That's a good start. You'll probably find even better spots in the days ahead. Just tell me if you decide to change your hiding places."

"Papa, you know I will."

It was May 10, 1940, when Annette heard the news that Germany had invaded Belgium, Luxembourg and the Netherlands. Shortly thereafter it was reported that France had been invaded. What Uncle Andre had told them at Christmas time was happening and survival was now becoming their most important priority. Several people throughout the day stopped in to buy bread and tell them of the news. Everyone was concerned.

With their wealth taken out of the country and hidden where the Germans couldn't get it, they felt more secure. Jacques hadn't moved their money any too soon and he was thankful to Andre for telling them about the pending trouble.

Annette would remember this day, since it was the day before her eighteenth birthday. Her father brought her a piece of pastry from the bakery and was planning a small celebration for her. He also bought her a set of earrings that the jeweler in the village told him Annette was admiring. When she opened the small box her face lit up and she put the earrings on immediately. During the private celebration Annette couldn't help but notice that her father's thoughts seemed to be elsewhere.

"What's the matter, Papa? You seem to be upset."

"I am, Child. I never thought this day would come in spite of what Andre told us."

"You should be pleased that you put your savings in a bank in Switzerland."

"I am. But I thought he was exaggerating. I decided to humor you and be prudent, just in case. It really was against my better judgment. Since my old friend, Martin, was going to Switzerland to put money in a Swiss bank, I thought that maybe I should do the same. I knew it would please you. I considered what I was doing a waste of time. Now I'm glad I did."

"I'm glad you did, too," Annette said as she put her arms around her father's neck and kissed him on the cheek. "Thank you for the lovely earrings. I will cherish them always."

CHAPTER 10

A sergeant was holding a sign that said **Fortier.** Paul noticed it immediately as he walked from the tarmac and entered the military airport not too far from London. There were several other military holding up signs for the other airman who were on the plane with Paul. The Sergeant introduced himself as Dudley Morrison. He took the smaller of Paul's bags, leaving him to carry the duffle. He insisted on calling Paul the Anglicized version of his name and Paul corrected him three times before he gave up trying to teach him the correct pronunciation. Paul couldn't understand why he couldn't say For-ti-ay.

Sergeant Morrison was a pleasant man and, on the ride up to North Yorkshire, provided Paul with a lot of information.

"We only have several Wellington bombers at present but we're expecting more," said the Sergeant.

"What's holding them up?"

"We've only started lengthening the runway. The bombers can land but with such a short runway they can't take off."

"Is that the only problem that is keeping us grounded?"

"Hell, no! I can't begin to tell you all the problems. That is probably the most obvious. We're short of personnel, the petro tanks need to be installed, the mechanics are in need of training and we don't have all our pilots. Each day it gets a little bit better. One day we'll be operational."

"I hope it's soon. Nothing is more depressing than doing nothing."

"Relax. Enjoy this time off, go into town with your mates for a pint or two, eat three meals a day, and try to enjoy this time off. We're see action soon enough. That's my advice."

"Thanks, Sergeant. I'll try to follow it."

When they arrived at the airbase at Skipton-on-Swales, Paul was amazed at how small it was. The runway was like that of a small plane airport back home. It was the kind of airport that weekend pilots could use to fly their two-seater planes. There was camouflage placed over most of the field making it seem like anything but an airfield. It wouldn't look like an inviting target for German bombers, which was the purpose of the camouflage.

Quarters were a series of Nissan huts. The curved, corrugated iron buildings with two small windows and a door in the front were to provide sleeping quarters to the expected airmen. There were thirteen of these and six other framed buildings for the mess hall, briefings, offices, first aid and repair. The airfield ran parallel to a small village and looked like it was an extension of the village. The few Wellingtons that were there were kept under camouflage.

Paul was anxious to get into action and found the inactivity frustrating. He met his fellow airmen but didn't get a chance to fly. He noticed that although work was being done on the base, nothing seemed to be happening. Air raid sirens could be heard occasionally at night but no bombers were heard near the airfield.

Several weeks went by and Paul was becoming concerned with his behavior. Whenever he got the chance he would go to town in a lorry with his crewmates for a pint or two of ale. He found all his crewmates friendly enough. They, too, were anxious to get into battle and down a Kraut or two. Several times he definitely had too much to drink and didn't like feeling drunk. He was not used to drinking. It took only a few pints of English ale to make him tipsy.

Going to town every evening seemed to be the only thing to do and Paul went into town with his mates to pass the evenings. He decided that getting drunk or even slightly drunk every evening was not the way he wanted to behave. Yet that was all there was to do. He attributed his drinking to his frustration with sitting around and waiting and he feared that eventually he would become an alcoholic.

At several of the pubs in town there would be some singing. Several of the men would play darts, but there was usually only one dartboard. The men sat and drank ale and talked of home. He, being the only Canadian, had no one to share his memories of home. There were some women who would come to the pub and the men would vie to buy them drinks. Several of the women were drivers for high-ranking officers. They provided most of the scuttlebutt. Paul never got to spend any time with the young ladies who would occasionally grace the table. The competition was just too fierce. What chance did a shy, eighteen year old Canadian airman have with all the boisterous Brits, some of whom were officers? Besides, he was still a lowly private.

Paul inquired about going to church and found that the village had a small Catholic Church and that two Masses were said on Sunday. He decided that one of these Sundays he would walk into town and go to Mass. But between getting tipsy on Saturday night and not having anyone to go to town with on Sunday morning, he never got to go. The expression of his mother's that 'the road to hell is paved with good intentions' invaded his consciousness more often than he cared to admit.

One day in mid June when the lack of action seemed to be getting the best of him, he decided to have a talk with the commanding officer, Wing Commander Hugh Holliday. The officer's secretary, Mrs. Dorothy North, told him Commander Holliday was out and wouldn't be back for the day. She suggested that tomorrow would be a better time. He was just about to leave when she asked him a question that he didn't understand. She repeated herself.

"When is the last time you've had a home cooked meal?"

"Probably… a month ago… back home," he stammered.

"Would you like a home cooked meal?"

Paul hesitated and slowly began to realize where the conversation was heading. "Yes, I would." Then he was at a loss for words.

"I'm inviting you for dinner at my home anytime after I leave here at five o'clock."

"How do I get there?"

"On the way to town, after you cross the brook, turn right at the first road and right again. I live on Inga Drive in the first cottage on the right.

It's white with yellow shutters. It's about two kilometers from here. You can't miss it."

"May I ask about Mr. North? Will he be joining us?" he inquired.

"No. Mr. North was killed several months ago."

"I'm sorry," Paul said and then after a moment's hesitation, "I'll see you probably about six thirty this evening,"

"Don't disappoint me. Food is not easy to get these days."

"I'll be there...and thanks."

With that Paul left the offices and returned to his quarters with a little more speed in his step. After five o'clock he took a shower and got into a clean uniform. Without saying anything to his mates he left the base. After five o'clock, their time was their own and they didn't have to sign out or report to anybody. They were required to be on base by midnight.

Paul had no trouble finding the cottage after a twenty-minute walk. It was small but quaint and nicely kept. Dorothy North came to the door in a very attractive flowery dress a moment after he knocked. The dress was covered with a blue apron. She invited him in but had to return to the kitchen to stir the gravy.

"Can I get you a drink, Paul? May I call you Paul?" she asked.

"Yes. What should I call you?"

"Here you can call me Dorothy. On the base I'm Mrs. North."

"That's fine. No, I don't want a drink just now. I found out recently that I'm not too good at holding my liquor. Several drinks and I wouldn't be able to find my way home."

The dress that Dorothy was wearing was red with white flowery prints. She was at least ten years older than Paul and had a nice figure. Her hair had once been blonde but was now a light brown. She wasn't what one would call a beauty but she was attractive. And she was nice and possibly the only woman on the base. Paul considered himself lucky.

Dorothy asked Paul to help her put the food on the table while she set the dishes, silverware and glasses. It was a meal of meat loaf, cabbage and mashed potatoes with gravy. It was a simple meal, cooked well. She poured herself another glass of white wine and Paul said that he would wait to have a glass after supper.

Paul enjoyed the home cooked meal. No matter how good the food, the military always seemed capable of cooking it to death. Dorothy had taken common food and made something nice out of it. After the meal they removed the dishes from the table and put the food away. After they retired to the living room, Paul asked for a glass of wine. Dorothy refreshed her own.

"Paul, I hope you aren't expecting a meal whenever you come here. You know everything is rationed for us civilians and food is a precious commodity," she began.

"Dorothy," Paul began with a measure of doubt in his voice. "Am I coming here again?"

"Only if you want. I sincerely hope you will want to."

Dorothy explained that she missed her husband who was killed in London in an air raid. He was a warden and was directing people to a shelter when a bomb hit nearby. She had already moved out of London.

She was hoping that someone would come into her life, even if only briefly. She said she knew that there was quite an age difference, but that maybe she could make his life just a little more pleasant until he moved to another base or whatever. The 'whatever' was better left unspoken.

Dorothy broke the awkward silence by getting up and putting on a record. She put on an album of Glenn Miller, the first track being "Moonlight Serenade." When she returned to the couch she sat closer to Paul than previously.

"Paul, I'd like your company, when you can visit me. I have no one else in my life and would like to be part of yours. I know this relationship will not pass the test of time but we can enjoy it for as long as we're both together on this bomber base."

"What will they say on the base when they find out we're seeing each other?"

"I don't really care. None of these airmen are from here and those that survive this awful war will not live here. So I don't bloody care what they think about me. How about you?"

"I like your company and I know we'll both take a lot of ribbing from my mates. At least I will. But I want to continue to see you. And I don't want to go into town every night for a pint or two." Switching to a British accent, he continued, "Since I'm not from here, I don't bloody care either."

"Paul, let's just say that I'm ten years older than you and I know this will only last while you're stationed here. Still…"

"If you are not unhappy with this arrangement, it's fine with me."

Paul moved closer to Dorothy on the couch and they kissed. Several moments later she took him by the hand, stopped to turn off the phonograph and led him into the bedroom. It was his first experience of complete intimacy but he didn't tell her. His only other sexual experiences had been with Celia. He wondered if Dorothy could tell.

CHAPTER 11

Paul returned the next day to the main office to speak with the wing commander. Dorothy announced him and ushered him into the office. Standing at attention, he waited while the commander completed the task he was doing. Since Paul had calmed down considerably from the previous day, he approached the commander with much more civility.

The officer asked Paul to stand at ease.

"Commander, this is not a complaint but rather an inquiry as to why we are sitting around doing nothing?" Paul began.

"Paul, that's your name, is it? We are not yet considered a fully operational base. All our bombers are not here, we haven't finished training all our squadron pilots and navigators and the tanks for storing petrol have not yet arrived."

"I'm not complaining, sir, but it isn't good for morale to be doing nothing when our services are needed. Most of the men feel that we came here to fight and they are anxious to see some action."

"I understand and fully agree," said the Commander. "Wasn't it Milton who said, 'They also serve who only stand and wait'?"

"I wouldn't know, Sir. I don't know who this Milton guy is, but I find it difficult to wait."

"Paul, I promise you that shortly you will beg for a few days off. Try to make the best of it for now, and you'll see action soon. I promise. Enjoy this time off, if that's possible."

Paul got a few of his questions answered and knew that he would be able to enjoy this time away from action by seeing Dorothy. That was the pleasant part. He was looking forward to another evening with her and as he passed her desk, she mouthed the word, "tonight." He nodded.

Paul went to evening mess as usual and was asked if he wanted to go for a pint at one of the pubs in town. He declined. While nothing was suspected, at the moment, it would be only a matter of time before his situation would be discussed. It would not be kept quiet. He didn't much care. Yet it was still wise to be discreet. He should not irritate his mates with his good fortune.

He enjoyed spending his evenings with Dorothy and enjoyed the walk home. It took him no more than twenty minutes and gave him time alone to think. He was supposed to be back in the hut by midnight but knew that discipline was lax and would probably remain so until they started flying missions. Because they both had to get up in the morning, he planned to leave her cottage at eleven-thirty at the latest. It seemed a suitable arrangement.

One evening Dorothy told Paul that she had to visit her mother and father in Sheffield over the weekend. She was expected and would be gone after work on Friday until Sunday evening. She told him that she would see him at work on Monday. At the time he thought that a weekend away from Dorothy wasn't a bad idea. It would allow him time to spend with his mates and maybe hit a pub or two.

When the time came, however, it was much more difficult than he had anticipated. Paul missed Dorothy. He missed her easy way, her gentle caring and her wildness in bed. Paul was falling in love with a lonely woman who was too old for him and would not marry him even if he asked. She would never be able to introduce him to her family. Wartime was wartime and this was a wartime romance. Two lonely people were helping each other survive these difficult days and lonely nights. His head told him to keep it that way, but his heart refused to cooperate.

It was difficult to wait until she returned and he was surprised at his emotions and his desires. Exercise and running and taking a dip in a small swimming pool were not enough to keep him occupied. The pool was too small for swimming but would allow the men to cool off. It was barely deep enough to allow one to dive off the small diving board.

On Monday morning Paul and Dorothy returned glances as she was standing her bicycle under the window of her office. They were able to communicate that he would visit her in the evening after mess. Not a word had to be spoken. That evening Paul told her how much he missed her. She told him that she was pleased but that was the price they would both have to pay for this time together.

"Paul, this is a wonderful interlude before the bombs fall and your mates get killed or maimed. Let's enjoy it but it's not going to last. I love the nights I spend with you but I know you won't be here forever. We just have to accept that."

Paul didn't know what to think as he began his walk back to the base. The strong feelings he was experiencing for this wonderful woman surprised him and he didn't want to let her out of his life. Yet he understood that if she were to love him and his plane was shot down and he didn't come home, she would experience a great loss. Even if he were transferred to another base, it would be difficult.

Could he do his job if he were this involved with someone? Approaching the base, he decided that she was probably right. He didn't want to lose her now. He would tell her that he would go along with her ideas. What he didn't want to admit, even to himself, was that he was having a relationship with a woman, and he had no intention of marrying her. He would not have believed that he was capable of such behavior six months ago, but he obviously was. Could he enjoy their time together but not make a commitment? Could he give up this woman who was the only joy now in his life? He didn't think so. With some conflicting thoughts resolved and with others germinating in his mind, he entered the hut and quietly climbed into his bunk.

The next week saw some progress on the base. Several Wellingtons were flown in with their crews and work was started on lengthening the runway. A week later two petrol tanks were delivered and installed near the repair shops. It was now the end of June and it appeared as if two squadrons would be housed at Skipton-on-Swale. One was designated #424 and the other #433. Paul was a gunner with the #424. Each day more mechanics were brought in to work on the bombers. Other construction workers arrived to build and defend the base. As soon as the runway was lengthened it was camouflaged and artificial trees were placed on the runway, weighed down with sandbags. It was amazing that in five minutes, what looked like an innocent meadow could be converted into an airfield.

The French Vichy government broke off relations with Britain. That came as no surprise to anyone since Great Britain didn't recognize the Vichy Government as the legitimate government of the French people. It did recognize Charles De Gaulle as the leader of Free France.

Paul continued to spend his evenings with Dorothy at least three or four times a week. Dorothy told Paul that it would be over soon enough and that they should enjoy every evening that they could. When Paul arrived after supper in the evening, they would frequently listen to the BBC broadcast until it was over. The war was not going well and most Brits believed that Hitler would invade England now that he had completed his conquest of France and the Low Countries.

CHAPTER 12

Paul saw the quartermaster crossing toward the office of Wing Commander Holliday and took that opportunity to walk in step with him.

"Sir, what's holding up our operation?"

"Oh, so I finally meet the Yank."

"I'm afraid you're wrong, Sir. I'm Canadian."

"Well, in any case, it's nice to meet you."

"What's the holdup?"

"It seems that the Jerry U boats have been sinking a lot of our ships from Canada and the States. We're short of petrol and bombers can't fly without petrol. In fact we're short of everything from food to ammunition."

"I'm sorry to hear that. We have to have supplies if we're to beat the Jerries."

"That's true. I hope America will join us soon. We need the help and not just with supplies. Germany will take over the world if something isn't done soon."

"Thanks for the information. Waiting is tough and I sure hope you're wrong."

As he continued his walk he realized that life at the base would have been next to impossible without Dorothy. He was certain that he would have gone crazy by now if he didn't have her to lean on and to share his frustrations. He was glad that he met her and was sharing his life and evenings with her, even if it would be temporary.

The German Luftwaffe flew nightly sorties over London dropping their bombs on civilian and military targets alike. Children were evacuated to homes in the countryside for the duration of the bombing, since there were fewer targets in the country. The Germans also expanded their target to the larger industrial cities like Birmingham, Liverpool and Leeds and attacked factories in those cities. They could be heard flying not many miles away. So far they were unaware of Skipton-on-Swale, or if they were aware of the base it was deemed too small to target.

As hard as they tried to get ready to fly, shortages kept pushing back the dates. Shortages of airmen, planes, mechanics, equipment, spare parts and petrol conspired to keep the bombers grounded. The men were told they would be going next week and next week and next week. The men listened to the BBC broadcast every evening and understood that it was not going well for the Allies. To a man, each wished he could do something about it.

Paul discussed his frustration with Dorothy. They had settled into a routine of listening to the BBC and music, talking, drinking wine and making love. Paul limited himself to one glass as he found that two glasses made him slightly tipsy and sleepy. He enjoyed the glass with his occasional meal at her house and asked Dorothy to buy him a certain kind of wine when she went shopping. He gave her several pounds each payday to keep them in wine and to help her with any meals.

CHAPTER 13

Andre paid Jacques a visit the first weekend in July. The brothers sat around the kitchen table, sipping tea while Andre smoked his pipe. Eventually Andre got around to the purpose of his visit. "This may be my last visit to Faymont for awhile, Jacques."

"Do you think the Germans will restrict your travel?"

"They will take away my automobile and make me fill out a travel request. They want to know where everyone is going. That could get you in trouble if somehow they thought I was causing trouble. They don't trust government officials and are keeping close watch over us."

"We don't see many Germans here. How about in Chaumont?"

"Since June they've been all over the place. They're definitely taking control. I'm sure you've heard that Marshall Petain, the French Prime Minister installed by the Germans, signed an armistice with Germany. Petain controls the southern part of France and the Germans the northern. In reality, the Germans control all of France."

The two men had plenty of time to talk on Saturday afternoon while Annette was still at the bakery, but when she came home the two men were unusually quiet. Annette sensed the discomfort and felt like she was not being consulted on something of importance. She didn't like the feeling.

After the three returned from church on Sunday, Uncle Andre suggested that all three sit at the table. "I have some things I must tell you."

"I've been wondering what you two have been up to. Whenever I'm around you get silent. What's going on?"

"The Germans have occupied the northern half of France and will control the southern half through a puppet government. They want to control everyone," Andre began. "We are in the occupied northern half. It has reached my attention that they will complete their move into the barracks north of town soon."

"We expected that when we heard that they were building barracks," said Annette.

Andre continued. "While they have not made it official as yet, they intend to round up Jews and send them to camps in the east. People are being asked to help the Germans identify the Jews in their village. Jews that speak French are harder to identify but those who immigrated to France and speak poor French, or no French, are being put into work camps. Right now many Jewish children have been smuggled out of Germany and are living in France. They need to be smuggled into Switzerland."

"I know most of that, Uncle, but how are we involved? We don't have any Jews in Faymont."

Andre continued. "My village, as well as several surrounding villages, harbors a number of Jewish children who speak little or no French. We have taken in all that we can. Our village has almost doubled in size. We cannot assimilate anymore without endangering the entire village. We would like to bring these to you and any others that we can't absorb. We want you to smuggle them across the border into Switzerland."

Annette's mouth opened and her heart began to beat so that she could feel the rhythm. If she craved excitement this would certainly be at the top of her list. Smuggling Jewish children into Switzerland under the noses of the Germans would be high drama. All of a sudden she experienced a moment of panic, replaced by a dozen questions.

Jacques interrupted her thoughts. "I will take two or three children at a time over the mountain. They will then stay in the woods all the way to the border. A stream separates France from Switzerland. About a kilometer on the Swiss side there is a very small shack where people will meet me to take the children to a nearby village and safety."

"Where will we get the children and how will we know on what day to transport them to Switzerland?"

"There is a reddish brown flower pot with a geranium in it by the back door of the bakery near where you park your bicycle. Every spring you have been planting geraniums in it and the flowers last until the frost," said Andre. "When the flower pot is moved to the opposite side of the door you can expect children to be in the barn that evening. That is the signal. Then you can return the flower pot to the left side of the door where you usually leave it. The children will arrive late in the afternoon but before it gets dark."

"Who will move the pot?" asked Annette.

"That's not for you to know. We tell you only what you need to know to do your job. That way if you get caught the operation isn't a total failure. The less you know the less you can tell. We hope that no one will be killed, but that is a possibility," said Andre.

"How will the children get there without being seen?"

"They will be transported to the woods near Henri Arsenault's place. Sometimes by car and sometimes a horse drawn wagon. They can walk through the woods unseen until they are near the barn. There is a secluded spot by the bend in the road where they can be dropped off near the path. They will be in the open field for only a hundred meters or so and when the hay is grown they probably won't be seen at all," explained Andre. "Once it is dusk you will lead them over the mountain. That requires Jacques or you, Annette."

"Papa, you'd be up half the night and would then have to get up just several hours later to be at the bakery. You are not as young as you used to be and you have gained several pounds. The trip over the mountain would be strenuous for anyone and it might be extremely difficult for you. Are you sure you could do it?"

"No, I'm not sure I can do it," Jacques admitted with a hint of annoyance in his voice. Then he softened his tone and addressed Annette. "Maybe this afternoon you and I can take that trip over the mountain and find that shack in the woods in Switzerland. Uncle Andre has a map for us that will be very helpful. Once we do it we won't need the map. Are you willing to take a hike this afternoon?"

"Yes. I think I know the best way to cross that mountain. Uncle Andre, may I see the map?"

Annette and Jacques studied the map. It showed the woods and mountains behind their property. The locals called it Jacques's Mountain because it bordered the LaVoie property but Jacques simply called it the mountain. The map didn't show how they would get over the mountain. Yet both knew how they would reach the border. The map told them where to go once they were safely in Switzerland. It looked like there would be a stream to cross, the boundary between the two countries. Part way up a hill would be a smaller stream that flowed into the larger one. They could follow the smaller stream to reach the shack once they crossed the border, according to the map.

After lunch Annette was anxious to get started. Andre said that he would remain at the farm until they returned. He told them that there was probably a checkpoint already at the border but he didn't think that the Germans were patrolling the border as yet, but he nevertheless urged them to be careful.

"Remember that this will involve risk for both of you. If one of you gets caught, they will most likely execute you both," Andre reminded them. "I know what I'm asking you to do is extremely risky. Consider this carefully before making a decision."

"We will, Andre," said Jacques. "I don't want anything to happen to Annette."

"Uncle Andre, we know it will be difficult. First we have to find out if we are capable of doing this."

"I'll hope you can give me an answer when you return," said Andre.

"We will," said Jacques.

CHAPTER 14

A short while after lunch Jacques and Annette set out for the barn. The house was set about two hundred feet from the road. The barn was another hundred feet from the house. Their field extended another three hundred feet past the barn before the tree line and the end of their property. The road in front of their house didn't go to the border but turned west to come out at Blamont. By the time it made the turn it was a dirt road not kept in repair and used infrequently by local farmers. Father and daughter would stay in the woods walking south to cross this road to reach the mountains that formed a barrier to the border. To reach the border by car it would be best to go back toward town about a kilometer and take a paved road several kilometers to the border.

Crossing the road they saw the mountains posing a formidable barrier about a hundred feet beyond. It wasn't that they were so huge but rather that they ascended vertically right out of the ground. A person would have to be not only a mountain climber, but a good one at that to scale the formations. Jacques and Annette decided to time their journey. The first five minutes were easy enough, but once they reached the mountain it looked like a wall of stone. Both were familiar with the way through the mountains, even though they had no reason to use the passageway.

The opening sloped downward and looked like it was only about twenty feet deep. Mountain laurel grew where the sun reached but rock covered with moss abounded. At the back of the passage there was an opening that doubled back and then formed an "S." The passageway was narrow and deceptive. It appeared to end and one would believe that they had gone as

58

far as possible. Few people traced it all the way through the "S." If they did they would be rewarded with a passage through the rock.

It was necessary for Jacques to squeeze through the narrowest part of the opening.

"I believe the passageway is getting narrower as I get older," said Jacques.

"I'm sure that's the problem," kidded Annette. "This will be no problem for children as long as none are afraid of confined spaces."

"I'm sure they'll do fine."

When they passed through, the path presented a series of ledges that reminded one of climbing stairs. Five strenuous minutes later they would be at the top of the mountain with an open rocky area in front of them. As they looked back at the passageway, it was almost invisible and the passage down to it looked steeper than it was. Both Annette and her father felt that no one would ever find this pass through the mountain unless they were shown where it was.

It was absolutely necessary to take that passageway to cross the mountain. Any who didn't know of that opening would meet a wall of rock at every turn. If they found what looked like a path they would meet a rock wall after a five or ten-minute hike. Every other passage came to a dead end or a drop-off. The passageway that Jacques and Annette took was the only way through the mountain for several kilometers either way where checkpoints were setup.

"Papa, do you remember which way to go once we reach the top?"

"Yes, we have to cut around that rock over there, to the right. The path to the left is a dead end. Remember, Annette, I've been on this property for at least twice as many years as you. Let's take a break."

Annette made a note of the time and they rested for five minutes. She was also concerned for her father and didn't think that he would be able to make many trips like this. After Jacques regained his breath, they continued on their journey. There were three or four choices still ahead of them, anyone of which would lead to difficulty if the wrong choice was made.

"I'd hate to have to make my way over this little mountain if I didn't know it so well. There are a lot of false trails and dangerous drop-offs," observed Annette.

"It's difficult enough when you know this mountain like we do. Let's stop again."

As they came down on the other side they had actually spent thirty-five minutes traveling, excluding the stops. The woods were now very thick and there was no path to be seen. They knew the general direction they wished to go and continued forward to the valley below. Soon they heard the stream that marked the border between France and Switzerland. As they got closer to the stream they stopped to make sure there were no border guards to detain them. The spot they chose was equidistant between two check points, about three kilometers from each according to the map. They walked next to the stream for a short distance looking for a way to cross without getting wet. Finally they found a narrow spot where the water ran deep and the land was close enough to step across.

"Little children won't be able to jump that far," Annette said.

"No, but they can cross if we make a bridge for them," answered her father. "We can keep a board hidden under leaves in the woods and bring it out if we need it. Just a flat board like we have in the shed."

"That would do, Papa."

They continued up the hill on the other side and after a short distance came across a very small stream that cut diagonally across the hill. They followed that stream until they came to the top of the hill. There they saw a small building that was abandoned and falling apart. They carefully inspected it and found it to be of little value except to shelter several people from a light rain. A short distance beyond they came upon a path that soon became wide enough to accommodate a car. There was a small opening to turn around. In all they had spent just fifty minutes with time for resting. The trip could probably be done in thirty-five or forty minutes each way.

Annette and her father talked on the return trip. They both realized what they were asking the other to do. They knew that they were risking their lives for children whom they never met and would never see again. They could very easily lose their lives if they made one mistake. Even if they didn't make a mistake they could be shot on mere suspicion of smuggling. From now on they would have to be very careful and make sure that they observed everything that was going on around them. The trip back to their farm looked so much different. The choices they made on the return journey made it seem like a completely different route. They were thankful that they were very familiar with the mountain, for this would be extremely dangerous for a newcomer. Annette observed that while her father could do the job, it was not going to be easy for him. If it was this taxing in the daylight, it would be more so in darkness. She knew that she would be the one making most of these trips.

Before they returned to the farm, Jacques spoke to his daughter. "Annette, I'm an old man and if I die, that's no terrible loss. I have lived a happy and full life, and without Marie I am just surviving until you are married and settled. But you are young and it would be a tragedy if you were to be killed at such a young age. I want you to have babies and tell them about their grandparents."

"Papa, I know what I'm getting into and I know how dangerous this can be. But consider all the children who will survive because of us. I want to do this and help as many children escape as I can. We have to do this. It is why we have lived for generations on this farm."

"I'm afraid that the bulk of the smuggling will fall to you. I'll be able to take children across in an emergency but not on a frequent basis," said Jacques as they came out of the woods and onto their property.

"I understand, Papa. I'm young and can do this. And I want to help children escape these evil people. Those actions would give my life purpose. I want to do it."

"Then let's tell Andre about our decision," said Jacques.

When they met with Andre they told him that they would take the job. They wanted to know how they would signal the people at the shack. Andre told them to use their flashlight and blink it twice. They would respond with two flashes.

"You will constantly have to watch for the Germans. They will not go down this road to the checkpoint but if they do use it, it will be so they can observe you and keep you from even considering smuggling. They will use this road to intimidate."

"Do you really think they will use this little dirt road?" asked Annette.

"They will be suspicious of anyone who lives near the border. They know that you are the nearest farm to the border and if they thought you were doing anything that even remotely seemed odd they would haul you in to interrogate you both. Get your stories straight now. We know this farm is a good spot to smuggle people into Switzerland and so will the Germans. They will watch your every move. They wouldn't hesitate to move you out of this farmhouse if they suspected that you might be doing anything remotely suspicious."

"You make the Germans sound like they have no compassion at all," said Annette.

"Remember that. They don't have compassion and will kill you at the slightest provocation. They are evil. Also, keep in mind that the Germans will have sympathizers in Switzerland telling them if people are being smuggled. That's why you will only take a few children at one crossing. This is a very dangerous operation you are undertaking. Keep to your schedule as much as you possibly can and be careful that you don't leave footprints. Also, walk through the woods a different path each time so as not to leave a trail."

"You make it sound extremely dangerous, Uncle Andre."

"It is, Annette. If you're very smart, you can keep them from becoming suspicious by sticking to your schedule. With luck, you may fool them. The Boche don't know there is a passageway through the mountains, and I hope they never find it. That is the most important thing you have going for you. One last thing. Even though I am a city official, my car will be confiscated. The Germans will not let me travel freely. This may be the last time I get to see you for a while."

We'll miss your visits, Andre," said Jacques.

"Just be careful. I love my only brother and niece. I don't want to lose you to those German bastards."

With that last bit of information, Andre got his hat and told his niece and brother to watch for the movement of the flower pot. He hugged them and gave each a kiss on both cheeks just before he opened the door to his car.

"Remember, this is important work. You will be saving the lives of many children. Jacques, curb your tongue. That is my last bit of advice. God will bless you," he said. Then he backed out his car to the road, waved and headed back to his home in Chaumont.

CHAPTER 15

Both Jacques and his daughter glanced at the flower pot daily, but it had not been moved. After the first week they almost forgot to look. In the middle of the third week the flower pot was moved to the other side of the doorway. Jacques noticed it when he arrived at the bakery a little after four in the morning but didn't move it.

When Annette showed up just before noon she spotted it immediately and moved it back to its usual spot. Since there was a customer in the store, neither she nor Jacques said anything. She waited until the store was empty before speaking with her father.

"I saw that the flower pot was moved."

"That means that we'll have visitors this evening. I may go home early," said Jacques.

"That might not be a good idea. We shouldn't change our schedule except when absolutely necessary."

"You're right, Annette. I'm anxious to meet the children and to make them feel comfortable."

"So am I, Papa. But the sun will be setting late and there is no need to change our schedule. I'm sure they won't bring the children until just before sundown."

"I suppose you're right. It will probably be around eight when we leave the barn. I'll go home my usual time and take a nap."

"That's a good idea. After your nap you may wish to check the barn to see if any children have arrived."

Jacques left at three, as usual. Annette stayed and closed up at six.

63

She then rode her bicycle back to the house. The roads were empty once she got out of town. Her father was asleep when she arrived home. After going upstairs to the bedrooms and searching for any signs of cars or other activity, she took some bread and cheese out to the barn.

When she entered the barn she didn't see or hear anyone. She stood in the entrance and let her eyes adjust to the light. Still there was silence. She called out, "Guten Abend," and heard stirring in the loft. Two boys stuck their heads over a bale of hay. She motioned for them to come down. They were dressed in dark suits with white shirts. One appeared to be about ten, and the other a year or two younger. Both looked frightened. Annette walked over to a bale of hay that was nearby and placed the bread and cheese on a cloth napkin. The young faces lit up and with their eyes they asked if it was for them. She gestured for them to eat.

Once supper was taken care of, Annette asked if they spoke French. The elder said he spoke a little and asked her if she spoke German. She replied that she spoke very little. That was not true but she didn't want anyone to know that she spoke German. She would have to think about whether she should speak German to the children. For now they would have to do the best they could with what they knew in French. Using hand gestures and pointing to the sun going down, she explained that she would return when it was dark. They nodded. She left the bread with them and returned to the house, watchful that there was no activity along the road or near the house.

Her father was up when she returned to prepare their supper of bread, cheese, wine and fruit. "Papa, two boys are in the barn. I can take them across the border by myself tonight.

"I know you can, Annette, but why don't we both go the first time? I want to meet those who will receive the children and I think they should meet me."

"If you're up to it, that's a good idea."

"Besides, this is for real and I want to know if I'm capable of doing this."

When the sun was near the horizon each took a flashlight and Annette tucked several apples into the pocket of her dress to give to the boys. She introduced the children to her father and they politely shook hands. He liked them immediately and he seemed to give them confidence. It was dusk and time to leave.

The journey to the mountain was easy and there was enough light to help them find their way. When they reached the woods behind the barn they made a left toward the mountains. They crossed the dirt road and walked directly to the narrow passageway. They passed through the passage, climbed the stair-like ledges and stopped for a few minutes at the top. It was now almost dark. They crossed behind the rock to their right using their flashlight to help the boys see their way and avoid getting near the edge. On the flat section of the mountain they could travel without the flashlight, but several places on the down slope needed illumination. At the bottom they again took a rest although neither Annette nor the boys needed the pause.

Making their way through the thick woods was more difficult at night than it had been by day. They kept their hands in front of their faces and a distance of about several paces to keep branches from snapping into the face of the person behind. Jacques led the way. Annette stayed in the rear. Soon, when they heard the gurgling water, they moved to the left to find the narrow part of the stream. Here they had to use their flashlights but kept them close to the ground and pointed away from the checkpoint. After taking a big step over the stream, Jacques lent a hand to the elder of the children. He told his brother that it was easy and so the smaller child jumped with no difficulty. After Annette crossed the stream the four continued up the hill.

They walked for a short distance along the banks of the small stream that crossed the hill diagonally before Jacques flashed the flashlight two times. There was a moment's hesitation and Jacques and Annette were starting to get concerned. Then two lights flashed in return. They continued their journey toward the shack at the top of the hill.

They were met by a man and a woman. They could not see their faces in the dark but were able to see the silhouette of the rifle held by the man. He had a medium build, and spoke with a very kind voice. He complimented them on being early and directed the children to the woman. The woman was short and heavy and very gentle with the children. She spoke fluent French to Jacques and Annette and German to the children. She told them thanks and left with the two boys. The man lingered a bit, said that he would see them next time. Having nothing more to say he followed the woman to the car. In a moment they heard a car engine and the children were whisked off to a new life.

The return trip went well but was much more difficult in the dark, especially coming down the mountain toward the passageway. Jacques led as they walked back to the farm. They used the flashlight very sparingly, always fearful that someone on the road could see the light. Annette made a quick check of the barn to make sure that it looked normal and that nothing was left behind. Then they headed for the house. Jacques observed that they failed to leave a light on and that a dark house so early in the evening might be considered suspicious by a patrol going past. Even though the road in front of the house didn't go to the checkpoint, they knew that German vehicles would drive this road just to spy on their house. Nevertheless, next time they would remember to turn on a light.

Annette also observed that her father was tired from this trip and that it had taken a lot out of him. He drank some water as soon as he came in the house and then excused himself for bed.

"Child, I'm going to bed. That trip was a bit more difficult than I anticipated, especially in the dark. Besides, I have to get up quite early." He gave Annette a kiss on the forehead before heading for the stairs.

Annette knew she would be the one taking the children across the border on future trips.

CHAPTER 16

It was two weeks before they saw the flower pot moved to the other side of the door again. The weather had been rainy for a few days and Annette considered that they probably would postpone the operation during inclement weather. Her father was aware that the flower pot was moved but he wasn't feeling all that great. Annette suggested that he go home early and get some sleep and she would take the children across the border that evening.

When Annette got home she went out to the barn after checking to see if anyone was within sight of the house. There were three children in the loft and when she called them, all three popped up. There was a twelve-year-old girl, a ten-year-old boy and a seven-year-old girl. The twelve-year-old spoke some French but with a heavy German accent. Annette told them that she would bring some food. They said that they ate a short while ago, but were thirsty. She communicated that she would be back with some bread and milk.

Back at the house her father was in bed. She heated up some onion soup that she had made several days before and made him some tea. He said all he wanted to do was sleep. Annette told him about the children and assured him that having the older girl would make her job easier. Annette brought a container of milk out to the barn, a loaf of bread and an apple for each. They put the apples in their bag with their possessions and drank all the milk. They then split the bread, ate some and saved the rest in their pockets.

When it was dusk, Annette did a check of the road from the loft. She could see well through the cracks in the wood. All was quiet. Just then she saw some dust up the road near town. She told the children to get up in the loft and she closed the door to the barn completely. She saw two German cars pass the farmhouse and continue on. In a few minutes, the cars returned, not wanting to chance a road like that in the dark. When she was convinced that they were gone for good, she called the children.

She told the older girl to go last and the youngest to stay behind her. The boy was in the middle of the three. She also asked them not to talk during the journey as voices could be heard a long distance. The trip went well for the first part and the children didn't have to stop to rest. When they got to the woods, Annette heard the youngest begin to whimper. She asked what was wrong in German. The child told her she was scared of the dark.

"Hold my hand. I will keep you safe," said Annette, again in German. That seemed to calm the child.

She then told the other two to spread out a bit so they wouldn't get hit by snapping branches, and to be as quiet as possible. The children obeyed willingly. At the stream, Annette noticed that the foliage had been trampled down along the stream on one side, the French side. She stopped, listened and looked both ways, anticipating that soldiers would not be as quiet or stealthy as were they. Maybe they had orders to patrol the border between the checkpoints. She would have to be careful.

The littlest child had no difficulty jumping across the stream. Annette had to turn on the flashlight, however, so she could see where to jump. They all walked up the hill, this time taking a slightly different route through the trees so as not to make a discernable path. At the little stream she flashed the light twice and got a return signal. The same two people were waiting beside the shack. A few words were spoken, the children said their thanks and Annette started back home.

The path that she found beside the stream disturbed her. It meant that the border was being patrolled between the checkpoints and could present a problem if they didn't time their crossing properly. Annette considered approaching the path from a different angle as she came through the woods so as not to leave a trace of their passage. She also wondered if she could find a place to cross in addition to the one she was using. Maybe she could cross at a shallow place by stepping on some rocks. She would talk to her father about these things and maybe he would have some ideas.

Jacques was up when she got home, nervously pacing the floor. "I'm feeling much better. I had some tea and should be able to fall asleep without any difficulty."

"Will you be able to work in the morning?"

"I think I'll be fine. All I need is a good sleep."

"If you don't feel well when you get up, wake me and we can switch jobs for a day." Annette decided to talk to her father at another time about what she saw at the stream. She stayed up and read for a while, drank a glass of red wine and was pleased with the evening's work.

CHAPTER 17

During the week of September 16 all sorts of necessary items arrived at the base. The Wing Commander called a meeting in the mess hall and told the entire base that they would be ready for action by the end of the week. He told them that a schedule of leave time was posted and that each person would get two days. He posted a schedule for the lorries to take people to town and the rail station and times for the return trip.

Paul was scheduled for Thursday and Friday. When he visited Dorothy in the evening he asked if she could get off at the same time.

"I'm afraid that's not possible. I have quite a bit of work lined up for the next few days while all of you are taking leave. It would be impossible."

"What will I do without you? It would be so much nicer if we could have some time away from the base."

"Maybe we'll get another chance soon. I would suggest that you spend time in Leeds. It has some quaint sections and I believe you'll like the people. It's a nice town."

He declined several invitations to join a group of his mates, preferring to be on his own. He climbed aboard the lorry for Leeds.

On Thursday he arrived at the railroad station about ten in the morning, and walked around that part of town, getting his bearings. He saw some bombed out buildings and a church that had been partially destroyed. The railroad station looked intact. He stopped at a pub for lunch and found a small inn nearby where he decided to stay for the evening. He dropped off his bag in a small room on the second floor and continued his tour of the city.

That evening he returned to the pub near the inn and had a pint of ale and a decent meal. There was a nice crowd. Someone sat down at the piano and soon the entire pub was singing. He was invited over to another table so he wouldn't have to drink alone. From his accent they asked if he was a 'Yank.' He told them he was Canadian. Several thanked him for coming from Canada to help them out. It was after eleven when he returned to his room, a bit tipsy but not drunk.

Shortly after midnight he was awakened by sirens, and when he stepped out in the hall the man in the next room told him to get dressed and head toward the shelter. He dressed and followed people out to the street.

"Where's the shelter?" he asked.

"Just follow those people there. Everyone's heading for a shelter."

He followed the crowd across the street and downstairs into the basement of a building that was probably a store. People were sitting on the cold cement with their backs to the wall. Some brought their own blankets and Paul was sorry that he hadn't. Paul's neighbor was a mother with a two-year old child who was frightened. Paul asked the mother if he could hold the girl for a few minutes and the child seemed to relax in his arms and was soon asleep. By this time all the lights were turned out except for a few small ones near the entranceway.

Paul managed to get some sleep even with the little girl nestled in his arms. He was impressed with how quiet and courteous everyone was. He heard some bombs burst but nothing was close-by. When the all-clear siren sounded, the mother took her sleeping child and thanked Paul for holding her. It was like this was a normal evening. Paul knew that night after night London was being bombed and that it had been going on for some time. This was his first experience of what the civilian population had to endure. He admired how strong the people of England had to be to survive this ordeal. He also could not make himself understand how the enemy could bomb civilian targets. It made no sense. It was barbaric.

The next day he saw some smoke and was told that the industrial section of Leeds experienced some damage but the area around the railroad station was not touched. He found it difficult to enjoy the city knowing that whatever he saw today might be destroyed tonight. Late in the afternoon he boarded the lorry at the railroad station for the trip back to the base.

CHAPTER 18

By Saturday the base looked very different. There were many new faces, all the huts seemed to be filled and there were twelve planes under camouflage near the runway. Mechanics were working on several of them. All the airmen were told to report to the briefing room immediately after evening mess.

The briefing was to tell them that their twelve Wellingtons would be joining another squadron of Blenheim bombers and would attack the German Navy in the North Sea. They would be awaiting word of the movement of the ships and would be on alert until further notice.

Paul observed that there were only twelve Wellingtons on the base at that time, so all would be participating in this operation. It rained Saturday night and all day Sunday with a forecast that the rain would be gone by Monday morning. Paul went to sleep on Sunday evening with a feeling that the time had finally come.

Monday morning dawned foggy and everyone was told that they would be taking off as soon as the sun was up. They walked to the mess hall in a heavy fog that seemed eerily ominous. After breakfast, they put on parachutes and boarded their planes. This was Paul's first flight in the Wellington. He toured several of the planes while they were being worked on, but had not as yet flown in one. He took his place in the front gunnery position and put on his earphones. Even before the sun was up, the Wellington was taxiing out to the end of the runway.

Paul was familiar with the two machine guns that were his weapons. He had fired ones just like them when he was in training. The weapons were arranged in tandem and could be fired singly or together. He realized that his position was fairly spacious and he occupied the entire nose of the Wellington. He didn't have much protection but he had a great view of everything in front of him, to the sides, above and below him.

The planes took off one right after the other with only a few seconds between takeoffs. Paul had heard that they could fly at 22,000 feet, which meant that flak from German guns could not reach them. Today they would be flying over the North Sea and not over German defenses. While their range was 2,200 miles they would not need all that range today. The plane was capable of 255 miles per hour. That was fairly fast for a bomber. They were well aware that the German Messerschmitt Bf 109 E was considerably faster and much more maneuverable.

They met up with the Blenheims just off the coast and flew at the same altitude but to the north of them. As both squadrons flew toward the east the weather began to deteriorate. The rain that had visited them for the past two days was in front of them. Once they reached the clouds, the squadron leaders made a decision. The Blenheims would fly below the clouds and the Wellingtons would stay above them. Once the convoy was located, the Wellingtons could come down for their run on the ships.

Another hour passed with nothing but clouds below and clear skies above. Suddenly the squadron leader for the Blenheims broke silence and said that he had located the German fleet. He gave their direction and the bombers changed course to that heading. The German convoy was not far from where they were expected. The squadron leader of the Blenheims said that they were going to go in very low. Then he broke off the communication.

The flight commander for the Wellingtons said that since the clouds were breaking up a bit he was going to try to find the convoy through the clouds. He headed a bit north to where the convoy was supposed to be and saw them at a distance through a break in the clouds. That was when a fighter escort of Messerschmitts came out of the sun.

Paul saw one heading toward the squadron but had to wait until it got in range. While he was waiting he was surprised at how many fighter planes he saw. He concentrated on one and squeezed off both guns at the same time. The fighter continued to come. Then it exploded in a ball of fire. He picked out another that was getting too close and trained his guns on it. The Messerschmitt was shooting from guns located in the wings and Paul knew that some of the fire was hitting the Wellington. Then that fighter also exploded.

Paul heard in his earphones the order to disperse and scatter. The bombers headed for the clouds as instructed by the Wellington Squadron leader. While he was anxious to shoot down a few more German planes he knew that they were sitting ducks for the Messerschmitts. The thick clouds were welcomed. They never got close enough to drop their bombs. Before the bomber got lost in the clouds, Paul saw two Wellingtons that were on fire and smoking. He knew they would never make it back to base.

When they got home they looked at the damage. Numerous holes were seen in the fuselage but nothing vital was hit. A mechanic said he would have her fixed up in no time.

"She'll be good as new in a day or two," was the pronouncement from the Cockney mechanic.

They stood around the plane with their eyes toward the sky, listening and looking and waiting for the two planes that Paul saw smoking. No one was surprised when they never showed up. In a debriefing Paul found out that five of the ten Blenheims were shot down as well, all as they were attacking at very low altitudes. Obviously, they were sitting ducks as they attacked from such a low altitude.

A debriefing was held and the men received all the bad news. Not one German ship had been hit, the Allies lost seven bombers and damage was reported on most of the others. Opinions were asked and several of the pilots said that flying in weather like that made the operation very difficult. Others said that they were surprised by the attack of the Messerschmitts. Most of the pilots were doing the talking. The meeting was about to break up when Paul felt the need to say something. He stood up and didn't wait to be recognized.

"Our bombers are no match for Messerschmitts. We are like fish in a barrel for them. It isn't even close to being a fair fight. They are fast and we are slow. They can fly circles around us. We need to avoid them or have Spitfire protection. It is the same way when our Spitfires attack their bombers. We always win. Maybe we will shoot down a few but the Messerschmitts will defeat us every time."

"Do others feel the same way?" the Wing Commander asked. Everyone agreed.

Paul had not relinquished the floor and asked if he could make one more comment. Given permission, he expressed doubt that Wellingtons should even be flying during daylight hours. "We can fly at 22,000 feet, have a big payload of deadly bombs, can survive being hit by enemy fire and can even limp back to base when we are badly damaged. We might do best if we flew at night, traveling by good navigation."

Paul sat down. Several of the pilots told the wing commander to pass that on to headquarters, as bombers are vulnerable to enemy fighters during daytime missions.

Paul and several other gunners were singled out for recognition at the mess that evening. The men also bowed their heads and observed a moment of silence for the twelve men from the base who didn't return from the raid.

CHAPTER 19

September weather was very pleasant in the foothills of the Alps. There were no incidents with the occupiers in town although the atmosphere was tense. The arrogance of the German soldiers was extremely annoying to the villagers. Some of the soldiers were polite and were not in the village to cause trouble. It appeared to the villagers that the German soldiers were everywhere. They frequently came into the shop to buy bread. Annette was more the object of their attention than the bread, but even when a soldier spoke French she would keep the conversation on a business-like basis. The message she wanted to convey was that she was not interested in their attention.

Two soldiers drove up to the farmhouse one evening. Jacques and Annette were eating supper when they heard the car. They quickly got up and went outside. They were not accustomed to having visitors after sundown and it was already dusk. The two soldiers spoke only German and Annette understood his question. She didn't let on at all that she spoke German but rather answered in French pointing to the road. They were looking for the checkpoint but she didn't know which one. She pointed back to the road that they just came from and directed them to go right. She counted on her fingers to five and added the word 'kilometers.' She pointed ahead and counted to eight but shook her head to indicate that they shouldn't go that way. They would have liked to stay longer but Jacques remained at the door and Annette turned around and went inside. After the car turned around and went back the way it came, Jacques rejoined his daughter in the kitchen.

"Annette, you handled that well."

"I understood that they were lost and were looking for the checkpoint but didn't want them to know that I spoke German. Do you think they were fooled, Papa?"

"Yes. Using your fingers to count was smart. They will find the checkpoint and we'll never see them again."

"I hope you're right, Papa."

On a Sunday morning, after they returned from Mass, Annette told her father that she was going for a walk and might be late. He cautioned her to be careful and she nodded that she would. She was dressed in slacks and dark clothes as the weather in late September was sometimes chilly. Jacques knew she was headed for the woods and the mountain. She fixed a lunch for herself and put a flashlight in her sack. They had been smuggling three or four children a week into Switzerland and hadn't encountered any patrols as yet. She wanted to know if there were patrols and how frequently they patrolled the border.

"Papa, I'm concerned about German patrols by the stream on this side of the border. I can tell that they have been using that path but don't know how often. I'm wondering if they patrol randomly, or every hour or two hours. That will be useful information."

"Yes it would, Child. But it will take time. I'm glad you like the outdoors and know your way around the mountain so well. Still, be careful. Don't let them see you."

"I won't. I can blend in and remain as quiet and still as a mouse. They won't see me."

Annette took her usual route through and over the mountain and as she walked through the woods she tried to discern a path. She made a conscious effort to go a slightly different way each time so as not to trample down the bushes and undergrowth. At night it wasn't easy to see small plants and bushes. She noticed a few small branches that were snapped but they were really unnoticeable and one might reasonably conclude that a falling branch could have been the cause. Only an experienced tracker could have spotted a trail.

She thought about her father calling her "child." She wanted to tell him that she wasn't a child anymore. Yet she was his child and would always be his child. He didn't treat her like a child and if she were to admit it, she liked the diminutive. It defined their relationship and was for her father an expression of affection. The more she thought about it the more she approved of being called "child" and it would hurt her father if she told him she didn't want him to call her by that name. So as long as he didn't use it to put her down or in front of others, she would enjoy being his child and he would be the only one who could call her that. That resolved, she put her mind to the task for the day.

When she came to the stream she walked along it for a way toward the west. It was full and running quite rapidly. She found a bit of mud and smeared it over her forehead, nose and cheeks. She had a dark bandana that she tied around her neck and she pulled her hat down to cover her forehead. A distance from her usual crossing spot there was a very shallow but wide place to cross. One could step on flat rocks and cross without getting wet. She tried it both ways and wished that there were one more rock in the stream. That would make it very easy for a little child to cross. That would be her next project.

She started back to where she had come and heard voices in the distance. They were coming from the checkpoint closest to their farm. She didn't have to go very far to find a hiding place in the woods. There was a big tree that would hide her well about fifty yards from the path. Behind the tree was a clump of bushes that she squatted behind. She was certain that she was invisible from the path the soldiers were on.

The two passed without even a glance in her direction. Rifles were slung over their shoulders and they continued to talk. She made note of the time. It was eleven-fifteen. She decided to stay where she was and eat some of her lunch to see if they would return. About a half hour later she heard and saw the same two coming back. After they were gone she returned to the path they had traveled. It now looked like it was fairly well used. It was obvious that these patrols traveled on it every day. She wondered if they patrolled at night. If they did, they would have to use a flashlight, which would alert anyone in the area. That would defeat their purpose in patrolling. Annette concluded that they wouldn't attempt to patrol after dark.

While walking along the stream Annette found a flat rock in the woods that she thought might make her crossing complete. It was heavy but she could carry it without too much difficulty if she kept it close to her body. She first got some leaves to fill in the place where the rock had been, making the area look very natural. It was a lot farther to her new crossing than she expected and the rock was heavy. She was forced to put it down and rest for a few minutes before she continued on.

When she reached the shallow place she saw that this rock would complete the crossing perfectly. Since it had been in the woods it had moss on it and was dirty. She took off her shoes and socks, rolled up her slacks and carried the rock to the place where she wanted it placed. She buried it securely in the sand and used sand to clean off the rock. When she finished it looked like it belonged and in a few moments the water was running clear again, giving the rock the appearance that it had been there a long time.

Annette went back into the woods to where she felt safe from any patrols and ate some lunch. The spot she found would allow her to see a very small portion of the trail and pine straw provided her a place to lie down. She closed her eyes and was asleep within minutes. The sound of men's voices woke her. It sounded like the same two who had passed earlier. It was now almost one-fifteen. She estimated that they were following a two-hour interval and if she knew the Germans they would be precise. Right on time they made the return trip a half hour later.

Annette spent the rest of the day enjoying the woods. She heard the three o'clock patrol pass by at three-fifteen and the five o'clock patrol at five-fifteen. When they were safely down the trail she started her journey home, pleased with her new crossing and with her understanding of the German patrols. She noticed that dusk came much earlier now and since she didn't get home from the bakery until after six, her trips across the border with the children would be later. The next time she smuggled children she would have to tell the handlers on the Swiss side about her new schedule.

She described to her father how she moved a flat rock into the stream to make a second crossing and said that if they went together again she would show it to him. That would be best done in the daytime. For now he should continue using the usual crossing. But even while she said the words she knew that the trip over the mountain and back was too much for her father. While he was only fifty-five years old his health had not been good for some time. He was also about thirty pounds overweight. He had high blood pressure and had suffered several heart attacks. Yet he refused to give up the work at the bakery. He was the village baker and would be until he died.

Annette anticipated that her father could make the trip in an emergency but that she would be the one who would be smuggling the children across the border on a consistent basis. She knew that if she got caught her father's life would be taken along with hers. It was rumored that the Bosch executed those on the spot who were violating their decrees. A public hanging in the town square was meant to deter others from similar behavior. A firing squad was an alternate form of punishment. Annette and Jacques both understood the risk and the consequences. Still they would not be able to sleep at night if they refused to help these children.

CHAPTER 20

It was dawn when the ten Wellingtons made their way down the runway and passed through thin clouds into a bright blue sky. The planes flew at its ceiling of 22,000 feet and were headed for Hamburg. All eyes were on the lookout for German fighter planes. They didn't encounter any until they approached the German coast near Bremerhaven. When they showed up they were as thick as mosquitoes. Even though Squadron #424 had teamed up with two other squadrons it was obvious that they were outnumbered and outgunned.

Paul shot down two more Messerschmitts and hit another. He saw it smoking and heading for home. This time there were no clouds to save them and the squadron commander radioed for fighter help, knowing full well that they already had all the help they would get. The Wellingtons dropped their bombs on Hamburg but didn't stay around to see how much damage they inflicted. They continued to be harassed by the German fighters and saw Messerschmitts attacking in large numbers any plane that was smoking or not flying as fast as the squadron. They were like hyenas attacking a wounded impala. Paul could see that their squadron would lose two more bombers.

In the post operation debriefing, Paul again expressed his opinion. "This is foolish to allow the Germans to shoot us out of the sky so easily, especially when we know what to expect. It's easy for them to destroy our bombers. Soon we won't have an air force to stop them."

It seemed to be the feeling of all the men that flying in daylight was asking for trouble and was stacking the odds in favor of the Luftwaffe.

Several pilots were chosen to speak with the wing commander, which they immediately did. The wing commander promised the airmen that he would make a protest as strong as possible and that he would advise the high command that the bombers should fly only at night.

Several days later, after losing two more bombers, new planes and crews were sent to replace them. Six of the original twelve bombers had been lost. The absence of their mates weighed heavily on the others. Finally the airmen were told that night flying was approved. The burden of reaching targets now became dependent on the ability of each navigator. It was he who had to plot distance, airspeed, wind, weather and topography to find the target. Anything was better than daytime flying.

The first evening that the bombers attacked Mannheim they were not expected by the Luftwaffe and so had a relatively easy time reaching the target. There was a slight moon and this helped them navigate and they left a flaming industrial city behind. The second night they met with more fighter planes than the first and resistance was a bit stiff. The Messerschmitts couldn't see the Wellingtons as well as they would have liked and the bombers couldn't see the fighter planes clearly. Paul got a clear kill as a Messerschmitt exploded in front of him, lighting up the night sky.

The bombers that were hit the most were those that couldn't fly high. Flak from antiaircraft guns was able to reach those planes with deadly accuracy. The Germans were also putting spotlights near strategic targets. A spotlight would search the night sky for a bomber and when one was spotted a dozen spotlights would be turned on and trained on it. That bomber became an easy target for the guns and for the fighter planes. The Wellingtons were able to stay above the flak and only had to contend with the fighter planes. By attacking different targets each night and using a variety of paths to get to the destination forced the Germans to guess where the bombers would show up. They were often wrong.

The Wellington squadrons would have liked to have more RAF fighter planes like the Spitfire to cover them but they were engaged in defending the country from the blitz. German bombers would drop their payload on London almost every night and the Spitfires would attempt to stop as many as possible. It was increasingly becoming an air war and air superiority would determine the outcome. There were only so many aircraft at the present time and many more were needed.

Paul was promoted to corporal in recognition of his successes shooting down six German fighter planes. Several of the men told him that they were proud that he spoke up at the briefings even though he wasn't an officer. He enjoyed the recognition but hoped that he wouldn't be labeled a troublemaker.

September turned to October and the successes of the Wellingtons increased. The German countered with an early warning system of radar to alert their fighters to the nightly raids and the British became more skillful at shooting the fighters down. Nevertheless, both sides were incurring serious loses and it was difficult to keep up morale when almost every few days a plane was lost. The Wellingtons had one big advantage over many other bombers in that they were built using a geodesic pattern on the fuselage. Bullets would often penetrate and pass through the plane, leaving two holes and doing no structural damage to the plane whatsoever. Some planes returned to base so chewed up and cosmetically damaged that it seemed like a miracle that they were able to survive. Two days later they would be patched up and ready for flight.

Paul's squadron was given leave for two full days the first week of October. Paul hoped that he could spend the time with Dorothy North. She wanted to spend the time with him but first had to get Wing Commander Holliday's permission. She simply told him that she too needed a break, and with the squadron gone this would be as good a time as any. She suspected that he knew about her relationship with Paul but never said anything to her about it. Her boss agreed that she should also take time off.

CHAPTER 21

The village of Faymont consisted of a town square with the main street running from north to south. There were six shops north of the village square and the same number south of the square. The bakery was between the wine and cheese shops. Across the street were the butcher, the tailor and the grocery store. These were all south of the square. On the north side was the hardware store, the cobbler, a barber, a furniture shop, and a small café. The jewelry store and gift shop, which was also the post office, completed all the businesses around the square. All other services and business took place in nearby Audincourt. The bakery was receiving more than its fair share of business.

"Annette, you are receiving a lot of attention from the soldiers."

"I know, Papa. What can I do about it?"

"You can stop being so nice." After a moment's hesitation he continued, "I'm afraid that would only cause trouble."

"Why don't you handle the lunch crowd?" she suggested. "That's when most of the soldiers come in to buy bread. I'll work in the back for that hour."

"That's a good idea. Once they find out that you are not available I don't think we will have as many customers."

Several days later Jacques mentioned to Annette that on more than one occasion a soldier would come into the bakery, and when he saw Jacques behind the counter, would leave. It was obvious they wanted to deal with the pretty one.

Annette handled the bakery from three to six and she would usually have several soldiers as customers during that time. Most of the soldiers didn't speak French and Annette never gave any indication that she understood a word they were saying when they spoke German. Sign language was the accepted form of speech. A few soldiers spoke some French, but they were usually polite and actually came into the store to buy bread. She did notice that several of the soldiers were very bold, and she was wary of them. One in particular would make smutty remarks, and while she understood what he said and wanted to say something sharp to him, she held her tongue and gave no indication that she understood.

One evening at closing time she noticed a vehicle down the street with two soldiers sitting in it. She suspected that their purpose was to spy on her. She didn't want them to know where she lived. She considered the possibility of sleeping in the shop but there was no way to notify her father. She didn't want him to worry. This was a situation that they would have to talk about.

Annette hatched a plan quickly. She decided to bring her bicycle into the back room and turn off the lights like she was closing. When the vehicle would leave to observe her leaving by the back door she would go out the front door. A very narrow alley across from the shop between the tailor and the grocery store would conceal her and her bicycle and she could observe what the soldiers intended to do.

She turned out the lights and in the darkness observed the vehicle move past the shop and around the corner. She quickly got her bike, and went outside and pulled the door locked behind her. It was a very short distance to the alley and she covered the distance in several seconds. She was able to quietly move an empty trashcan into the opening and crouch behind it.

It was several minutes before the soldiers realized they had been deceived. They continued driving without lights. They headed south on the road that Annette would usually take. Five minutes later they returned through town with the headlights on, obviously headed for their quarters north of town. Only then did Annette feel safe to come out of hiding and ride her bicycle home.

After supper she spoke with her father about the incident. He was furious and threatened to shoot every last one of the "Boche bastards." But Annette had another plan.

"Papa, if you shoot one of those soldiers you will only bring repercussions on us and what we are trying to do to help the children. Maybe we can get some identification as to who they are. Perhaps we can get a vehicle number and their rank and report them to the German major."

"That could possibly work. The Boche don't seem to want to cause trouble with the villagers and maybe a sympathetic commander will understand that we are just trying to survive."

"I have an idea as to how to get the identification. I know them from their rude behavior in the store and they are of low rank. If I don't come home at the usual time you can be certain that I'm locked in the store. I'll bring a blanket and can sleep on the sacks of flour. It won't kill me for one night. Once they're gone, I'll come home."

"Annette, you're brave, but please be careful. I don't want you getting hurt. If you do, I'll just have to shoot as many of those bastards as possible," Jacques said with a twinkle in his eye as he placed a hand on her arm.

Annette knew that her father would do everything in his power to keep her from harm and would visit vengeance on those who harmed her. His life would mean nothing if he could kill those who harmed his little girl. Of that she was certain and it was up to her to make sure that she remained safe. It would mean saving the life of her father as well.

The following day was normal until about a half hour before closing. Annette saw the vehicle waiting in its usual spot. She had no customers and so busied herself with moving the bread from the back room to the display rack. Several times she went into the back room and each time stayed a bit longer. The soldiers in the vehicle could only see a portion of the store and would have to move closer to see the entire bakery.

After being in the front of the store for a while she disappeared into the back room, left out the back door, raced behind other stores to the corner and to the street. She came out on the square about twenty feet from the rear of the vehicle. The license plate was clearly visible. Annette memorized the number and raced back to the store, bringing her bicycle in with her. She wrote the license plate number on a piece of paper and hid the paper in the cash box.

At quitting time she went through her usual routine, locking the door and turning off the lights. She observed the vehicle go only as far as the corner where the soldiers could watch the main street and a side street. But they couldn't watch behind the other stores. After a few minutes she heard someone try the back door and in a moment the vehicle turned around and went back through town. She knew that she would be able to dupe them only so many times and that they were getting increasingly frustrated. It was time to consider going to their superior.

CHAPTER 22

Jacques and Annette rode their bicycles to the barracks and requested to see the commanding officer. The guard on duty didn't seem to understand French. They waited while the guard went inside to find out how he should proceed. Obviously, not many French civilians came to visit the barracks. The guard returned with a soldier with three stripes on his arm and he introduced himself as Oberfeldwebel Wilhelm Schmidt. He was a tall soldier who spoke excellent French and escorted them to the main building directly ahead of them. Annette recognized him as having visited the bakery. She remembered that he bought several loaves of bread. They waited for a few minutes and were then ushered in to see the commanding officer, Major Fritz Decker, according to the nicely handcrafted wooden nameplate on his desk.

"How may I help you?" inquired the major in perfect French.

"I am Jacques LeVoie and this is my daughter, Annette. We own the bakery in town. Several of your soldiers have been stalking my daughter and even went so far as to attempt to enter the rear door of our shop, after hours," Jacques began. "It happens when my daughter is taking care of the store by herself, usually at quitting time." He allowed an uncomfortable pause, and then continued. "Do you have children, Major?"

"Yes, two."

"Is one a girl?"

"Yes."

"Then you would understand my concern if something were to happen to my daughter. And my concern would extend beyond me to this entire village. Annette grew up in this village and is known by everyone. The villagers have all had a hand in watching her grow up. Your soldiers would find themselves hated and in danger because of the actions of these two. We are simple country people who make bread for our fellow villagers. We don't want to make trouble…but your men will not harm my daughter." He said the last eight words slowly and with conviction.

Annette reached into the pocket of her dress and pulled out a piece of paper with the license number of the vehicle the two soldiers were driving.

"I can identify the two soldiers who were driving this vehicle and parked outside the bakery waiting for me to leave," said Annette. "It was the taller of the two who is causing most of the trouble."

The major waited until he was certain that they had nothing more to say. "I can assure you that this matter will be taken care of and that you will not be bothered again. I also appreciate that you didn't take matters into your own hands."

"That's all we want, Major," said Jacques.

"And we want a good relationship with the village. We are here in a spirit of brotherhood and don't want to cause any harm. This matter will be taken care of."

He asked his secretary to escort them to the gate. The baker and his daughter walked with their bicycles to the gate where they got on their bicycles and started the journey back to town.

Annette and Jacques pedaled back toward the bakery in silence. About half way to town they stopped under a tree, and Jacques asked Annette how she thought the meeting had gone. She expressed the thought that the major was sincere, and that they might not have any more trouble.

"I was pleased with your diplomacy, Papa. You were eloquent and I believe the Major thought so, also."

"Thank you, Annette. As you know, I love my little girl and don't want any harm to come to her. I wanted the Major to know that."

"I know that, and always have." After a moment she added, "I think that one of the soldiers can be trusted but I'm not so certain about the tall one. He has a mean streak in him."

"I'm glad you recognize that, Child. Some people just never learn."

"I'll be very careful, Papa."

"I don't want to have to shoot every Boche in town," he joked as they continued their journey back to the shop.

Annette knew that he wasn't kidding.

CHAPTER 23

Dorothy picked Paul up at the entrance to the base shortly after seven that evening. She drove her 1937 Jaguar SS 100 that she had not used in several months. It had been her husband's car. Petrol was rationed and she was saving her coupons for an occasion, and this was it. An evening spent at Dorothy's cottage was a treat for Paul, not having to return to base by midnight.

In the morning they drove to a mountain hideaway that belonged to Dorothy's friend. All it took was one phone call to her friend and she was told where the key was hidden. No questions were asked. Dorothy had been to the cabin previously. She had no trouble finding her way. Paul wisely made no comment about her being familiar with the cabin location.

They stopped in a nearby village and purchased a few provisions. Eggs, bread, sliced ham and cheese, and several bottles of wine were bought. Then Dorothy drove the Jaguar up a dirt road to a cabin nestled deep in a stand of pines at the top of a small mountain. It was a beautiful spot for a retreat.

For both Paul and Dorothy the afternoon and evening in the cabin was precious. They began to unwind and to tell each other so many things that they couldn't express while they were involved with work on the base.

Sitting before the fire with a glass of wine in their hand, Dorothy said, "Paul, do you have any idea how much I worry about you?" She waited for an answer that never came. "If your plane is not one of the first four or five to return, I fear the worse. I hear another plane land and I have to look out to see if it's yours. If it isn't, I start to shake."

"Don't let it get to you like that. I know that this is dangerous business, and one of these days my plane might not return. We have to be prepared for that."

"I don't believe I could handle it if you didn't return."

"Yes, you would," said Paul as he reached for her hand. "You are strong and you would miss me for a time but you would get on with your life. We knew that before we got involved with each other. Besides, if I get shot down I'll find a way to swim or crawl home."

They talked late that night, finished the bottle of wine and made love until they were exhausted. After breakfast the next morning, they stood on the cabin porch to watch the sun rise while they drank coffee. Later, they talked while they roamed in the woods and reached a high rock that gave them a good view of the valley below. They sat there and talked some more. Speech flowed freely for both of them, having been deprived of intimate conversation for so long. They were comfortable in each other's presence. They knew that this was as close as they were going to get toward a commitment. It was all either of them knew that they could have or wanted.

That evening Dorothy cooked up a nice meal from the food they bought in town. After supper they sat on the rug in front of the fire and drank the second bottle of red wine. Then they made love without moving from the rug. When they were exhausted they covered themselves with a blanket and slept until sunlight flooded the room. Then they made love again.

The two days of being together did wonders for them. They could feel the tension go out of their bodies and the rest and relaxation made them feel alive. Their lovemaking was wonderful. The time moved all too swiftly and soon they were packing their belongings to head back to the base. Dorothy dropped Paul off at the gate shortly after dark. Both were sorry to be parted.

All the other bunks were filled with sleeping airmen except his bunk. That was a bit unusual for so early in the evening. Paul wondered if they had been alerted to a change in schedule. He suspected that they were told earlier to get some sleep since they might be called into action during the night. Without turning on a light, relying on the sparse light from outside, he removed his shoes, shirt and pants and climbed into his bunk. Moments after his head touched the pillow he was asleep.

It was a little after midnight when the lights were turned on in the Nissan huts and everyone was awakened. It seems an opportunity had come up and the squadron was pressed into action. They didn't return any too soon from their two-day leave. Paul was thankful that he got at least several hours sleep. While the crew prepared for their jobs, the navigators and pilots got briefed. Then they told the rest of the crew what was going to happen. This raid was a bit unusual.

The squadron was to fly southwest over the Channel and south out over the Atlantic until they reached Nantes. They would then fly east, just south of Nantes, till they reached their target. The Germans had a new weapon called radar but its use was limited at this time and this city was not equipped with one. The weather was wicked over Germany and no resistance was expected. The front was moving south and the squadron was anticipating some clearing about the time they reached Stuttgart. The navigators on each bomber were busy calculating the time from the Rhein River to the target. Paul was told that they were to attack a factory just south of Stuttgart that was making tanks and armored vehicles.

The trip over the channel and then south parallel to the coast of France was uneventful. The Germans didn't expect any activity because of the weather but everyone expected it to clear about four in the morning, just before dawn. If that prediction held, they should have little trouble hitting their target. As they flew across France the weather became more turbulent and when they neared the Rhein the clouds were only starting to break up. The front had not moved in as quickly as predicted. There was no resistance but they would have to lower their altitude if they were to find the factory.

Under the clouds, coming into the first light of dawn, they saw Stuttgart dead ahead. Paul could see everything in front of him and soon found the location of the factory. The flak from antiaircraft guns was light until they almost reached their target and prepared to drop all the bombs. As the flak became heavier the plane shook as they dropped their load and started to climb into the clouds.

A burst from an antiaircraft shell hit the plane in the rear section of the fuselage. The plane bucked and dropped several hundred feet before the pilot could regain control. There was a second burst behind Paul, close to where the bombs had been stored. He was thankful they had been dropped.

Paul was told to get out of his forward gunnery position. He grabbed a fire extinguisher along the way and used it to put out the fire in the bomb bay, holding on to make sure he wasn't sucked out. One of the doors to the bay was no longer in place.

The pilot managed to steady the plane and it started climbing but ever so slowly as the pilot turned it toward the south, away from the guns and into the clouds.

"Is anyone hurt?" asked the co-pilot.

Several answered that they were all right but there were two big holes in the plane. One shell hit the bomb bay and the other shell damaged the tail and just missed the rear gunner. The plane was filled with smoke but now that the fire was out it was becoming less as clean air moved through the open bay and out the hole in the fuselage.

The co-pilot left the cockpit and came to see the damage for himself. "We're heading south toward Switzerland but the storm is directly in front of us. We're being forced to go west over France. That area is under German occupation. Get ready to parachute, just in case."

The four not flying the plane buckled their parachutes a bit tighter as the chutes were put on several hours before. Now they waited for further orders. The plane was not stable and was barely under control. The weather was playing havoc with the bomber making it difficult to gain altitude. Paul wondered how much longer it would remain in the air. The rudder was damaged and the pilot had to fight just to keep the plane flying. The bomber was enveloped in heavy clouds and there was no visibility.

The pilot was having trouble keeping the plane on course even though the western course was not as turbulent. Gradually the plane began to gain altitude. Paul's assessment did not change. He was certain that the bomber could not make it back to England.

"I'm flying west as there is too much weather south of us," echoed the voice of the pilot through the speakers. "We won't make Switzerland. We are minutes from France, someplace south of Mulhouse, not too far from the Swiss border. Head southwest to get into Switzerland. We're going to try to make it back to England but our chances are not good. Your best chance is to try to make it to Switzerland. I'll tell you when we are out of

Germany. It's up to you whether you want to jump or try to make it home with the plane."

Two of the men, the bombardier and navigator, said they would stay, at least until they determined if the plane would make it home. The other gunner, a corporal by the name of Harold Dickson, said he would take his chances on the ground. Paul said that he would, also.

"Jump about a minute apart so if you're caught you won't be able to tell the Germans where the other person is. We're about two minutes from being in France if our calculations are correct."

Paul and Corporal Dickson moved toward the bomb bay. There was a big hole in it and one of the doors was torn off. The noise from the rushing air outside caused them to shout in order to be heard.

"Dickson, do you want to go first? Paul yelled.

"No, I'd rather be second. I want to make sure I'm in France."

"I'll go first, then. Stay away from the opening where the door was so you don't snag yourself on the cut metal," Paul suggested.

"Thirty seconds till we cross the Rhein!" shouted the co-pilot.

In the heavy clouds the river was invisible from the air. "What's our altitude? Paul inquired.

"About four thousand feet. That's not too high so pull the cord when you're free of the plane. The ground can be very rough if you hit a hilly spot. There are mountains and it is heavily wooded according to the map. Good luck."

"We're in France. Go whenever you're ready," said the co-pilot's voice over the speakers. The two who were about to jump waited another minute.

Paul looked at Harold, gave him the thumbs up sign, made the sign of the cross as he dropped off into the darkness below.

CHAPTER 24

The noise of the plane was fading even as Paul pulled the ripcord and felt the harness tighten around him. He could see absolutely nothing but could feel the wet moisture of the cloud on his face. He didn't know when he was going to reach the ground and so was straining to see through the dense fog that enveloped him. The world had become eerily silent. He prepared himself for the landing, his eyes searching for a tree line or the darkness of the earth but it didn't come. As he began to relax, the ground surprised him and hit him hard.

His first instinct was to scream when he experienced pain in his left leg. He didn't know it but he could have screamed until he was hoarse, and he would have been the only one who would have heard. He drew himself into a fetal position and tried to recover the parachute. He was fortunate in that there was little wind and unfortunate in that it was raining.

As he pulled the parachute together and escaped from the harness, the pain in his calf was starting to subside. It hurt when he attempted to put weight on his leg, and he knew for certain that he would have difficulty walking. For the present, he simply pulled the parachute over himself to keep off the rain. He was also cold, and the cloth of the parachute was the only hedge against the cold and wet.

Paul slept, but only for a short time. The rock beneath him made for a very hard bed. His airman's jacket provided some warmth and cushion to the rock but his trousers did little to keep his hips from hurting. When he finally did stick his head out from beneath his cover, there was some light, no rain and less fog. At least there was some visibility, but not enough to allow him to explore. He returned to his makeshift bed, changed his position and promptly fell asleep.

The next sensation was of warmth and bright light. He peeked out and was greeted by blinding sunshine. The sun was a good bit over the horizon and had burned off the fog. He tried to stand but found that he needed assistance. He crawled to a nearby rock and leaned on it to get himself upright. He could stand and even take steps as long as he put down only the toe of his left foot. He had pulled or torn the calf muscles and he could feel pain from his ankle to just above his knee. The leg was swollen.

Paul gingerly walked back to the parachute and saw puddles of rainwater in the folds and creases. Carefully lifting the corners of the parachute to make the puddles run together into one big puddle, he was amazed at how much water was collected. Using his hands for a cup, he drank deeply. He found that he could raise himself if he used only his right leg. He realized that it would be a lot easier if he had a stick for support.

A heavy forest with some very tall pine trees surrounded the slab of rock which now comprised his world. Paul felt fortunate that his parachute didn't land high up in one of the pine trees. What is a pulled muscle compared with being stranded high in a tree swinging in the wind for the enemy to see? His was not the worst predicament.

An overhanging rock near the edge of the woods offered some protection from the elements. He found a stick that turned to a ninety-degree angle and used his knife to cut off the part that wasn't useful. He tucked it under his arm like a crutch. It took several tries to get the height correct. It would do until a better one could be found. As he searched around his little area of rock, he wondered if he was truly in French territory and was thankful that he didn't land outside a German barracks. At least here he was safe while he searched for food. His leg needed time to heal if he was to do any walking.

Paul returned to the parachute and moved it over to the overhanging rock, all the while taking care not to spill the water. He found a small depression and used his knife to cut up the parachute. He cut a three-foot square piece of nylon and lined the depression. Then he poured the water that was on the parachute into the hole. He used some of the rope to tie the top of the lining, protecting the water from the bugs. At least he wouldn't be thirsty for a few days.

He took the remainder of the parachute and cut it in half. It was quite large, much more than he had anticipated. He placed half the parachute on the overhang and secured it there with a few rocks. The rest of that piece draped over the front of the overhang and a few small rocks neatly held it in place. His tent, of sorts, was sufficient to shelter him from the elements. The other half of the parachute would be his blanket.

Paul's leg was throbbing and he was in serious pain when he finished rigging up the shelter. Yet the inside of his makeshift home was cool since the rock had stored the cool from the night before. For October the weather was still quite warm. Paul was forced to rest his leg for a while before he limped to the nearby woods to cut some pine bowers for a bed.

He also found the remnants of several wild berries but the birds had gotten to most of them. He found some ferns and cut one that was just emerging. It was edible and satisfied his hunger. While in the woods he searched around and found several wild pear trees that had some fruit left on them. With his homemade cane he was able to knock down three pears that had not yet fallen.

Late that afternoon, having nothing to do, Paul made a net from the nylon cords attached to the parachute. He had seen several squirrels and rabbits on his travels and felt that a net might be just the tool to capture one. He realized that getting food for his body might be his biggest challenge while his leg healed. There was plenty of cord and even with less than two inches between the openings, he knew he would have plenty left over. He began by attaching the strands of the parachute to a long stick and then knotting a horizontal cord every few inches. By nightfall he had a nice sized net completed and attached to a second stick. He ate a pear for supper and fell asleep just after the sun set. He was happy just to be alive.

CHAPTER 25

Dorothy arrived at her desk several hours before the first four planes landed. She had been awakened in the middle of the night by the sound of the Wellingtons taking off. After she left Paul at the gate she presumed that everyone would get a good night's sleep and would resume duties in the morning. Once she heard the roar of the bombers she knew she was wrong. She didn't like the ominous feelings that she was experiencing.

With her third cup of coffee in her hand, she went to the window and nervously watched as two more planes landed. Paul's bomber was not among them.

The words, "Paul, where are you?" escaped ever so quietly from her lips.

A half hour later, a plane that had been severely damaged, landed. Another landed with just one landing gear and skidded to a stop at the end of the runway. That was eight of the ten planes that returned and still Paul was not among them.

With each passing minute she knew that the chances of Paul returning were diminishing. By noon she had accepted the worst. Her stomach was in knots and her heart was breaking. Her boss, Commander Hugh Holladay came out from his office and spoke to Dorothy.

"Please take the afternoon off, Dorothy. I can get along without you. I know that Paul meant something to you and I really don't need you here this afternoon."

"Thank you, Commander. I will. And thank you again."

Dorothy rode her bicycle home with tears clouding her vision. She could barely see the road. She leaned her bicycle against the side of the house, fumbled for the front door key and had difficulty placing the key in the lock. Once inside she locked the door and took out a bottle of sherry from the cabinet. She poured three fingers in a tumbler and downed that in one gulp. Then she poured the same amount a second time. She held up the glass before her first sip and said, "To Paul. I wish you well." Then the tears came and she sat down on the sofa and cried loudly into the pillow. Between crying and drinking sherry she passed the afternoon and didn't bother to make supper. She just continued drinking until the bottle was empty, and she had passed out on the sofa, still in her clothes.

She awoke in the morning with a dreadful headache. That was no surprise. She took three aspirin, let the hot water wash over her in the shower, put on fresh clothes and had a breakfast of toast and coffee. She pedaled her bicycle to work as if nothing had happened. Her boss greeted her as usual and she went about the day as if it were a typical day. What she did was done without thinking or concern. She was enclosed in her own world and was experiencing her own private loss.

She spent the next few days depressed and barely able to type and file. She wanted to go home and sleep. Her boss understood and was tolerant, not requesting that she do more than she was capable of doing. Finally, four days after she realized that Paul was gone she found that her work was returning to her standards. She didn't know that she would take the loss so hard. She was beginning to understand that she would have to pick herself up and get on with it.

A week later the wing commander was making an inspection of several new planes when a young airman asked to see him.

"I'm sorry. The wing commander is gone for about an hour. Could you return about eleven?"

"Yes, I suppose I can.

"May I tell him who called?" asked Dorothy.

"Tell him that Charles Nottingham wished to speak with him concerning a better route to one of our targets. I'm a navigator and I think I know of a safer route to Frankfurt. I'll try to be here at eleven.

After Charles Nottingham had his meeting with the wing commander he stopped for a minute to thank Dorothy for her assistance.

"I did nothing. But I'm glad you got to see the wing commander. Anything we can do to make the trip over Germany safer would be helpful. If your suggestion saves one plane it will be well worth the visit."

"You were very helpful," he said nervously, looking for words that would allow him to keep talking to this nice lady.

"Do you mind if I ask you? When is the last time you've had a nice home-cooked meal?"

"Not recently," the navigator replied.

"Would you like a home-cooked meal?"

"I sure would. How can I get one?"

CHAPTER 26

Heavy fog covered the countryside. The sun eventually broke through, and burned the fog off earlier than the day before. Paul searched for food in ever widening circles. He found an apple tree about a third of the way down the hill, and noticed several more in the same vicinity. The tree he reached first still had quite a few apples on it. These he truly enjoyed and he filled his pockets with them. He also found a straight stick that bent and tucked up neatly under his arm. It gave him better support and he spent most of the morning whittling away to make it fit. He was sitting and whittling on the overhanging slab that had become his home, when he noticed a rabbit below. When the rabbit saw him move, he ran. Paul went under the overhang and got the net that he made, put some pear and apple cores where the rabbit had been and brought the net to the top of the overhang. He tried throwing the net and after a few tries was able to cover a considerable area. All the exercise tired him considerably as walking with his leg constantly bent was a strain. But at least he could get around. It was time for some rest.

Paul awoke from a short nap and saw the rabbit eating the cores. Just raising himself on his elbow scared the animal away. He ate an apple and dropped the core with the others. He remained quiet on the overhang. It wasn't long before the rabbit returned. Paul waited until he was engrossed in eating the cores before he threw the net and it landed perfectly.

"Now, that was a good throw," he said out loud.

He used a rock to kill the rabbit. After skinning and gutting the critter, he made a small fire and cooked him. While he didn't smoke, he carried a cigarette lighter just as every airman would carry a knife. The meat tasted wonderful and he even had enough left over for another meal.

Before the sun went down, Paul made a mental note of the points on the compass. He found a spot where he could see a bit of the countryside and saw some smoke rising from what he presumed were houses in the east. He had glanced at the navigator's map when they were in the plane, but that map was of little use now. He needed to know exactly where he was. He would let his leg heal, and when he could walk he would go southeast. He was concerned that he might walk right up to a German barracks or a checkpoint and spend the rest of the war in a POW camp.

"Where will I find a map?" he asked himself. "How can I get from wherever I am into Switzerland without ending up in a camp?"

The next two days were much like the two before except that it rained one evening and Paul was able to collect more rainwater using his parachute as the collector. He also caught the mate to his first rabbit. His stomach felt satisfied with his meal of rabbit, pear, apple and fresh ferns. His leg didn't hurt as much and he was getting around fairly well, even though he still couldn't extend his leg. He would have to walk on the toes of his left foot for a few days longer. He suspected but didn't want to admit that it might be quite some time before it would be completely healed.

On the fifth day of self-imposed exile on the slab of rock, that was more a hill than a mountain, Paul decided that it was time to make his way southeast toward Switzerland. He wanted to know where he was and just how far it was to the border. Getting across the border would be his next achievement. He buried the parachute under pine needles, saving the piece that he used for a blanket. He also took the water with him. Several quarts were left. Getting down off the slab was difficult but he took it slow and used his crutch to good advantage.

Eventually, he came to a road that went east and west. It was early afternoon. Rather than walk on the road he stayed in the woods and walked parallel to the road. He saw two German military vehicles going east and one horse and wagon going west. He was glad that he wasn't walking on the road, as he wouldn't have had time to get off the road and hide. He rested for a while and in the late afternoon continued traveling east. He came to a crossroad and saw signs on it. From the woods he couldn't read the signs. He listened for the sounds of vehicles for a moment then hurried to the wooden sign. There was just enough light to read the faded directions.

He saw an arrow pointing east that said, "Della 7km." A second arrow pointing south read, "Beaucourt 2km." It looked like there had previously been several more signs on the post but these were missing. Paul was fairly certain that he was in France and decided to go south because the road was much smaller and likely to be less traveled. He also wanted to walk on the road instead of in the woods. Once it became dark, walking in the woods would be difficult.

A beautiful harvest moon presented itself on the horizon and soon gave Paul plenty of light to see his way on the roads. He saw the lights of Beaucourt in the distance and was surprised at how large the town appeared. He knew that he would have to avoid the village, being dressed in his airman's uniform. His greatest fear was that dogs would signal his presence by barking. But the village was dark, and everyone seemed to be inside their homes. He found a small dirt road that appeared to skirt the town, and was able to pass the one house on that road with caution. On the far side of town the road took a turn to the west, and Paul knew he didn't want to go that way. A dirt road that continued south was his other choice if he was to avoid the town. Since he didn't see anything ahead of him except fields on one side and woods on the other, he took the dirt road. He felt so lost without a map.

The dirt road was only about a kilometer long before it met with another road that was going southeast. After a few meters the road forked and Paul had to make another big decision. So far he had been taking the smaller of the two roads and it worked out well. So he did it again and continued south on a poorly defined dirt road. He felt a lot safer on the smaller road and it appeared to be deserted. After about an hour his leg was in considerable pain and needed some rest. The moon was now high overhead. He was able to read the hands of his watch and saw that it was just past ten-thirty. He had been walking for several hours. When he came to a stand of pine trees, he piled up some of the straw and made a bed, using the small piece of parachute as a blanket.

It was the cold that woke him several times during the night. His jacket kept him warm when walking but it didn't provide enough warmth for sleeping. As the sky was getting light, he brushed himself off, yearned for a cup of coffee, but settled for a drink of water and started walking. Keeping to the woods and heading south and east and parallel to the dirt road, he saw neither cars nor bicycles. What he did see was a wall of rock formations to his east, forming a formidable barrier. He wondered if he was getting close to Switzerland.

Several hours later he heard a car motor a short distance in front of him. The car was not visible because of the bushes and trees. He suspected that he was getting near a major road and possibly a checkpoint. His senses were on alert. He moved forward to where he could see a road and stopped behind some bushes. From there he saw another vehicle pass, going in the same direction but he still wasn't sure it was a German vehicle. He walked forward cautiously, keeping his head down in the tall grass and bushes. A few moments later it appeared that the same two vehicles were returning. Standing behind a pine tree, he recognized the German markings on the sides of the cars. Paul was certain that they were coming from a checkpoint and that he was close to the border.

After making sure no vehicles or soldiers were nearby, he crossed the road to the woods on the other side. There were woods on his right as well as his left with the rock formations behind the woods on his left. He felt safer in the woods and continued walking west. He passed several fields on his right that were fallow but the rock formations still loomed up on his left. Several times he moved toward the mountains to see if they were passable. He concluded that they weren't.

Eventually he reached a field next to the woods. A dirt road separated the field from a farm. He was looking for something to eat and hoped the farm would provide some food. He found a small turnip that had been overlooked. He used his knife to cut off the skin and while it didn't taste good, it did provide food for his growling stomach. While sitting on a rock and eating his breakfast he observed a barn and farmhouse in the distance. He sat in the shadows at the edge of the woods and decided that he might need some assistance getting across the border. Behind him were the woods and the ever present wall of rock. The brown barn off in the distance looked inviting.

Paul remained in the shadow of the woods walking parallel to a dirt road that was badly in need of repair. Several times he went deeper into the woods looking for an opening. Each time he was met by rock formations that didn't allow access over the mountain. Once he found an opening, but it led to a dead end in a narrow canyon. He continued, moving along the dirt road toward the woods behind the farm. When his leg began to tighten, he found a downed tree in the shadows and sat on it to rest. From there he observed to see if there was any activity in the farmhouse.

The field around the farmhouse appeared to be about forty acres and it was harvested and ready for the next planting. The house was set back from the road about two hundred feet, and a dirt driveway went past the house to the barn which was another hundred feet beyond the house. There were steps and a vestibule at the back of the house and a nice sized window faced the south. He presumed that was the kitchen. Around the house and barn were several maple trees and a small grove of fruit trees near the road. The house was painted white with brown trim. The barn had also been painted the same color brown as the trim. While he sat there finishing the last of the turnip, he observed no activity but realized that he had made several trips toward the rock formations and had been careless in his observations of the house.

The barn looked like it was in good condition. Paul stayed in the woods walking in the shadows to the back of the acreage and to the area directly behind the barn, where he couldn't be seen from the house. He walked the final hundred yards to the barn, pushed open the big doors enough to get inside and closed them behind him.

After his eyes adjusted to the darkness, he noticed that the barn was a good size and held some of the implements to plow, make furrows, rake and bale hay. The loft was half filled with loose hay and there were about thirty bales of hay on the floor of the barn. The loft looked like the perfect place to rest. But first, hearing chickens, he followed the sound to the chicken house. He found six eggs which he promptly devoured, dropping both the yoke and white of each egg directly into his mouth and swallowing it whole. He took the shells and buried them under some leaves by the side of the barn. With a full stomach he returned to the barn. It took more of an effort than Paul had anticipated climbing to the loft. It was not easy to climb when he couldn't put weight on one leg. He was forced to use his arms to keep the weight off that leg. Once there, he pulled a mound of hay in front of him and was asleep in minutes.

CHAPTER 27

Jacques returned from the bakery in the early afternoon. He made himself some lunch, had a cup of tea and rested on the couch for a short nap. The sound of the chickens making more noise than usual awakened him and he wondered if possibly a fox or snake was in the chicken coop. He'd check later. But he couldn't get back to sleep and so decided to check on the chickens.

All was quiet when he got to the barn. The hen house stood next to the barn and near a shed that Jacques built to house his tools, and provide a work area to do some of the chores that needed to be done. He checked the eggs, but didn't find any. He was certain that Annette must have gathered them before she left for work. Right now he had something else on his mind. He went about trying to find the knife he knew was in the shed. Below the working surface, on a shelf, he found it, hidden among his tools. It had a substantial blade of about four inches. He used a whetstone to sharpen it, snapped it closed and released the snap that opened the spring-loaded blade several times. He put a drop of oil on the release and repeated the procedure several more times. He then put the knife in his pocket and returned to the house.

Paul was listening and looking through the openings between the boards from his position in the loft. His stomach welcomed the six eggs but his head told him that he had made a mistake. He realized that he should have left several with the chickens. He saw the farmer go from the chicken coop to the shed and back to the farmhouse and he wondered if the farmer was suspicious. Paul decided that he would have to be more cautious in the future. He was pleased to see that the farmer didn't appear to have a dog with him. While he was looking through the openings between the boards, he saw that the farmer had a vegetable garden. There were some peppers visible and tomato plants that were well past their prime. The cabbage, cauliflower and brussel sprouts were not yet mature. He decided to wait until dusk when he would be able to sneak out and get a few vegetables. He also saw that there were still some apples and pears on the trees in a small orchard near the road.

After dark he ventured to the garden and gathered just enough to eat for the evening. A pear and an apple from the orchard were stuffed into his pockets. He promised himself that he wouldn't be greedy, as that would only make the farmer suspicious, if he wasn't already. While he was crouched behind a pepper plant he was surprised when a person on a bicycle drove up to the back door of the farmhouse, moved the bicycle under the porch overhang and went inside. Paul could see that it was a young person and from her size and movement, he was certain that it was a young woman. After a few moments, with a pear and an apple in his pockets and a tomato and a pepper tucked inside his jacket, he made his way back to the barn. In the dark he had to be extremely careful when he climbed the ladder, especially favoring his bad leg. He found that he could climb if he used his right leg to raise himself a rung and then bring his left leg to that same rung. It was slow but effective.

Annette and her father had soup, cheese and bread for supper with some red wine. Jacques wanted to broach the subject of Annette protecting herself and wanted to make sure she had a knife on her person at all times. At the same time he didn't want to alarm her.

"Annette, do you really think those soldiers will leave you alone?"

"The one probably will. But the tall one is a bully, and I expect that after a while he might try something."

"I believe you're right. Don't be deceived by the Boche. We know they can't be trusted."

"I won't trust them, Papa, I'll just outsmart them."

"Annette, I want you to take this knife and keep it in your jacket. If you are alone in the store it will fit in your smock. Especially when you are riding home at night in the dark you need to keep it in your pocket. I want you to have the knife with you at all times."

"There have been times when I wished I had a weapon with me. Most of those times were when I was riding my bicycle home," she said. "I will keep it with me. How do I use it?"

Jacques showed her where to push to snap open the spring-loaded blade. "Once the blade is open, it locks in place. It will stay open until you press the button on the side and manually close it. The blade is very sharp and can kill."

Annette practiced a few times until she felt comfortable with the operation. She then pressed the button and closed the blade and put it in her dress pocket. Jacques felt better and was glad that it wasn't all that difficult to convince his daughter that she needed protection.

"Annette, if you kill a German soldier, there will be severe repercussions, maybe even French deaths."

"I understand, Papa. I'll do everything I can to avoid any confrontation." Jacques went to bed early in the evening as usual and Annette several hours later.

The slamming of the back door awakened Paul. The light above the back door provided sufficient light for him to see that it was the farmer. Between the boards in the barn he could see the farmer get on his bicycle and ride to the road. Paul checked his watch and could hardly believe that it was only a quarter to four. He wondered what the farmer did for a living since he didn't seem to work on the farm. Several hours later the farmer's daughter, letting the door slam on her way to the chicken coop, awakened Paul a second time. The sun had risen and she had a basket in her hand. Moments later she picked some vegetables and added them to the eggs before returning to the farmhouse.

Paul could not believe his eyes. She was young and beautiful, about five feet four inches tall. Her long brunette hair and dark eyes highlighted her beauty. She moved with grace and confidence. She had a lovely figure and from his vantage point, she looked like a model out of a magazine. He wanted to leave his spot in the loft and introduce himself to her immediately. That wouldn't be a wise thing to do. He still hadn't planned his next move and didn't know if involving a French family into smuggling him across the border into Switzerland was smart. He believed, however, that he had chosen the right barn to visit.

CHAPTER 28

After the young lady left for town near noon, Paul found four eggs but ate only two of them. A bell pepper that was turning red completed his lunch. It wasn't much of a lunch especially without coffee, but at least his stomach wasn't making noise. He fell asleep after his meal and slept for over an hour. It was the slamming of the back door that woke him. He observed from the loft that the farmer was headed toward the barn. Paul ducked down in the hay. The farmer opened the big doors wide and let his eyes get accustomed to the light.

"Mes enfants," he called. When there was no response he called a second time. Then he closed the doors, leaving them open slightly, and returned to the house.

This puzzled Paul. He had seen no children. Who was he calling? It was something he didn't understand. He stayed in the loft, and with the warmth of the day he grew sleepy.

About two hours later, three boys dressed in dark suits, awakened him. They looked around the barn and then sat on a bale of hay to munch on apples. One of the children started to explore the barn and started climbing up the ladder to the loft. Paul saw the ladder shake and he wondered how he would handle this situation. The oldest boy shouted something to the child and the young one climbed back down. Paul remained silent and listened. It was almost four o'clock.

Soon, the farmer came out of the farmhouse and opened the barn door. He was obviously expecting the children and they were expecting him. He led the children back with him into the house. Darkness came and the young lady returned home after six. She was only in the house about fifteen minutes when she emerged with the three boys. The children waited for her as she stopped by the shed and picked up a board. She led the children past the barn, through the field and into the woods. Paul didn't know what to make of all this but the pieces of the puzzle were starting to fall into place. These had to be Jewish children being smuggled across the border into Switzerland. He thought that was a courageous and dangerous thing to do. Somebody would bring them to the barn and this old man and his daughter would smuggle them the rest of the way. He surmised that the board would be needed to cross a stream.

Sometime after eight the young lady returned home. Paul didn't see her but heard the closing of the back door. The light went off inside the house about an hour later. Feeling the need for some exercise for his leg, he climbed down the ladder and walked the length of the barn several times. He could now place weight on that leg and could almost put the heel to the floor. He massaged the calf and walked some more and was convinced that the torn muscles in his calf were healing.

Paul woke the next morning with a deep thirst. He would love to have a cup of coffee but for now would be happy to have some water in addition to the vegetables. The water that he carried in the parachute was gone. He knew the schedule of the farmer and his daughter fairly well by now. The father left before four in the morning and the daughter left before noon. He returned in the middle of the afternoon and she after six. No one was home from when the girl left until the old man returned, about three hours later. From what he could see they didn't lock the house and the thought occurred to him that maybe he could get some water and food after she left for work. He began to suspect that they owned a store in town but still couldn't figure out why the man left so early for work. Paul considered that he might be a milkman.

Paul watched the beautiful young girl go about her chores. He very much wanted to meet her and get to know her. He wondered how her father would take to him if he knew that he was living in his barn. He suspected that he might be met with a shotgun. The farmer seemed like a no nonsense kind of man.

When the young lady left on her bicycle for town, Paul watched until she was out of sight. Then he walked to the back door and opened it quietly.

Inside, he filled himself with water from the faucet in the sink using a cup from the cupboard. He dried out the cup and replaced it. He found a good supply of bread on the counter and used a knife from a wooden block to cut himself a large piece. That's when he considered that the old man might be a baker. There was a good supply of apples so he figured one would not be missed. He cut the apple in half with one of the knives in the block and left the knife on the sideboard. While he was eating he looked around and saw that it was a fairly large house, comfortably furnished but not at all ostentatious. It was neat and clean and Paul suspected that father and daughter lived comfortably and worked hard. There was a bottle of red wine, about half full, on the counter. He removed the cork with his teeth and took a drink from the bottle and remembered to put the cork back in it.

The kitchen window above the sink faced the south and the back door faced the west. There was a large pane of glass in the back door that would allow the room to be filled with sunshine in the late afternoon. The big kitchen window allowed the southern sun to brighten the room the rest of the day. There was a shade on the back window to keep out any unwanted sun and to provide privacy. The kitchen was large, and besides a lot of counter space and cabinets, there was room for a round table and four chairs. Paul especially noted the quality of the cabinets. They were simple in design but well made and very old. Off the large kitchen, near the back door, was a door leading to the cellar.

The living room occupied most of the ground floor in addition to a bathroom with a bathtub. There was a door that went out to the front of the house and stairs that went up to the bedrooms. Paul suspected that the front door was seldom used.

On his way back to the barn he stopped in the chicken coop to see if there were any eggs. There were three. He took only one and ate it raw before he returned to the barn. The shells were disposed of outside and buried under some leaves in the garden. While he was outside he walked in front of the barn and did some exercises, gently stretching his calf muscles. He kept looking down the road toward town so as not to be surprised if someone came by. Feeling the effects of the wine he decided he needed a nap.

When Jacques returned home that afternoon he knew instantly that someone had been in their home. The crumbs from the bread on the counter, the careless way the cork was only half placed in the wine bottle, the water spots in the sink and the skin of apple on the knife that was not returned to its block, were all signs that someone had been in the house. Annette was a fastidious housekeeper and wouldn't tolerate such carelessness in doing her chores. It had to be an outsider and obviously a male.

Jacques went to the cellar and got his shotgun. He opened the barrels and put a shell in each chamber. He closed the barrel and dropped several more shells in his pocket. He left the house, closing the door without making a sound, and walked directly to the barn. Now that he suspected that someone was inside the barn he looked for signs. He noticed scuffmarks by the doors and the large doors were not totally closed. He squeezed in and moved into the shadows, allowing his eyes to adjust to the light.

With deliberate steps, making absolutely no sound, he searched the lower portion of the barn. He knew he would have to climb to the loft to investigate before he could return to the house. As he did, the first rung of the ladder made a creaking noise. Paul heard the noise and knew he was in danger.

"Arête," Paul said. "I'm coming down."

Jacques stepped down and retreated from the ladder. He knew that he would have had a hard time shooting from the ladder if it came to that and was pleased that the intruder was being sensible. But then he did hold the upper hand with the shotgun. Jacques saw a young man in a RAF airman's jacket raise his body above the hay and raise his hands over his head.

Paul spoke in French, "Don't shoot, I'm from England and my plane was shot down."

"Come down, slowly," Jacques demanded, as he observed his captive straddle the ladder.

Paul turned his back to his captor and slowly descended, one rung at a time. His leg forced him to descend slowly. The man was sitting on a bale of hay with a shotgun on his lap with his finger on the trigger. He motioned for Paul to sit on a bale of hay opposite him.

"You are English?" Jacques inquired.

"No, Canadian...from Quebec. I was sent to England to fly with the RAF. Our plane was shot down a week ago," Paul explained.

"You speak French, but a bit strange."

Paul understood the statement to be actually a question and told the man that he grew up in Canada, immigrated to the United States but returned to Canada to fight against the Germans.

"That is why you speak with a strange accent."

"I guess it must sound a bit strange, as does your French to me. You are definitely not from Quebec."

That little bit of humor pleased the old man and he relaxed just a bit. "I don't think you understand that your presence here could put us in danger. If the Boche were to find you they would probably execute us for harboring you and send you to a prison camp. Beside we are already suspected of suspicious behavior because we live so close to the Swiss border."

"I was hoping that when my leg got a bit better and had less pain, I'd be able to make my way to Switzerland."

They spoke for a time about Paul's injury and that it might be another week or maybe even two weeks before he could travel. Paul suggested that he stay in the barn but Jacques said that would not be necessary. "You will sleep in the house. We have a spare room in the attic."

"The barn will be fine. I don't want to inconvenience you."

"No," said Jacques. "You will sleep in the house."

"Is it because you don't want me to know you are smuggling Jews into Switzerland that you don't want me here?"

Jacques now understood that he didn't have to keep this secret anymore. He wanted to know just how long Paul had been living in the barn.

"Several days. I've been eating eggs and vegetable and fruit from the garden.

"And bread and wine from the kitchen," said Jacques.

"Just this one time. I needed water and went into the house to get a drink. I just..."

"I understand. You need not explain. You will live in the house. The first place that the Boche would look would be in the barn and they would do it with bayonets, jabbing the hay wherever there was a sufficient amount of hay to conceal someone." This last sentence was spoken with appropriate gestures using the shotgun as a prop.

"I don't want that to happen," said Paul.

"Did the Boche see your plane go down?"

"No. I parachuted out of a bomber before dawn about a week ago and landed on a rock formation on the top of a hill, north and west of here. They have no idea that anyone landed in this area. I don't know if the plane made it back to base."

"If you're caught with us you will be treated like us. They are known to execute on the spot those who don't cooperate with them. And those who harbor Jews are considered the most despicable of the French. Do you understand?"

"Yes. I would consider it a privilege to assist you in any way I can in helping children get to safety."

"Then welcome to France. My name is Jacques LaVoie. My daughter is Annette and if you are to stay here you are not to touch her. I would consider it an act of betrayal if you were to attempt to…"

While he was searching for the right words, Paul answered that he would indeed behave like a gentleman and would treat his daughter with the utmost respect.

"I am Paul Fortier." Paul extended his hand and Jacques accepted it.

"Then we have an understanding. You don't touch my daughter and we will get you to Switzerland when your leg heals."

CHAPTER 29

Annette was visibly shocked to see an airman sitting with her father at the kitchen table. She was not only surprised but disturbed. Who was he and what did he know? Were the Germans looking for him? Her eyes asked those questions.

"Annette, I would like to introduce you to Paul Fortier," her father said.

"Father, who is he? Isn't it dangerous to have him in our house?"

Paul stood up and spoke in French, "Annette, I'm an airman with the RAF. I know that you smuggle children into Switzerland and when my leg is better I hope you will smuggle me with them."

She then extended her hand reluctantly. "You are welcome. I didn't mean to be rude, but I was concerned that your presence will bring the Boche to our home. We do everything we can to be above suspicion."

"Sit down, Annette, and let's talk for a moment," her father began. "Paul will live in the attic. His presence here will only be for a week, perhaps two. He is most anxious to get out of France."

Annette's fears were allayed when she became convinced that Paul would soon be leaving and that the Germans did not know that he was in the area. He told Jacques and Annette about his adventures to date and they were both captivated by his accent, his modesty and his courage.

Annette showed a little bit of her sensitivity when she delicately told Paul that his accent would fool the Germans but not the French. "A true Frenchman would immediately detect the accent and use of different words.

Unless a German was truly bilingual, he would probably not recognize that you were a foreigner."

"It is not my intention to have anything to do with either the French or the Germans. I'm just glad that I met you and will be able to escape into Switzerland and get back with my squadron."

They talked for another hour and Paul was treated to several glasses of wine. Jacques told Paul of the work that Annette was doing bringing the children across the border. They spoke of their work at the bakery and their desire to keep the Germans from becoming suspicious of their smuggling.

Jacques also told Paul about the German soldier who had a fascination with Annette. Paul told Jacques, when Annette was busy elsewhere, that he suspected the soldier would try to take advantage of Annette in the future.

"When your daughter is alone, and the soldier is most likely not to get caught, he will attack your daughter."

"I know that, but don't want to alarm and frighten Annette. I did give her a knife and have insisted that she keep it with her at all times. Yet I believe, like you do, that he will not stop until he is transferred from here or killed."

Jacques felt that he had an ally in Paul, and Paul did not believe that Jacques was overstating the danger to his daughter.

Annette returned and suggested to her father that they get clothes for Paul. He was most conspicuous in his airman's uniform. He thought that it was a good idea but knew that his clothes wouldn't fit Paul. Jacques was short and heavy and Paul was tall and thin.

"I'll visit Henri tomorrow afternoon," Jacques suggested. "He had a son who died last year and he was about your size. I'm sure he'll have some clothes for you. We'll make you look like a Frenchman, at least."

Jacques took Paul upstairs to the attic and showed him a canvas cot, pillow and blanket that Paul could use. He left Paul a candle and told him that he would be going to the bakery very early in the morning and that he could sleep as long as he wished. Paul was asleep very quickly, the result of many days sleeping on less than ideal beds. He thought for a brief moment, in the time before he was completely asleep, that the wine had something to do with making him drowsy. Then he was asleep.

Annette was busy cutting bread for toast when Paul reached the kitchen the next morning.

"Bonjour," she said.

"Bonjour."

"Would you like a breakfast of eggs and toast?"

"Yes, please. And I would like a cup of coffee."

"Pour yourself a cup. I'm finished and I made some extra."

Paul poured a cup of coffee and could immediately smell the chicory. It was a taste he was familiar with from Canada but a taste he had never acquired. The coffee was strong, unlike what he was used to drinking. Yet it tasted surprisingly good. He was pleased, however, to have good food and someone with whom to talk. Paul was overwhelmed with Annette's poise and couldn't help but appreciate her beauty. She was extremely pleasant to be with, even when they were not speaking. Paul was nervous in her presence and this surprised him.

If he were to be true to his thoughts, it was the fact that Paul was extremely attracted to this young lady and he had never met anyone who affected him the way she did. She was pretty, smart and talented. She was also gentle, kind, considerate and humble. Although she seemed to be of school age, she acted more mature. These were the obvious qualities he immediately saw. He had a fleeing thought that maybe this was a young lady that he could love and cherish. It was a shame that he couldn't remain here. He told himself that he should be thankful for the blessings that he was experiencing and be grateful for being rescued by this family. He needed to forget any romantic notions.

As Paul made small talk and ate breakfast, he thought to himself that this woman was much too good for him. In her presence, he was ashamed of his relationship with Celia and was having second thoughts about the time spent with Dorothy. This was the kind of person he always wanted to meet. He was intimidated by her sincerity and goodness and felt that he didn't measure up. He didn't trust himself and remembered that he had promised her father that he would always be a gentleman. That would have to be one promise he would keep or he would surely lose her trust.

The morning passed all too quickly and Annette left for work. Paul took a tour of the house and wondered what would happen if Germans came to the house while he was there. He looked around starting in the cellar and found some of the fruits, vegetables and wine that were stored for the winter. Nor were any hiding places apparent and he couldn't see where one could be built. The heavy stonewall would show if any work was done on it. Likewise, there were few places where a room could be hidden on the first floor. The closet under the stairs was small and an obvious place to look. On the second floor there was also little opportunity for a hidden room.

Paul went up to the attic and looked at the construction. The attic had two vents, one at each end. That wouldn't allow for construction, as they were needed for ventilation. There was a dormer window facing the back of the house and one facing the front. Unless someone paid very close attention to the construction of the house they probably wouldn't notice that there were two dormer windows. From the front of the house only one could be seen and from the rear only one could be seen. It would take someone looking critically to observe and note that fact, and that very observant person would also have to be the person who inspected the attic. What were the chances of that happening, he speculated.

Paul studied the attic and rear dormer carefully. The roof slanted all the way to the floor. He was fairly secure in his knowledge of carpentry and believed that he could close the dormer area so that anyone checking the attic from inside the house would not be able to tell that there was a room behind the slanted roof. Mentally he planned how he would build it and what he would need. His biggest problem would be to get wood that was as weathered as the attic wood.

After he came down from the attic he went out to the shed to see what materials Jacques had on hand. He found some boards but most of them were relatively new. They looked like they were bought to repair wood in the barn that needed replacing. Paul made a note of the size to see if possibly a few substitutions could be made. In the barn he found only a few boards that needed to be replaced. The boards were painted on the outside but unstained or untreated on the inside and would match the lumber in the attic. He planned on substituting a few of these boards, painting the new ones on the outside and staining the inside to make it look like the other boards in the barn. In a dark barn a few new boards placed indiscriminately wouldn't be noticed.

When Jacques came home from the bakery, Paul could hardly wait to tell him what he was thinking. They ate lunch together and while Jacques was eating his sandwich Paul laid out his plan, sketched on the back of a paper napkin. He expected some opposition but all Jacques had were questions. He wanted to know if Paul was certain he could make the dormer room match so that it couldn't be detected. He also wanted to know how Paul planned to close the wall from the inside.

Paul and Jacques climbed the stairs to the attic and Paul noticed that it wasn't easy for Jacques to climb stairs. He wondered how he was able to shepherd the children through the mountain into Switzerland. Then he showed Jacques what he proposed. Jacques was impressed and thought it would work. He was most impressed with Paul's idea of how the panel would be pulled into place after a person or people were inside the dormer room. "Let's see what Annette thinks," suggested Jacques.

"Do you think she will approve?"

"Yes, she has concerns about the children when they are in the house. She's as nervous as a cat about to give birth to kittens. She can hardly wait to get them out of here and on their way. We have not had to keep any children overnight. She'll be pleased to have a place for the children to hide should a German car pull up outside. Believe me."

Paul and Jacques looked at the wood in the shed and knew that it couldn't be used in the attic. He did find lumber that he could use to make a frame. But the wood on the walls of the barn was perfect on one side and Jacques agreed with Paul that it would be a good match. The new wood could be used to replace the wood that Paul would take from the barn and use upstairs. The two men spoke of the tools that were available and the paint and stains that would make their project perfect.

"When this project is finished, it will be possible for a child to close the panel to this room. Maybe not a five year old but a child of seven or eight should have no difficulty securing the room. If they remain quiet they will not be detected."

"I hope you're right. I'm anxious to see the room finished."

Jacques asked to be excused so he could take a little nap since his day had begun so early. About an hour later Jacques told Paul that he was going to ride his bicycle to Henri's house to see if he could get some clothes for

Paul. Paul used this time to plan how he would complete his project and the schedule he would follow. He liked planning his projects. That way there were no surprises. It pleased him that he was using his talents and being useful.

The clothes that Jacques brought back with him fit Paul well and made him much less conspicuous. Jacques told him that Henri had plenty of clothes and would put together a second set. Paul was reluctant to part with his boots but was willing to follow Jacques suggestion that he scuff them and dirty them so that they didn't look military and keep the trouser legs over the boots. Looking in the mirror Paul almost felt French. He considered growing a beard to appear more native. He thought that Annette might have some ideas about how he could appear less conspicuous.

When Annette arrived home she smiled at the Frenchman standing in front of her.

"Now you look like a Frenchman. Perhaps a goatee and a mustache would complete the picture," was her comment.

"You might be right. I'll start growing one tomorrow," was Paul's reply.

"It would make you look older," said Jacques, "and with the limp you could pass for an old man."

"You grow the beard, and I have some makeup from a school play that would put a bit of gray in the beard," Annette offered. "It will make you at least twenty years older."

"I would have to be a lot older than forty to escape the notice of the Germans."

Paul liked all the attention and was pleased that they thought they could work up a suitable disguise for him. Young Frenchmen were not seen in France. If found, a young man would be sent to a concentration camp or into forced labor or executed on some charge or other. Most fled France to fight with Allied forces in North Africa or England. Only old men, woman and children were reasonably safe. Paul knew that the time might come when he would have to make himself into an old man, complete with cane, limp and some gray in his hair.

At the end of supper Paul gave Jacques a knowing look and Jacques took the cue.

"Annette, I believe that we need to make a place to hide our little charges should the Boche come when they are here."

"That would be very useful, but where?" Annette asked.

"Paul thought that we could take the dormer window in the attic and enclose the one that faces the backyard. No one sees it and he's convinced that once it is pulled closed it would be virtually impossible to believe a room was hidden there."

The two men explained how they proposed to do it and why it should be done soon. Annette listened carefully; asked questions that helped her make sense of the project. She said that she thought it would be a great idea.

"You sure have been busy since I left this afternoon. I can see that I'm going to have to be careful that you two men don't come up with too many crazy ideas."

The three of them smiled and toasted the success of the project with the remaining wine left in their glasses.

CHAPTER 30

Paul was excited about the project, and that caused him to have trouble sleeping. His brain just didn't want to shut down. After he blew out the candle in the attic, he sat on the cot, planning how he would get started in the morning. There was still a generous moon, several days past being full. Paul walked to the window and searched the countryside. He could see a faint glow on the horizon, the lights from town. While he was watching he saw a car coming slowly down the dirt road that passed their house. It was a German car, the kind made by Volkswagen and used by the military. About a half kilometer from the farmhouse it turned off the lights while the vehicle was still moving and rolled to a stop, still a good distance from the house. Paul continued to watch knowing that he couldn't be seen since the moon was casting a shadow on that side of the house.

His first thought was that he should wake Jacques and Annette, but on second thought, he knew it best to tell them in the morning. He continued to watch. Paul knew that he could wait out the soldier, even if he stayed there all night. He saw the light of a lighter and the glow from a cigarette. After about fifteen minutes the car turned around and moved very slowly without headlights back toward town.

Only when the vehicle was well down the road did the headlights come on and the car increased speed. Paul had little doubt that this was the same soldier who was stalking Annette. He was surprised that he found himself so protective of her. The soldier was probably going to the checkpoint at the border either because he was on duty or had to deliver a message. And he just happened to decide to stop for a smoke along the way. Paul couldn't get his mind to believe that story. It was the soldier who wanted to rape Annette and who had caused trouble at the bakery. He was again stalking her as Jacques believed he would. He was positive that he was correct, in spite of the fact that he didn't have an ounce of proof.

In the morning both father and daughter were in the kitchen, as it was a Sunday. The two would go to Mass at eight. When they returned Paul told them about the incident the night before and they discussed the problem over breakfast.

"Annette, I believe that the most dangerous time is when you leave the shop at six to return home. Your father and I agree on that," said Paul.

"I don't think the soldier would try anything while it is daylight," said Jacques.

"Once you arrive home, we'll be able to protect you. You must be extremely vigilant as you're closing up the bakery."

"What more can I do? I'm already making sure they are not outside, sitting in their car."

"After turning off the lights, stand in the dark and watch the street for traffic. Check behind the bakery before going outside. Don't leave the safety of the bakery until you're sure it is safe. They are impatient and if you don't show up when they expect you to, they will start searching for you. You might bring your bicycle in earlier in the afternoon," suggested Paul.

"I'll do those things. I don't believe they have much patience and if I don't come out, they'll start driving around or checking the doors or looking in the windows. I'll be careful."

"It's the ride home that concerns me the most. Check to see if there are any hiding places, trees, bushes, rocks or a hill you could hide behind. Go from one safe spot to the next. Take your time and observe everything."

"Those are some good ideas. I'll be careful. Thank you for the suggestions."

He would have liked to walk the road to see if there were any hiding places. He wanted to see if there was a grove of trees, some bushes, a big rock or houses along the way that could give her a place to hide or a place she could flee to safety. Henri's house was the only possible place once she left the village.

Paul, dressed in his new French clothes, took a day off and he and

Annette took a short walk in the woods. It was pleasant but because of his leg, he could not walk far. They sat on a rock for a while, but there was a nip in the wind, and they didn't rest for long before going back to the house. Their eyes searched the road, the tree line and the fields whenever they were outside. It was becoming a habit.

The following morning, shortly after breakfast, Paul started to gather tools and materials for the project. Annette was impressed with the fact that Paul was industrious and handy with tools. She could see that he was smart and gave a lot of thought to the planning of this project and to her protection. If she would allow herself the thought, she was glad he chose their farm for his recovery.

Paul opened the doors to the barn to let in as much light as possible. With a tape measure he found in the shed, he measured and selected eight boards to be replaced, all randomly spaced on the backside of the barn. Jacques's ladder was used to reach the higher boards. He thought of his father as he did this and heard his father's voice in his head, "Measure twice and cut once." A smile crossed his lips.

After carefully measuring the boards to be replaced, he cut eight boards the length he needed from the new wood in the shed. Jacques's saws were sharp. Carefully removing the old lumber and replacing it with new lumber, he procured the needed eight pieces of seasoned lumber. It took two trips to the attic to carry up all the lumber for the project. Walking on the toe of his left foot was awkward but not impossible. He could tell that the muscles in his calf were healing.

The work moved at a good pace, due mainly to Paul's experience and good planning. After making the frame that would not be seen, the boards were hammered in place. By lunch time the opening was completed with only the detail of how to remove the opening and how to lock it closed when someone was inside. Paul found all the hardware that he needed in the shed. He staggered the lumber so that pieces were of different lengths and no vertical line was visible.

Paul then put a strip of wood on the floor to keep the bottom of the door aligned properly. He also matched the trim at the top by taking trim from the far end of the attic. It wouldn't be missed there and he needed it to disguise the opening. He used eye screws and hooks on the inside to keep the door snug and two stripes of trim on the outside to keep the door in place. The weight was surprisingly light although he wondered how easy it would be for a child to manipulate. It would probably be too heavy for a small child. An adult would have to accompany children under ten. He knew that while he lived here he would be that adult. By the time Jacques returned from the bakery he was finished.

"Paul, I'm not feeling well. I'm going to lie down," Jacques said almost immediately as he entered his home.

"Let me get you a glass of water," Paul suggested and didn't bother to wait for an answer. "Can I fix you lunch?"

"No. The water will be fine. I just need a rest. I'll be fine by supper."

Paul ate a sandwich by himself, and then cleaned up the mess he made upstairs. He gathered the tools and returned them to the shed, closed the barn doors, got out the paint and brought it inside to warm up for the completion of the task in the morning.

When Annette returned home, Paul told her about her father who was resting comfortably on the sofa.

"Annette, your father had nothing to eat and wanted to sleep immediately after he arrived home. He is definitely sick. I think he needs a doctor."

Annette looked at her father on the couch but didn't wake him up. She put her hand to his wrist and took his pulse.

"Paul, he doesn't look well. His color is bad and his pulse is erratic. I need something to eat and then I'll ride into town to get the doctor."

"I wish you didn't have to go out. It's dark and I know you're tired."

"It's what I have to do. Thank you for taking care of Papa while I was working."

Annette left fifteen minutes after she had arrived. She returned home within the hour. "Paul, it would be wise to stay out of sight. The doctor can be trusted but the fewer people who know about you, the better."

A few minutes later they heard a car drive to the side of the house. Paul went upstairs and Annette went out to greet the doctor. He spent about ten minutes with Jacques and told Annette that Jacques's blood pressure was elevated and his heartbeat was irregular. With his history of heart trouble, he should be in a hospital. He told Annette to stay home, as there was nothing that she could do. She reluctantly agreed. She knew that she would probably have to do two jobs for a day or two.

As she assisted in helping Jacques out to the car, she asked the doctor, "Would you stop by the bakery in the morning and let me know what's happening?"

"As soon as I visit Jacques in the morning, I'll let you know of your father's condition."

She kissed her father after he was comfortably seated in the car and closed the door. Once inside the house she called Paul and told him what she knew. They both agreed that her father didn't look good and appeared very weak. They spoke of the busy days that were in front of her. She told Paul that there was a lady who could do the work in the afternoon and she would do her father's job. That meant getting up at three in the morning and making the bread for the next day.

"Annette, if there is anything I can do to help, please don't hesitate to ask. I feel helpless not being able to assist you now that you need help."

"Paul, don't feel like that. If you weren't here this would still have happened. Father hasn't been feeling well for some time. I've been concerned about him even before Mama died."

"Please let me help. I'm here, and I want to be useful while my leg heals."

"I will. By the way, making that room in the attic was a great idea. How is it coming?"

"I've finished it but have to paint the boards that I removed from the barn. Then I'll add a little stain to the inside to make them look like they were there for twenty years. Of course the new boards need to be painted on the outside but that shouldn't be a problem. Your father has plenty of extra paint. Tomorrow I finish it. I'll show it to you then."

"Great. I'm exhausted tonight, although I would like to see it. Tomorrow will be soon enough. I'll set the alarm and try to get to the bakery before four o'clock."

Paul stayed up a short while but not having anything to read or to do he thought it wiser to get to bed. He lit his candle and retired to the attic. When he got there he thought it might be a good idea to put a curtain on the window to block any light from the candle. He wouldn't want the soldier who watched the house to know that someone was living in the attic. When the moon was full, the light wouldn't show but the moon wasn't always full. A curtain was needed.

He blew out the candle and went to the window to see if the soldier was spying on the house. The moon was moving in and out behind clouds but he could see no vehicle on the road. He stayed at the window for some time, expecting a car to stop. It didn't happen at least while he was watching. He retired to his cot and was asleep in minutes.

CHAPTER 31

The alarm made its annoying noise at three and Annette silenced it. She washed, made breakfast and prepared to leave fifteen minutes before four. As she left the house she checked both directions on the road to see if she was alone. Then she got on her bicycle and pedaled toward town. The sky was very cloudy and she expected rain during the morning. For that purpose she kept a raincoat hanging on a peg at the bakery.

At the shop, she parked her bicycle, noticing that the flower pot had been moved. With all her troubles today she didn't feel that she needed another responsibility. She felt overwhelmed about her ability to handle everything. She wondered if she would have enough physical and emotional strength to fulfill this obligation.

She worked until eight, mixing, knocking down the rising dough. While it was rising a second time she hung up her apron and locked the store, leaving a sign that said she would return soon. She left the shop to walk to the home of the lady who frequently helped her. Jeanne Cartier invited her to sit and have a cup of coffee. Annette gratefully accepted.

Annette explained about her father's condition and asked Jeanne if she would be willing to work while her father was sick.

"Of course, Annette. I'm glad you asked me. Michelle is also available after school to help. Should I ask her?"

"Please. That would be wonderful. Papa might need me these days when he comes home from the hospital." When the two finished coffee, Annette asked Jeanne to come as soon as possible. "The doctor is going to pick me up and drive me to the hospital. I'll leave the door open if I have to leave," she told Jeanne.

When Annette returned to the bakery and was putting out the fresh loaves for the customers, the doctor arrived. He told Annette that her father was in very serious condition and had asked for her to come see him.

"Annette, I hate to tell you this, but I don't expect him to pull through."

That statement sent a shock through Annette. She knew her father was not feeling well, but didn't believe that it was that serious. "Doctor, can you drive me to the hospital?"

"Yes, but who will mind the store?"

"Jeanne Cartier will be here in a short while. The store will be safe. We can go now."

On the way to the hospital, the doctor explained that her father not only had blockage to his heart but also had a mild stroke. The tests revealed possible blood clots that could make matters worse. It was a fifteen-minute ride to Audincourt and the regional hospital. The doctor dropped her off at the entrance. At the front desk the receptionist told her to wait a moment for someone to escort her to her father.

Jacques was in a private room that was sparsely furnished with a bed, a table next to the bed and a chair. The room was painted a cream color. There were no pictures on the wall and the room had no windows. A crucifix hung over the door.

A nun, who was a nurse, escorted her to the room and explained that her father was comfortable and in no pain. She also told Annette that he was seriously ill. When Annette saw her father, she was surprised how old he seemed to have become overnight. He opened his eyes when she kissed his forehead.

"Papa, how are you feeling?"

"Not well, my little one. I'm not going to survive this."

"Don't say that, Papa. You'll be as good as new in a few days," Annette encouraged.

"I asked the nun to get Father Gilbert. I want to go to confession and receive the last rites."

"Good, I'm glad that you want to go to confession. And people often get better after receiving the last rites."

"Yes, but I don't have much time left. There are a few things I need to tell you."

"What, Papa? Can't it wait?"

Jacques ignored her question and in a weak voice said, "You are a wonderful daughter and a fine woman. Your mother would be very proud of you, as I am." He took a deep breath and continued. "When I leave, the house, farm and bakery belong to you. If the house is too much to handle, you can rent it to someone and live in town near the bakery. That might make life a bit easier."

"Papa, let's not talk about this now. We'll have time to talk when you come home."

"Annette, I'm not coming home. I know how sick I am. There is one last thing I have to say. Paul is a very good man. I do not know if he is the man for you…" Jacques needed to take a breath. "Maybe Paul would stay in this country or maybe you would go across the ocean to be with him." He paused again. "I do know that he is a hardworking, honest and dependable man. Give him some consideration."

Just as Jacques finished that last bit of advice, the village priest, Father Robert Gilbert, tapped on the hospital door.

"Good morning, Father. I'll wait outside," Annette said as she moved toward the door.

Father Robert Gilbert was a tall, thin, ascetic looking priest. He was almost gaunt with black hair that was graying at the sides. He had been the pastor in this village for more than twenty years and was loved and respected by the entire parish. There were those who said that he would give you his shirt if you needed it. All who knew him loved and trusted him. He was a no nonsense pastor who was truly concerned about his flock.

The priest was with Jacques for about fifteen minutes preparing him for his journey. He heard his confession, gave him communion and invited Annette into the room when he was anointing him with oil. When he was ready to leave, he gestured with his head for Annette to come with him outside the room. He told her that Jacques was a good man and would soon be with God. He told Annette that she would have to be strong especially in the days ahead. He put his hands on Annette's head, made the sign of the cross on her forehead and asked for God's blessing for her. Then he left.

When Annette returned to her father's bedside, he was having trouble keeping his eyes open. He told her he needed to sleep. She stroked his hand briefly and told him to get some rest.

Sitting in the chair by his bed holding his hand and alone with her thoughts, she considered her father's words. Moments later, while Annette was deep in thought, her father started to struggle for breath. She ran out in the hall and called for the nurse whom she saw at the other end of the hall. Her father continued to struggle for a few more seconds and then, just as the nurse entered the room, stopped breathing. The nurse checked the pulse in his neck, put her cheek to his mouth and shook her head. She gently closed his eyelids, blessed herself and left the room. Annette returned to the chair she had been sitting in. Tears filled her eyes. She knew that she was going to miss this gentle man, this man who had worked his whole life with her interests always before his own. After a few minutes, she slowly pulled the sheet up over his face.

Her last words were, "I love you, Papa, and I will miss you. Thank you, Papa."

CHAPTER 32

Paul had just finished painting and staining the new boards in the barn and had returned to the kitchen when he heard a car drive up outside. He retreated to the stairs going to the bedrooms. Annette got out and said goodbye to whomever drove her. Then she came inside and the car left.

"I just left the hospital," she said in a raised voice. Paul descended the stairs. After a moment, she continued barely audible, "Papa is dead."

The message surprised Paul as he wasn't expecting that to happen. "I'm so sorry, Annette. Your father was a good man."

Annette came to him and he put his arms around her and held her while she cried. It was the most natural thing in the world for him to do. He wanted to help her carry this terrible burden, if he could.

When the tears stopped, Paul asked, "What can I do to help?"

Annette gathered herself, wiped her eyes and said that a lady from church was going to pick her up after lunch to take her to town to make funeral arrangements. She told Paul that children would be arriving in the barn sometime that afternoon and she would have to take them across the border. She would also have to make the dough and bake bread for the next day.

"What a terrible schedule. I need to help. Is there something I could do?"

"I have to take care of the children. You would get lost trying to get them into Switzerland. Even if you could find the way, it would be too dangerous. If the border guards didn't shoot you, those waiting for the children probably would. No, that is something I must do."

They talked of how they would handle the evening. Annette would go to town to make funeral arrangements; Paul would provide a snack for the children in the barn. When Annette returned, the two of them would take the children across into Switzerland. Paul felt that if they didn't go too fast and if he paced himself, he could make it, even with his bad leg. As for his staying across the border, he wouldn't consider it. This was not the right time to leave Annette. She needed him, even if both of them would not admit what they were feeling. She would admit that she was glad he was here, and for his part, he would not have wanted to be anywhere else. He felt needed and he liked the feeling. That was enough for now.

Three children arrived late in the afternoon. There were two small girls about six or seven and a ten-year-old boy. None of them spoke French. Paul brought them some bread and jam. Apples were tucked into their pockets for later. Paul waited with them in the barn for Annette's return. She arrived home about dusk. After her friend left to return to town she went out to the barn. She spoke with the children in German and told them they would soon be safe in Switzerland. She had decided that it was foolish to hide from the children the fact that she spoke German.

Annette led the way and Paul followed last in line. When they got to the pass in the mountain, Annette cautioned everyone about talking. She told Paul to pay close attention to this passage, as this was the most difficult part of the journey. Paul memorized the signs and frequently looked behind to become familiar with the returning view. He was pleased that his leg was holding up even if he could not put his full weight on the heel. In the darkness he had to walk very carefully. The pace, because of the small children was slow, and for that he was grateful.

They stopped short of the stream and listened. All that could be heard was the gurgling water. Annette got the board from under some leaves and put it over the stream for the little ones. Paul returned it to the woods and covered it with leaves. He rejoined the group and started up the hill. At the smaller stream Annette flashed the light two times and the response came almost immediately. They continued up the hill and turned the children over to the two waiting Swiss friends.

"Paul is my companion, and he might bring children on the next trip. My father died this morning," said Annette.

"We are so sorry," said Marie as they both embraced her.

"Paul, I am Pierre and this is my wife, Marie. We are pleased that you are willing to help."

"I'll do what I can. I don't know how Annette can work and transport the children," said Paul.

"We have only started moving children out of harm's way and so far it has been very successful. We hope you will be able to continue," said Pierre.

As they said goodbye to Marie and the children, Paul shook Pierre's hand. That handshake told both men that the other was trustworthy. To both it was a meaningful gesture, much more than a formality.

Annette and Paul made their way back to the farm. Annette suggested that Paul lead the way and he did fairly well. Several times, however, she tapped him on the shoulder to alert him to the fact that he was going in the wrong direction. He wondered how long it would take him to memorize the route. He also recognized that anyone unfamiliar with these mountains would have difficulty making the passage through them. They could easily get hopelessly lost if they didn't kill themselves by falling off a cliff.

They arrived home in the early evening and made some tea. Annette confessed that she was emotionally drained. She knew her father was sick and had been lost without his wife. She was happy that he had the priest prepare him for death and that she was there for his peaceful death. But she knew that she depended on him and would miss him terribly. He had been a good, loving father. She was not yet eighteen and she was without parents. She went to bed soon after she finished her tea, thinking of the last words her father said to her but not yet willing to share them with Paul. She closed her eyes and willed sleep to come, knowing she would be going to the bakery in the middle of the night, as usual.

CHAPTER 33

The next few days were emotional ones for Annette. She posted a sign that the bakery would be closed on the day of the funeral and her friend, Jeanne Cartier, offered to be her driver. Paul was lost during this time, wondering what he could do to help. He wanted to be with her and help her through her grief but knew he would endanger the entire village if he were caught. It was best that he remain in hiding. He wished it could be otherwise.

At the Funeral Mass the church was filled with almost every villager. Annette was surprised by how many were packed into the church. The people in the village told her over and over that he was a good man and asked if they could help. She thanked them all.

Paul decided to use the day to explore the mountain that he would have to travel if he was to help transport the children across the border. He found the passageway with a little bit of difficulty and in the daylight was able to study just how hidden it was. As he looked at this opening in the mountain he would see about twenty feet of a crevice and then the passage would apparently end. Only when he got to the deepest part could he see that the passage doubled back and continued on through curves to what Paul liked to think of as stairs. It was well hidden.

He made his way to the rock at the top of the stone step like formation. There he sat for a few minutes to give his leg a rest. Minutes later he continued on, remembering that he had to go behind the rock before continuing forward. He took a pine branch with him to leave sprigs of pine to guide him back, just in case he got confused. It was considerably easier in the daylight than in darkness. He tried to memorize landmarks that he could recognize in the dark and continued to drop sprigs to assist in finding his way home. As he was coming down the mountain he was certain that he was following the path from the previous evening. In the woods, just as he heard the rippling of the water, he also heard voices. He hid behind a thick clump of wild rhododendron bushes and watched as two soldiers routinely walked along the bank of the stream. They had probably done this several times each day and were paying no attention to anything except their conversation. He noted the time. Paul patiently waited for their return about thirty minutes later. When they were gone Paul made his way back to the farmhouse.

While he tried to develop the habit of leaving nothing of his belongings in sight, he felt the need to check both the kitchen and the living room to make certain there was no trace of his presence. He went upstairs and put his airman's jacket in a cardboard box and his other clothes in another. He either had to find a place to store them or would bury them. For now he put them by the dormer window. While he was in the attic he heard the kitchen door shut and he knew Annette was home. He heard several voices and understood that he would have to remain out of sight for a while. He suspected that her driver and friend, Jeanne, stopped to have tea with Annette. He took a nap on the cot.

When he awoke, Annette was kneeling beside him.

"You must be hungry. Are you ready for supper?" she asked.

"Yes. Tell me about the funeral."

"I will, over supper."

"While you're here I want you to look at your new dormer room."

Paul showed Annette the dormer room. She was surprised that it didn't give any indication that a room was hidden behind the boards. Unless someone knocked on the ceiling and heard the hollow sound, it was not visually detectable. Paul showed Annette how easy it was to close the opening and make it snug from the inside. She was impressed. Paul also suggested that she make a curtain for the front and back dormer windows to hide any light from the candle.

"That would be a good idea. I have plenty of flour sacks that will suit that purpose just fine."

In the kitchen Annette admitted to being relieved that the funeral was over. She told Paul of the kindness of the men and women in the village and of all the children from her school that attended the Funeral Mass and sang the offertory hymn. She spoke of the eulogy that Father Gilbert delivered and was especially pleased that he was very honest in his praise. She told him how difficult it was at the cemetery.

"Annette, I went over the mountain today. Paul began. "I thought it would be easier in daylight and it was. I left sprigs of pine so I wouldn't get lost returning."

"I'm glad you did. That will make it easier when you take the children to Switzerland," she said.

"I believe that I can do it in the dark, if I'm careful. I also saw two Germans on patrol along the stream."

"They seem to follow the same time schedule. Did you notice that?"

"Yes. I saw them go one way and the time was fifteen minutes after the hour. They returned a half hour later."

"If you are able to take the next group of children, it will take a heavy burden off my shoulders. It will give me a chance to recover from Papa's death.

"You know I'm pleased to help. It makes me feel needed."

"And I couldn't have survived these last few days without you."

Annette went to bed early because of emotional exhaustion and because she had to get up so early. Paul sat in the kitchen, turned off the light and lit a candle. He wondered about their future. This was the first time that he thought of his future as being tied somehow with hers. This war was complicating and destroying so many lives. He wondered how long the war would last. Would they survive? What did the future hold? And would the Germans find out what they were doing and shut down their operation? Would they be killed? Would this be the last year of his life, the last month, the last week? These questions filled his thoughts and he wondered if he would change anything even if he could. He knew he could escape to Switzerland and resume his role as an airman. But wasn't what he was doing now more important? Would he leave even if he could?

When he reached his attic bedroom, he looked out the window and noticed the German car a good distance from the house. He was certain it would not be long before the soldier would make a move. Paul hoped that he would be ready when he did. For now, all he could do was watch and wait.

CHAPTER 34

The two German soldiers sat in the vehicle at the far end of the street, just down from the bakery. The bold one whose name was Obersoldat (private first class) Herman Hess was waiting to see if Annette was working in the store. The other, Obersoldat Conrad Westphal, didn't want to have anything to do with stalking a civilian, even if she was pretty. They had been reprimanded and were forbidden to have anything to do with the girl from the bakery.

Hess told his companion, "Her old father died and now she lives alone outside of town."

"How do you know that?"

"I heard that the old man who owned the bakery died. I assumed that he was the man who spoke to the major. One day I followed her home. I stayed back a good distance as she rode her bicycle. She didn't see me and I didn't turn the car lights on. I also watched her house several nights. She lived with her father before he died. Now he's dead and she's alone," Hess said with mock pity in his voice. "The corporal from Barracks C who broke his leg and was in the hospital when the old man died, told me the baker had a heart attack. I just put the facts together."

"Leave me out of this. Don't invite me to go with you if you're having anything to do with that girl. Count me out of anything you want to do that involves her," said Westphal, showing a backbone for the first time.

"I won't involve you. But you won't have any of the fun. In another few days she'll be begging for some company. Don't worry. I want her all to myself. You won't be involved."

The bold one said that he was just going to drive past the bakery to see who was working there and then they would return to the barracks. Seeing that it was the older woman, he pretended that he was upset but believed that Annette was home by herself. It was her schedule that Hess was attempting to deduce, and according to his calculation she would be home in the early evening. One of these evenings the time would be right. He turned the car around and drove back to the barracks.

It was several nights later that he had to go on duty at checkpoint #2 at 2200 hours. He left the barracks early but signed out a half hour later. Discipline was usually ignored when soldiers worked during the night and no one would even notice that he was gone. He did this several nights in a row.

He had turned off the lights long before reaching his usual spot. The farmhouse was dark and he felt himself getting excited just thinking about the fact that she was asleep inside. He had fantasies about having sex with her and that she wanted him and was waiting for him. He would change his duty time with someone to be at the farmhouse when she was still up. He knew it would be unwise to attempt to break into the house when she was asleep. If she heard him she might be waiting for him with a shotgun.

The soldier thought he understood how he could get away with this crime. He considered the possibility that she would welcome his advances. And if she didn't she would be too afraid of losing her reputation to report it. Finally, he wanted to believe that the major would stand behind him if she did report the act since she was the enemy. In his mind, he thought that he could do what he wanted and she would be helpless to stop him. After all, isn't that what conquering armies did? That's what he wanted to believe. He had no fear for his safety since he was twice her weight and considerably bigger and stronger. He easily convinced himself that she wasn't going to be a problem and would welcome his advances.

Paul happened to look down the country road, as he was accustomed to do each evening and saw the dark silhouette of the car. He watched for about ten minutes until the car turned around and drove to the larger road about a kilometer back toward town. There he turned right to go to the checkpoint.

He continued to watch and in about ten minutes he saw lights on the larger road and a car returned traveling at a faster speed. He surmised that the soldier just replaced another soldier at the checkpoint. Paul knew what the soldier was planning; he just didn't know when.

The following afternoon when Annette came home, Paul asked her about her knife. She had it in her dress pocket. That pleased Paul. He told her about the visits at night by the soldier and that soon he wouldn't be satisfied to just sit and watch. He would drive up to the house and come in. Paul strongly suggested that they keep the doors locked and keep the knife handy at all times. Annette said that she would.

Paul told Annette all of this, not to scare her, but to help her prepare for the inevitable. What Paul didn't tell her was that he was hoping the soldier would attack Annette in the house when Paul was there and could protect her. He was also planning how he would cover up the killing. He realized that there were a lot of things to consider if he was to prevent any suspicion from falling on Annette. He would have to make it look as if the soldier was never there. He was also making plans as to how he would handle such a situation.

Four children arrived in the barn the following night and Paul led them across the mountain and to the waiting car on the other side. The trip took place without incident. Paul spoke with the two friends who were escorting the children and asked them if they could get a message to British authorities that he was alive. They asked for the necessary information. He gave his name, rank, serial number, squadron and location. Paul also spoke to them of Annette's situation and wondered if they might get permission for Paul to stay in France. Paul explained that Annette couldn't do the escorting alone. The couple agreed that many lives would be lost if Paul could not assist Annette. They told him they would see what they could arrange.

The trip back to the farm was uneventful. Paul was extremely pleased with his navigation because he made only one false turn and recognized his mistake immediately. He arrived just moments before Annette retired for the night. Annette told him that she had a gift for him and showed him a paper bag with a second set of clothes. She told him that Henri was the gift giver.

"Henri stopped by while you were gone," said Annette.

"What does Henri think?" Paul inquired. "He must know that a man is living in the house."

"Henri knows all that he wants to know. If he wants to know more, he'll ask. When he speaks with the Boche, he'll be a dumb farmer who only knows how to mow hay and milk cows."

Paul told Annette to tell Henri thanks when she next saw him. He would wear the clothes in the morning. He made himself some tea after Annette went to bed. As he sat in the kitchen and nursed the tea, he wondered what life would be like with Annette. They were living like brother and sister and that couldn't go on forever. Yet he felt fortunate to be a part of her life and to be involved in transporting the children into Switzerland. He really felt that he was doing something worthwhile with his life.

CHAPTER 35

Conrad Westphal remained concerned about the threat made by his commanding officer. Being associated with Hess bothered him and he didn't want to be painted with the same filthy brush. Nor did he want to lose his rank, what little he had. His main concern, however, was that he sure as hell didn't want to be sent to the eastern front where he could lose everything, including his life. Patrol duty was fine with him.

"Aren't you concerned that the major will find out that you're not obeying his orders?" asked Westphal.

"That's what the major is expected to say," said Hess. "He knows that Germans are in charge and that France has surrendered. To the victor belong the spoils. He knows how soldiers behave and if I'm not the one to sleep with that bitch, it will be some other soldier. I don't intend to let that happen. I'll let it cool for a bit and then we'll see what will develop," he said, moving his hand between his legs.

Westphal tried to avoid Hess but Hauptmann Schlayer would frequently request the two of them. Recently, however, Hess was volunteering to patrol at night and he didn't invite Westphal along. That was fine with Westphal since he suspected that Hess was planning to visit the bakery girl. At least he wouldn't have anything to do with whatever was happening.

Westphal watched Hess, even as he tried to avoid him, over the next few weeks. He could tell that the soldier was getting weird. He considered going to the major and telling him what he knew but he thought the major might consider the flimsy evidence as insignificant. Maybe if he had just a bit more evidence, he could talk to the major. What Westphal feared most was Hess's anger if he found out that Westphal reported him. He knew that he could make life miserable for him if he wanted to do so. Nor did he want it to look like he was trying to kiss the major's ass. And it didn't look as if Hauptmann Schlayer had any control over Hess or for that matter didn't even know when he was driving the vehicle.

One night late in October, Hess was on duty at ten but signed out at nine. Westphal just happened to be passing by and after Hess left he looked at the log. He signed out at 2100 hours but wrote 2145 hours in the log. That gave him forty-five minutes that wouldn't be accounted for. No one would pay attention to Hess's movements, especially during the evening and night shifts. Westphal wondered if he waited too long.

When he saw Hess the next day, his instincts told him that nothing had happened. Westphal was glad of that. He didn't want anything to happen to that pretty girl. Maybe he would get enough nerve to tell the major. If he weren't so afraid of Hess's reaction and his anger, he would tell him now. But he didn't.

CHAPTER 36

It was Halloween in the United States and All Saints Day Eve in France. Paul and Annette had just finished doing the dinner dishes when they heard a car pull into the drive. Paul grabbed the biggest knife that was in the block on the counter and disappeared into the living room and partially up the stairs.

Annette looked out the window and saw the tall German soldier. She turned away from the window and shouted to Paul, "It's him. The tall one."

The soldier came to the back door and tried to open it. He didn't bother to knock. Feeling that the door was locked, he put his shoulder to it, and on the second try the jam broke. Annette moved as far away from the door as she could. She fingered her knife in the pocket of her dress, hoping that she would not have to use it. He stood leering at her then slowly came toward her. He grabbed her around the waist in one quick motion and started kissing her. His free hand was in her hair, pulling her toward him. She could smell coffee on his breath. She tried to fight him off but with little success. He reached down with his free hand and put it under her dress. She attempted to withdraw the knife from her pocket but his body prevented her from moving her hand. When he thrust his hand between her legs she cried out. His body wouldn't allow her to withdraw her hand out of the pocket.

Paul was at the foot of the stairs and in three steps was in the kitchen. The German was facing toward the window and away from Paul. With the force of his movement, he plunged the knife into the soldier's back, just below the shoulder blade. Hess let out a long string of what surely must have been profanity as he spun to face Paul, his eyes wide with pain and understanding. Paul kept his hand on the knife handle and removed the knife as the German turned.

Annette pushed away from him as he reached for the pistol in the holster on his belt and unleashed the leather strap that covered it. His eyes were big in agony. Fear covered his face. Annette cried out that he had a gun as Paul plunged the knife into his chest. He turned the knife just enough to slide between the ribs and into his heart. The soldier crumpled in a heap, his hand still on the pistol in its holster. There was no doubt that the knife pierced his heart.

"Take off your dress and throw it on the floor. There's blood on it," Paul ordered. Annette pulled her dress over her head and dropped in on the floor. "Change into dark work clothes and wear strong shoes. We have work to do."

Paul turned the soldier over and saw that the bleeding was flowing slowly. His heart was not beating. He had thought out numerous times what would happen if they were forced to take the life of the soldier. Paul understood that they had but two choices to escape execution. They could flee to Switzerland or make it look like the soldier was never at their place and take their chances. Paul's decision was to make it look like the German was never at their farmhouse. He knew that Annette would never agree to discontinue the smuggling and he had committed himself to this cause. When Annette returned, he asked her to get a rake and the wheelbarrow. He used her dress to clean up the blood on the floor and dragged the soldier outside on his back, leaving a trail of blood from the kitchen to the grass outside. Together the two were able to lift him into the wheelbarrow and Paul wheeled the body a short distance away.

"Do you have some old towels or cloth so we can clean up all the blood?"

"I'll be right back," she said as she hurried back into the house.

Annette returned with several old towels and began to wipe the kitchen floor and the stairs from the door. Paul got the hose and rinsed the steps and the grass and area near the steps. They put the stained towels and the bloody dress in the wheelbarrow and Paul wheeled it into the barn.

"I'm going to back the car out to the street and you should rake up the tire marks. Then we'll drive the car almost to the checkpoint. Do you know where it is?" he asked.

"Yes, the road makes a sharp turn to the right and it is only a few hundred meters beyond that."

"You'll have to come with me as I might go too far and end up at the checkpoint."

"What about the body?"

"It's fine for now. I'll bury it after we get back."

Paul found the keys still in the ignition, as he knew he would, and backed the car out to the road. He left the motor running. He would have to leave the car on the road for a few minutes while they completed the task of erasing the tire marks. They both knew that it was highly unlikely that another vehicle would come down the road.

As Annette finished raking, Paul got a dead tomato plant and went over the rake marks to make them look less recent and obvious. He threw the dead plant in the compost heap and climbed in the car. Paul drove back to the main road and toward checkpoint #2. When Annette told him that they were getting close, he turned off the lights and drove slowly. There was sufficient light from a sliver of moon to see the road. When Annette told Paul that she could see the final curve, he shifted the car into neutral and turned off the engine, letting momentum take them as close to the curve as they dared. Just before the final turn he pulled the car off the road and both got out. Leaving the keys in the car and taking care not to slam the car doors, Paul entered the woods and quietly broke a few branches on bushes and made a mess of the leaves giving the impression that a struggle had taken place. In the soft earth he made some tracks into the woods until he reached hard ground and walked backwards on his way out. He did his best to make it look like several people were fighting in the woods. The two then started their trek back to the farmhouse,

Paul had time to explain what he had been doing, although some of it was obvious. They needed to get the car away from the house and he wanted it to look like there was a struggle in the woods near the checkpoint. He also wanted to give the impression that there were two men making tracks, not just one. That should keep them wondering as to what actually took place.

They headed back toward the farmhouse. Paul still had the task of burying the body and fixing the door jam. Several times they wanted to run but Paul's leg wasn't up to it. He did walk faster than he thought possible. They walked and listened for the sound of an automobile and their eyes were alert for any headlights. They were prepared to jump into the ditch on the side of the road at the slightest provocation. To save themselves about two kilometers of walking they cut through the woods. It was a bit slower walking but they were off the road and wouldn't be seen by anyone.

"When we get to the house, you need to go to bed," said Paul. "Your day starts early."

"Yes, but I need to help you."

"That would be nice, but I really don't need help. I have time and I can sleep tomorrow, if I need to. Get your sleep. They will be inquiring if you were at work early in the morning. I'm certain of that. And they will probably visit the farm later in the day to see if there is any indication that the vehicle was here."

Once they reached the farmhouse, she headed for her bedroom and he to the shed. He gathered the rake, a long handled shovel, a pickax and some gloves. These he put on top of the dead soldier in the wheelbarrow and wheeled them to the farthest end of their property. A section of the field that had recently been harvested was chosen for the burial. He raked the leaves that had fallen from nearby trees and made a pile of them. Then he began the digging.

The earth was soft and he made steady progress. It had now been less than an hour since the soldier was killed. Paul didn't have to worry about how the pit looked. His only concern was that he not hit any rocks. The earth got progressively harder as he continued to dig. He had to use the pickax once he was beyond three feet.

He encountered quite a few rocks beyond three feet but they were mostly the size of a loaf of bread. These he piled up on the edge of the pit. When the pit was shoulder deep, he dug just half the hole another foot deeper. One part of the hole looked like it was over Paul's head, which meant it was over six feet. He threw Annette's bloody dress in first and the bloody towels and cloths. He then dumped the body unceremoniously out of the wheelbarrow and kicked it in place to fit into the deepest part of the grave.

149

The soldier's pistol was still in the holster on his belt. As he shoveled the dirt on top of the soldier, he stomped it down with his boots. He didn't want the earth collapsing any time in the near future and he didn't want extra dirt when he was finished. Then he placed a layer of rocks, hoping to discourage anyone from digging any deeper if they got this far. Stomping down the earth was a welcomed change in activity as his muscles were experiencing the strain of digging.

Once all the dirt was replaced and stomped down, he set about to make it look like the rest of the field. The rake made it smooth, and a branch from a nearby bush erased any marks. Leaves scattered randomly over the area made the site look natural. Even though it was dark, he was pleased with his handiwork. He might have time in the morning to make adjustments but for now, by the light of the dim moon, it looked normal. He had no intention of telling Annette where he buried the German soldier but thought that he might have to add some dirt to the hole if it started to sink, possibly several weeks or months in the future. Approximately three hours had elapsed since the soldier had been killed.

Paul got a bucket of water and rinsed the wheelbarrow and tools and put them away. He also rinsed his boots. Then he took a look at the door jam. He noticed that it broke easily and that glue would make it look normal until he could replace it. It wouldn't withstand any weight, but it wouldn't have to bear any, at least for now. He got the glue from the shed and several clamps and temporarily repaired the door jam. He sat at the kitchen table in the dark with only a candle for light. After an hour Paul took off the clamps on the doorjamb and put them back in the shed, carefully locked the door and went to his attic room.

Paul had one more task and that was to get out of his dirty clothes. They could be washed in a few days after the commotion died down. For now he would pile them in the dormer room. There was no doubt in his mind that they would be receiving a visit from the Germans the next day or very shortly thereafter and he didn't want a man's trousers and shirt to be hanging on the clothesline.

He looked out the front dormer window for quite some time. From that vantage point he could tell if any cars were moving about. He couldn't see the cars but rather the light from the headlights. Sometime after one o'clock, he saw the lights of two vehicles going from town toward the checkpoint. Evidently the car had been found and the Germans were attempting to find out what happened or the car was missing and they wanted to find out where it was. They were gone for a long time and still they didn't return. He knew that they had found the vehicle and were investigating the disturbance in the woods. Paul was extremely sleepy. He finally saw the vehicles return about an hour later. It was just after two o'clock. They continued on their way toward town and to the barracks. Paul considered that one danger had been eliminated.

CHAPTER 37

When Annette returned home shortly after lunch, she and Paul had a chance to talk. Paul told her of the vehicles that passed by in the middle of the night and that he expected company soon, probably this afternoon. He explained that he walked around outside and could find no indication of the vehicle having been there and that nothing seemed out of place. He mentioned that he would fix the doorjamb permanently as soon as possible.

"When the German officer comes to investigate, he will insist on searching the house. I'll be in the dormer room and will take the radio with me. Tell them that you keep your radio at the bakery for music. They wouldn't believe you if you said you had no radio."

"Will they confiscate the radio at the bakery?"

"Probably. It's best that we lose that one than the one here at the house."

She agreed that losing just one radio was the best they could do and her candor might go a long way with the Germans. They could also see that she couldn't handle a big soldier like the one that was missing and she couldn't easily dispose of the body. Paul didn't think they would really suspect her. But they would insist on searching the house and that included the attic. Paul said that he would leave the cot out but would move the bedding into the dormer room.

"Make sure the officer knows that you are not too pleased with his visit and you wish to go with him as he searches the house."

"I will. That would be the normal thing to do."

"Is your conscience bothering you about last night?" Paul inquired.

"No. I knew that if he attacked me, he would have to be killed. My father told me that he would have killed me after he was finished with me."

"I agreed with your father. He was warned and he couldn't allow you to tell his commanding officer. So he would have killed you. There is no doubt about that. I'm glad you see that once he raped you he would have had to silence you."

"I'm just sorry that you were the one who had to kill him. He grabbed me so quickly and held my arm against his body so hard that I couldn't get the knife out of my pocket. I didn't expect that."

"I'm a soldier and he was the enemy. That was my job. It is just an awful thing to have to take someone's life. I'm glad it was his life and not yours. I hope that there will be no repercussions toward the villagers. I believe we did everything we could to confuse the Germans."

"Paul, I'm still a bit scared that I'll be nervous when they get here."

"You should be a bit nervous. No one likes being questioned especially by people as ruthless as the Boche. You'll do fine."

It was in the middle of the afternoon when the soldiers came. Seeing the officer and soldiers in their gray uniforms with green collar, intimidated Annette, as they were intended. She had to take a deep breath and convince herself that she would not be panicked. Paul hurried upstairs and secured himself in the dormer room before the soldiers were even out of the vehicle. There were three of them. One was an officer and the other two stayed outside next to the vehicle with rifles slung over their shoulders. The officer introduced himself as Hauptmann Horst Schlayer. The officer was polite and spoke good French. He told Annette that a crime had been committed and he wanted to know where she was last evening.

"I work at the bakery in town and was there at four this morning. I was in bed by eight or eight-thirty," she lied.

"Did you see any vehicles last evening?"

"No."

"Are you the same person who complained to Major Decker that a German soldier was harassing you?"

"My father and I both spoke with the major. Since then my father had a heart attack and died. We were trying to avoid trouble with the soldiers."

"Who owns the bakery?"

"I now have total responsibility. Our family has owned the bakery for several generations."

"Do you speak German?"

"I understand a few words in German."

"When did you arrive at your work this morning?"

"At the usual time. Four o'clock."

"Would you have any objection if I have a look at your home?" questioned the officer.

"You mean you want to search my house?"

"Yes. That's what I mean."

"Not if I may accompany you," responded Annette.

"That would be fine. Your presence would be welcome. We will also search the barn and shed."

He didn't wait for permission. Hauptmann Schlayer went to the door and barked orders at the two soldiers waiting by the car. They immediately headed toward the barn. He turned his attention back toward Annette.

Hauptmann Schlayer noticed the shotgun the moment he reached the cellar. He didn't say anything but continued to look. Finally he asked, "Do you shoot?"

"No, but my father used the shotgun to scare away the occasional fox that thought he would like to eat our eggs. The shells are in the cabinet over there."

"Have you fired the gun recently?"

"No. I don't remember the gun being fired for several years."

He picked up the shotgun, sniffed it and replaced it on the floor. He climbed the stairs to the living room and looked at the living quarters, opened the closet door, looked in the cabinets under the sink and counters and asked to go upstairs. Annette nodded. He searched her father's room, looking under the bed and in the closet. Next he entered her room and followed the same procedure. He saw the door to the attic in the hall and asked where it went.

"It goes to the attic."

He opened the door and climbed the stairs but didn't go all the way, seeing that it was empty except for the cot.

"Why the cot?"

"In case we have visitors. We haven't had any recently."

"You always say 'we.' Who is the we?"

"My father and I. I'm not used to his being deceased. I guess it will take me a while before I adjust to that."

"When did you learn to drive a car?"

"I don't know how to drive. I've never even sat in the driver's seat of an automobile. We never had a car and I would have been too young to learn to drive. I don't know why you asked me that question?"

"I had my reason. Thank you for answering my questions and for your cooperation."

Schlayer was silent as they continued downstairs to the kitchen. Annette had the distinct impression that he was disappointed.

"Oh, do you have a radio in the house?" he asked.

"No, but I do have one at the bakery for music. It makes the work a bit more pleasant."

"I will send someone to the bakery to pick it up tomorrow. You should have known that radios are not permitted." She acknowledged his statement. Then he clicked his heels, turned and walked out. He climbed into the passenger seat and the driver and other soldier piled in, placing their rifles on the back seat.

A few minutes later Paul came out of hiding and they discussed the visit. "I don't think he suspects you and they know that they had an undisciplined soldier on their hands. I don't believe they'll blame any Frenchman. Maybe they'll believe that he left the vehicle to urinate in the woods and was attacked by smugglers or people trying to escape into Switzerland. They may increase their night patrols."

"Paul, my heart beat fast when he wanted to look in the attic. He didn't suspect anything. Wasn't it great having a room to go to when they came?"

"Yes, and I felt very comfortable and secure. I could hear him when he climbed up the stairs and asked about the cot. Annette, where did you learn to act like that?" Paul asked.

"Oh, I guess there was always the actress in me. I often played parts in school skits and liked to sing at school functions. My mother encouraged me."

"You played the part very well. Remember, the Germans have no right to the truth. If it keeps us alive to lie or will keep others alive, then, by all means, lie."

"Paul, I know it would be wrong to tell them the truth if I were to endanger someone else. They are doing evil things and it is our obligation to oppose them, each in our own way. That's what we are doing. If what is called lying will help us oppose them, then we lie. My father told me that evil people like that don't deserve the truth."

CHAPTER 38

Annette and Paul ate supper and remained at the kitchen table for a while after the meal, sipping tea. It had been a very emotional twenty-four hours and talking seemed to help. Both agreed that this was the only possible outcome that was best for everyone. Maybe the outcome was not best for the soldier who died, but it was for everyone else.

"In a few weeks this may be forgotten and they will leave you alone."

"I hope so. It is a bit frightening. You have to be forever on your guard. I'm glad we live far enough off the road so that when we hear a vehicle you have time to get out of the kitchen and upstairs."

"We are fortunate."

They discussed how they would handle children during the winter months. Annette pointed out that leaving tracks in the snow would be the biggest problem, especially if it didn't continue snowing for a good while. Their trail would be easily spotted by a patrol either that night or the next day. She suggested that they talk with the contacts in Switzerland to find out what would happen if they were delayed for a day or two and what should be done if it snowed.

Paul told Annette that he gave Pierre and Marie his name, rank, squadron and location and asked them to alert the British that he was alive. He explained that he didn't want the British to think that he was deserting. He also asked them to use their influence to allow him to stay in France in order to continue this successful and dangerous operation.

Annette agreed that her ability to smuggle the children would be hampered and probably would need to be shut down, if Paul were not able to remain with her and help the children cross to safety. She knew that making bread for the community was an important obligation, but most of all, it was great cover for her. So far the Germans didn't suspect that she was engaged in any illegal activity.

"Paul, I don't want you to leave," she began. "I would miss you and we couldn't continue to transport the children. What's going to happen to us?"

Paul took Annette by the hand and moved his chair closer to hers. Taking both her hands in his he looked earnestly at her.

"I've wanted to bring up the subject for some time. The first day that I met your father, he made me promise that I would always treat you with respect. I promised him that I would always be a gentleman. Now, even though he's gone, I still respect that agreement. I've wanted to kiss you many times, and I love being with you and enjoy just sitting here and talking. But I don't know what the future holds. I've wanted to be intimate with you for some time. But if we have a future together I don't want to do anything to jeopardize our relationship."

"Paul, I feel the same way. I, too, want to be romantic. Yet, I feel it is too soon after my father's death. Then I wonder if you will be here beyond the war? We don't even know if we will survive this war. We could both be killed because of our activity."

"We know the chance we are taking. Could we do otherwise?"

"I know that I couldn't live with myself if I were to refuse to help these children. Without us, they will be sent to camps and death. I believe that you share the same feelings."

"I do. I just hope the British will see the situation as we do."

"What bothers me, Paul, is that if you stay here you are confined permanently to this house. The Germans can't find out that you live here or even exist. Just two or three kilometers from here you would be free to continue your life as an airman with the RAF. What you have now isn't much of a life."

Paul recognized that Annette was posing a serious question that would have to be addressed. He realized that she had been giving their situation a lot of thought as he wondered how long he would be able to live cooped up in the house.

"This is a major decision in our lives," Paul admitted. "Maybe we are at a crossroad and what we do in the next month or so will affect our lives permanently. I am content to live with you as your brother until such time as we can change that. Maybe the military will not require me to return to England. What they decide for me is important. I couldn't live with myself if they labeled me a deserter. Let's wait and see what happens. You're not unhappy, are you, Annette?"

"No, but I feel the frustration that both of us are experiencing. I'm not ashamed to admit that I have strong feelings for you and want to sleep with you."

"And I for you, Annette. I believe that I love you but the war has put our lives on hold. We don't know what tomorrow holds for us and that is no way to begin a life together. I want this to be permanent and not just for a few nights."

"And I love you too, Paul. Let's see if we can get the British to agree to let you remain doing what we're doing."

They talked openly during their evening meal and after supper, until Annette left for sleep. All the talk of intimacy and friendship and possible romance left both of them aroused, yet too much was at stake for either of them to act on their emotions. Both understood that acknowledging that fact, however, didn't make living together any easier. But they had reached an understanding and both were pleased that each was looking at the other in terms of a long term relationship.

Paul remained in the kitchen thinking about all that they had discussed. He felt that being able to talk about their situation was important and was pleased to know that Annette was serious about him, personally. It wasn't just so that he could assist her in bringing Jewish children into Switzerland. She had feelings for him. He was also pleased to know that she understood his frustration with being cooped up in the house so much of the time.

CHAPTER 39

The week after the soldier was killed was active for both Paul and Annette. On Monday, Paul escorted four boys, all ten or eleven years old, across the border, with no difficulty. The children saw the journey as a great adventure and were most cooperative. He had a moment to talk with Pierre and was able to tell him about the incident on Halloween night. Pierre said that he heard a German soldier was missing but so far the Germans haven't figured out what actually happened. Pierre told Paul that he would keep listening and would pass on any information.

On Wednesday there was one boy about eight and two girls, one seven and the other just five. The five year old was very frightened and had fears of the dark. Annette spoke with the child before they left for the border but it looked for a while as if the trip might have to be aborted. Then Annette asked the child if she would be less afraid if Annette took the trip with them. She said that she would like that.

The child balked a bit when they got to the passageway through the rocks. It seems she was also claustrophobic. The darkness may have helped a bit in that she couldn't see very far and Annette was right behind her, whispering encouragement. As the group started down the mountain to the valley below, she began to cry. She was frightened by the shadows and the dark trees.

This next phase of the journey was critical and silence was essential. Paul suggested to Annette that he carry the child. The child wanted Annette to do the carrying but she said that she wasn't strong enough. The child reluctantly accepted Paul. Annette told her that she needed to be absolutely quiet when they crossed the stream and went up the hill. A cry from the child could be disastrous. The child promised that she would not cry.

It was a severe test for Paul's leg. With all his senses on alert and the fear that the child might cry, he didn't experience any discomfort. He stepped across the stream and the group continued to remain exceptionally quiet. At the small stream half way up the hill he blinked the flashlight and received the customary two blinks in return. They were very happy to deliver this group of children to the escorts.

"Paul, I'm glad you and Annette are here. I have some information that requires you to make a decision," began Pierre.

"What kind of a decision?"

"I've notified my contacts as you requested and they got word to the British. The British wanted you to proceed immediately to Bern and there they would arrange for you to return to England. I explained that we are smuggling Jewish children out of France and you have the only successful operation in this part of France. I told them that recently we were forced to reroute two other operations in the area. Now with the death of Annette's father, we need you more than ever to escort the children. They still didn't want to let you remain," said Pierre.

"Don't they understand how important it is to get these children out of France and away from the Germans? The alternative is that they would all be sent to concentration camps and most would die," explained Annette.

"They know that, but that is not their concern. So I told them what they should be concerned about. We have a British pilot, shot down several weeks ago, hidden in the area. I told them that I knew of several other airmen in the area and I bargained with them to keep you where you are. In return we will ferry the airmen across the mountain just like we do the children."

"Do you really have other airmen?" asked Paul incredulously.

"No. Not at the moment. But we will," Pierre replied with a grin. "We do have the British pilot and will keep him until the British show some sense."

"Paul, what do you think?" asked Annette.

"I think it will work. We'll be helping the British get some of their airmen back and they won't destroy our operation. I think it's a good trade.

Whether we get caught smuggling an airman across the border or several children, the consequences are the same. Should we agree?"

"I agree," she said.

Paul turned to Pierre and said, "Tell the British that we would be happy to help smuggle airmen out of France and back to England. But the deal is that in return they cannot interfere with this operation."

"I'll tell them," said Pierre. "I think this is a good deal for them since they give up one airman and will probably get three or four, maybe a lot more in return. Let's see what they say."

Marie returned at that moment and told Pierre that they would have to leave, as the child was getting upset. Pierre shook their hands and said he would give the Brits the results of their conversation in the morning. The two watched the car drive away and believed that they had made an important decision. Each life was precious and they just couldn't allow this operation to be terminated. Smuggling soldiers across the border to fight again was equally noble, and Paul told Annette that doing so was a small price to pay for being able to stay with her.

In the darkness she kissed Paul. "I'm proud of you that you are willing to stay and face the chance that we might be caught and executed."

"You are the courageous one. You give me the strength to continue doing this dangerous work."

Together, side-by-side, they walked down the hill, across the stream, through the woods and up to the rock formation. Paul didn't even notice how tight the muscle in his left leg had become.

CHAPTER 40

Annette went to church on Sunday, by bicycle. She was usually very faithful and had been going until the death of her father. She attended the funeral Mass, but had not attended since, mainly because of the weather. She told Paul that she wanted to go to thank God for all His blessings but also because it was important to keep a routine. Paul agreed and wished that he were free to go with her.

Annette spoke with the pastor after Mass.

"How are you doing, Annette?"

"Good, Father. I miss Papa very much but I know that he is happy with Mama in heaven."

"Is there anything I can do to help?"

"There might be, Father, but I have to give it some thought first. I appreciate the offer."

On the trip home she wondered about Father Gilbert's question. She sensed that he knew about her and Paul killing the German soldier. It was the look that he gave her. It seemed to penetrate her, as if he knew. Maybe it was her conscience that was causing her to behave as if she were guilty. She would have liked to go to confession, but for now, she didn't think she should tell anybody. She knew that what she told the priest in the confessional was sacred, and he couldn't reveal what was confessed. However, she didn't want to confess. She hadn't done anything wrong. She thought about the killing and concluded that they were only defending themselves, and she couldn't have acted differently. She felt sorry for the dead soldier, but her conscience told her that her act was not unreasonable or reckless. It was unfortunate.

Yet she would have liked to talk with Father Gilbert. Reassurance would have been nice.

Paul greeted her when she returned and made her breakfast. She had been fasting in order to receive the Eucharist, and he thought that making breakfast was the least that he could do. Annette suggested that they fix a picnic lunch and go for a walk. Even though it was November, it was a nice day and not too cool. They knew the cold weather would settle in soon enough.

It was a pleasant walk. Annette showed Paul another part of the mountain that was very rugged and scenic. The problem was that without scaling the mountain there was no pass to the other side. It was a wonderful place for a picnic, quiet and secluded. They found a rock covered with moss where they sat and ate a slice of bread spread with liverwurst and washed down with some wine. It was a perfect setting.

Annette waited until they were finished eating before she broke the silence. "Paul, I was speaking with the pastor after church today, and an idea came to me."

Smiling and curious, Paul responded, "What kind of idea?"

"He could marry us," she said hesitantly.

A moment of silence passed. Paul knew what his answer would be.

"Nothing would make me happier than to live with you the rest of my life. The only force that could hurt us now is if the British refuse our offer or if the Boche find out what we are doing. The British would be foolish to stop us and the Germans would be evil. We can't do much about the Germans but we can try to bargain with the British."

"If the British accept your offer, you wouldn't be a deserter, and you would be free to marry me," offered Annette.

"Exactly. I still won't be able to be seen with you and no one can know we're married. I don't have any trouble with that. We can still go on smuggling children and airmen until the war is over."

"That is unless the Boche become too suspicious and determine that I shouldn't live here."

"That would be a disaster. We would most certainly be separated and your movements would be watched closely."

"Have you thought about what you would do after the war?"

"I'd stay here with you and make furniture. I know how to make cabinets and I'd learn what the French need and want and will make quality furniture. You have a big barn that could be converted into a workshop. Henri really doesn't need all the barn for the hay and storage, and it could be a good work area."

"I can see you've given it some thought."

"I must admit that I have. After the war I would need to take you to the United States to meet my family. They are living in New York now. And while we are there we would visit my aunt and uncle in Quebec. Then we'd be free to live our lives on this little farm here in France."

"Paul, that would make me very happy. Just knowing that you want to marry me and live with me brings me happiness."

"How will we be able to get married? I can't be seen in town or at a public ceremony. What do you have in mind?"

"I'll talk to the pastor. He can be trusted. He would come here and marry us, and Jeanne and her husband could be our witnesses. They would be the only people who would know. I'm sure the paperwork can be handled without the Germans knowing about us. The Church can be discreet when it needs to be."

"I see that you've done some thinking, also."

"I have. Now tell me that you want to marry me," she said laughingly.

Paul took both her hands and looked into her eyes and said, "I fell in love with you the first day I saw you from the barn. I'd consider myself the luckiest man in the world to know and to spend my life with you. Annette, will you marry me?"

"Paul, I will. I want to spend my life loving you."

The two continued discussing their plans. Annette told Paul that she would arrange things with the pastor and after that she would talk with Jeanne. She stressed that she and Guy could be trusted and would not tell anybody. Paul said that he was expecting the British to agree to his deal and it was possible that they might hear something the next time he crossed the border. Paul told Annette that waiting was going to be difficult but she said that under the circumstances waiting a week or two would be nothing compared with waiting until the end of the war. Paul had to agree with her.

As the evening shadows began to lengthen and the sun was setting behind the mountain, the two leisurely started home, oblivious to the falling temperature. The sky put on a show for them as they made their way back to the farmhouse. Both were experiencing the joy that comes from being truly in love for the first time.

CHAPTER 41

It was a cold Tuesday when Annette arrived at work at four in the morning. The flower pot had been moved. The geranium had long since died and all that was left of it was the dried stems. She was anxious to get inside where it would be warm to start the day's work. She appreciated the heat from the ovens warming up the back room. Her mind was replaying yesterday's pleasant picnic with Paul. The morning seemed to pass quickly.

After Jeanne came in at noon, they talked for a few minutes. Then Annette was free to leave. She pedaled home with the cold wind pushing her and hoped the children would be dressed sufficiently warm. She told Paul that he would be traveling that evening.

Paul went outside and looked at the weather. The clouds were lowering but he thought that the rain might hold off for a few hours, but one could never be sure. He told Annette that he would leave as soon as possible after the children arrived.

Paul, standing by the kitchen door, saw four children enter the barn about four o'clock. Annette suggested that they bring the children some milk, apples and bread. Her presence never failed to reassure the children and make them feel that they would be safe. She told them that she was not going with them but that they were in good hands. They were all either seven or eight years old. Two were boys and two were girls. Paul spoke with the children before they went, but since none of them spoke French, he knew they wouldn't understand. Still it was important for the children to hear him and know that he cared for them. His intonation was kind and gentle and they understood that he would protect them. Sign language was used to communicate anything of importance.

They left before the sun was behind the mountain and were able to negotiate the passageway and the trail over the mountain before it was completely dark. Paul had the children wait at the start of the forest and he went ahead to make sure there was no late patrol. He listened carefully for a few minutes and then returned to the children. He put his fingers to his lips, and the children did the same in the universal sign that said they would be silent.

All crossed the stream with little difficulty and Paul blinked the flashlight halfway up the hill. The return signal was slow in coming. Paul thought that they might not expect him that early. That was the case. Marie took the children while Pierre and Paul talked business. Pierre told him that the British didn't want to go along with the deal. Paul's spirits fell. He didn't realize how important this was to him but now it took on much more importance since he considered it the biggest obstacle to marrying Annette.

"I told them the name of the pilot that we have in our possession, thanks to the Resistance," Pierre began. "I told them that unless we have the agreement that we suggested in writing, the pilot would remain in France. I also told them that no other airmen would be smuggled out of this sector of France unless they acquiesced. If they want to play rough, we can also."

Paul was extremely pleased that Pierre was fighting so hard on his behalf. He told Pierre that he was disappointed that the British wouldn't be reasonable. He appreciated what Pierre was willing to do for him.

"Paul, we appreciate all that you are doing. This work is dangerous and you are doing it very well. I don't know where we would be without you."

"And I appreciate that you are fighting so hard for me to remain where I am. Annette couldn't do this without me, or at least not for very long."

"Paul, you and Annette have the best cover, provide the best access to the border and are accessible by woods from an isolated location. You have smuggled more children across the border and have not had an incident that would require us to use a different route and more dangerous connections. We need you and will do everything we can to keep you. Don't worry. The British are being unreasonable. Eventually they'll come around. They know we are playing for keeps when we asked for the deal to be in writing. If it isn't in writing, I told them that we can't deliver the pilot. They'll agree. We hold the cards. They have some say about what happens to you but they have no power over me. Be patient, my friend."

Paul thought that this might be the time to ask what would happen if the weather was too inclement or if it snowed and a trail would be visible in the morning.

"When the flower pot is moved, I receive a message that children are being moved. I don't want to tell you how I get the message, but we do. Once we receive the message we come here at dusk and remain until the children arrive. If the weather changes or we suspect that the children can't come that evening, we will be here every night until they do come. You can be assured that Marie and I will be here every evening and will stay several hours if necessary."

Pierre emphasized that it was up to Paul and Annette to determine if they could move the children across the border safely. He told Paul that they were doing an excellent job and that was why he didn't want to lose this operation.

With all this information, Paul made his way back home. Yet there was the vague feeling of disappointment. He felt that his life was depending on a favorable decision by the Brits. Just as he arrived at the mountain it started to rain, and in a few minutes, it was raining hard. His coat, a gift from Henri, absorbed the water and got surprisingly heavy. He was also surprised at how slick the path was when it was wet. This was especially true when he was going down the mountain. He made a note to remember that fact should he have to take children over the mountain in the rain. He was pleased that he had no children with him at the moment. They would have to avoid rainy nights.

Paul told Annette all the news. She listened carefully and at the end she smiled and said, "Paul, they want that pilot and all the other airmen much more than they want you. Pierre is smart and getting you a piece of paper with the agreement on it is worth a month of waiting. Why didn't we think of getting it in writing? This has turned out to be a blessing in disguise. Just wait, you'll get the agreement."

"I hope you're right. It will be nice to have a document so they can't come back later and say that I deserted," Paul said as he sipped his tea.

Annette came over to Paul as he sat at the table and put her arms around him and kissed him on the mouth. "Paul, it will be worth it. We are doing things right. I want you very much, but the work we are doing is God's work, and we have to be patient. We need his protection and blessing, and he will reward us for being faithful."

"That doesn't make it easy. Until we marry, I'll remain your brother. Now get to bed," he kidded as he pulled her close to him for another kiss.

She kissed him again and left. Paul was pleased that she trusted him and was not afraid to show her true feelings. He spent time considering Pierre's words and couldn't help but agree that getting the agreement in writing, duly signed, would be invaluable.

He sat at the table and considered what could be if everything worked out like they wanted. There were so many 'ifs,' and at this moment, they didn't know if the various problems could be solved. So many confusing scenarios presented themselves that he began to get sleepy and knew that it was time to lay them to rest.

CHAPTER 42

On Friday of that same week the flower pot was on the right side of the door. The weather had been cold and it snowed lightly several nights earlier in the week. Paul was surprised when Annette came home and told Paul that children would be coming.

"I'll watch the weather carefully, but my feeling is that we'll have snow before supper," he said.

"I think you're right. If we have to keep the children overnight we can do so. Let's see how it goes."

The children arrived about four and the first flakes arrived minutes later. Big, fat flakes covered the ground in a garment of white in just a few minutes. Annette brought the children in from the barn and sat them around the kitchen table. They were three of the cutest girls that Paul and Annette had seen. They were all seven years old and two were twins.

Annette was not afraid to speak German with the children. She had long ago decided that she could speak with the children, but would not let the Germans know how much she understood. Sign language continued to be the speech of the day, especially when Paul was present. Sometimes Annette would translate for Paul if something were important or humorous. For the most part everyone seemed to get along well and understand what needed to be communicated. As the evening grew dark, and the snow continued, it became obvious that the children would be forced to stay the night.

Annette got two goose-down comforters and pillows from her closet and placed them on the floor in her room to make the girls comfortable and warm. They giggled a bit and seemed to like the sleepover. Paul kept an eye out on the snow and noticed by around eight that it was barely snowing but had turned colder. He was glad that the children stayed. They were asleep about the same time as Annette usually went to bed.

After a nice breakfast in the morning, Paul took the girls to see the chickens and gather eggs, which they enjoyed. He kept looking toward the road to make sure no German patrol cars were in the vicinity. He also took them for a tour of the barn and they liked climbing up to the loft. It was a bit dangerous but they were nimble and careful and it was a real treat for him to hear their laughter.

After lunch Annette arrived home and the children were pleased to see her. They gathered around her, pulling on her skirt and vying for her attention. They were children separated from their parents and in need of motherly affection. Annette instinctively knew that and gave the children the attention and affection they craved.

About three-thirty in the afternoon both Paul and Annette took the children for their walk in the woods. There was no rush and they didn't want to get to the stream while the soldiers were still on patrol. So they went slow, stopped at the top of the passageway and played with the children before they began the rest of the journey. On the way down the mountain they cautioned the children about silence. Paul saw that the warmth of the day had melted all but a bit of the snow. He had the children follow him single file and he avoided any patches of snow or slush, and stayed away from low spots that might make footprints.

In the woods above the stream they stopped and listened for about five minutes. It was dusk and this was the time to be most careful. They then proceeded cautiously and he and Annette noticed some footprints left by the patrol in last night's snow. They didn't say anything, so as not to alarm the children, but exchanged glances that said, "Did you see that?"

They easily passed over the stream and up the hill where they blinked the flashlight. It was not yet dark. It took Marie and Pierre by surprise, and they had to get out their flashlight to signal in return. They were friends now and it was nice to see them.

"We're glad you didn't come last night. Your footprints would still be visible in some places," Pierre acknowledged.

"I'm glad, too. It could have tipped off the Boche," Paul agreed.

The children were reluctant to leave. In just twenty-four hours the adults had become attached to these little urchins, and the children needed them even more. Paul and Annette gave the children long hugs, and Marie was gentle with them. Annette assured them that they were safe and would have more fun in the days ahead. One child walked with Marie to the car, turning back several times. The twins walked together hand in hand and didn't turn back.

"What's the story from the British High Command?" Paul asked.

"They have so far refused to budge. So I was forced to give them an ultimatum. I told them that we have three demands. One, we want everything in writing, especially that they recognize your work and authorize you to remain in France to do it. Two, back pay and monthly pay will be sent to a bank in Bern. I've given them the account number and only you or I can get the money. By the way, I need your signature. Three, they have a week to agree or they will be forced to raise your rank every six months."

Paul could not help but smile. He had never known anyone as tenacious and wise as Pierre and he was pleased that Pierre was his advocate.

"Remind me to hire you as my lawyer, should I ever need one," quipped Paul.

As Paul signed the bank's signature card and was about to commit to memory the account number, Pierre said, "They have no choice. We are holding the pilot and he has information that the British are eager to have. We also have two other airmen in our custody now, and I've told them that the only way to get them out is through you."

"How long before you will know?"

"They will have to decide before the week is out or they will pay dearly in rank and salary for your services. I think they are only now beginning to understand that we have them by the short hairs. They're bluffing with no cards, and we're sitting with four aces. Oh, here's a copy of the account number and the password that I have chosen. Memorize them and destroy the paper."

"Thanks, Pierre. Maybe the next time we meet this will all be settled."

"They will realize that we are not unreasonable. Patience, my friend, and everyone will win."

The two men shook hands, as did Annette. Paul was glad that she heard the conversation and was anxious to have her understandings of the negotiations. They were forced to wait until they arrived at the mountain for fear their voices would be heard. They still kept their voices barely above a whisper.

As they walked back to the farmhouse in the crisp cold air they both had the feeling that they were doing something important. Silently they walked behind the big rock, down the stairs and through the curves that made up the passageway. They walked through the woods, crossed the dirt road after they searched the field and the road. Seeing nothing they continued to the house.

Annette felt that Pierre was acting in the best interests of all parties. The British just didn't realize how much they needed Paul and how much they would lose if he returned to England. Pierre couldn't operate the most successful smuggling operation in that part of France without Paul and Annette. And Annette couldn't do it without Paul. The result would be that Paul would be given the freedom to risk his life to save little children from extermination and to rescue airmen from the Germans and would continue getting paid. He would also be allowed to continue living with Annette, albeit as brother and sister for the time being.

A hot cup of tea helped them overcome the cold. Paul was not at all certain if Pierre was going to win. Annette's assurances helped him to settle down and to recognize the reasonableness of their proposition. They sat in the living room with only a candle for light until Annette said she needed to get to bed. Paul was also tired and decided to go to his attic room a few minutes later. Paul noticed the curtain made out of flour cloth on the window. He checked and saw that one was in the other dormer window as well. He didn't know when Annette had the time to sew but saw that it would do the job just fine.

CHAPTER 43

The mornings were especially cold those last days in November. Even though Annette was bundled up, she hurried to work on her bicycle. She was pleased to arrive at the bakery, and get inside away from the cold wind. She started one of the ovens both to warm the shop and to prepare them for use. Then she went about the task of mixing the dough for new loaves. Her thoughts turned to Jeanne and how grateful she was to her and her daughter. If she had to stay until closing time she would have an exceptionally long day. Jeanne and her daughter, Michelle, were lifesavers. They told Annette that they could continue helping her for as long as they were needed. That gave Annette tremendous peace of mind.

It was in the middle of the morning when the tailor, Monsieur Girard came into the store. He seemed a bit uneasy as he waited for the lady who was talking with Annette to leave. The customer didn't appear to be in any rush to get out into the cold. When she was gone, he spoke.

"Annette, I am with the Resistance. Listen carefully. The Boche will be putting twenty-four hour surveillance on the farm. They suspect that you are smuggling children across into Switzerland. I have a source within the German garrison that told me this. Hauptmann Schlayer has been suspicious of you but can't prove anything. If he went to the major with the little information he has he would be laughed at. He wants to find some evidence that you are involved."

"If they watch the house twenty-four hours a day they will find out what they want to know. We are involved. What can we do?"

"Just listen for a moment. The airman is in danger. I don't believe you

175

are. It will probably take most of today to get organized so they will most likely start tomorrow. But they could start this afternoon. The airman has to leave as soon as possible. They found a wooden board that they believe you use to cross the stream. They also found some small footprints near that crossing and Schlayer suspects you are involved with smuggling children. Now that Major Decker is in Berlin for two weeks, Schlayer can do what he wants. Remember, he is just suspicious. He has no proof."

"How do you know about the airman? I didn't think anyone knew about him."

"Only those who are involved in this operation know about him. Your secret is safe with us."

"Thank you. I know it is. I'll get Jeanne to come early so I can go home and alert Paul and urge him to flee to Switzerland."

"No, Annette. Stay here. I'll get things going, and I'll have someone tell Jeanne that you need to go home early."

"What about the children?"

"They will be held here in France until this is over," said the tailor. "Now I have to go. You will get a visitor soon who might be able to tell you more." With that cryptic remark, he left.

It was about an hour later when the pastor, Father Gilbert, entered the bakery. Annette was using a wooden paddle to take loaves out of the oven. She stopped for a moment to give the pastor her attention.

"Annette, how are you?"

"Fine, Father. What can I get for you?"

"Are we alone?"

"Yes. How may I help?"

"Annette, I'm the person who moves the flower pot."

"You,...Father? I don't understand."

"There are many of us who are helping with smuggling the children and we are so grateful for what you and the airman are doing. We don't want the Germans to shut down this successful operation."

"But what about the children?"

"We can keep them for a week or two. It is impossible for you to smuggle the children now. Usually when I come into the bakery there are people here, and I can't wait until we are alone, like today. If I buy white bread I'm telling you that the danger has passed. Dark bread means it is still dangerous. We'll still use the flower pot to tell you the day children will be arriving."

"Father, I didn't know that you knew about Paul. I've wanted to talk to you about him for some time. After this crisis is over, would it be possible for you to marry us? We love each other very much and have wonderful plans for the future. Jeanne and Guy Cartier can be our witnesses. We just can't keep on living as brother and sister when we love each other so much and want to show each other how much we care."

"Yes, Annette. I can make those arrangements. Let's talk about this after you are no longer in danger. Now is not the time. Tell Paul to leave immediately and you must keep to a strict schedule, like you always do. Pierre has been notified that he is coming and has made arrangements to meet him this afternoon. He must leave as soon as you can notify him. Now let me buy that loaf of dark bread. We'll talk again about matrimony after this crisis is behind us."

"Thank you, Father."

"Jeanne will be here soon. She doesn't know what you are doing or about this entire operation. You might want to ask her about being witnesses but then you will also have to explain what you are doing. She and her husband can be trusted. Also, I have a letter for your airman to post in Switzerland. Annette, it's important that no one see this letter. Lives depend on it, including yours," he said as he handed Annette the letter. She put it in her smock.

"I'm beginning to understand. I'll give it to Paul and explain how important it is." After a moment's hesitation she continued, "It's nice to know you're involved in this business, Father."

The pastor smiled as he left with his loaf of dark bread. Annette had very mixed feelings. She didn't feel so alone knowing that her pastor was her contact with the Resistance. And it was nice to know that he had connections within the German barracks. She wished Paul could stay. She didn't want him to go but knew that if he was found in the farmhouse or if any item that belonged to him was seen, their life would be over. She was concerned that something as small as a boot print would give away his presence and be cause for German retaliation. Would it be like this for a week, two weeks or a month? She didn't know and didn't like the uncertainty.

After Jeanne arrived, late in the morning, she left for home.

CHAPTER 44

It had warmed up considerably since her trip to work in the middle of the night and the bicycle ride was comfortable. Paul had fixed the doorjamb and was working in the shed. She kissed him affectionately and he immediately suspected that she had something on her mind.

"Paul, you have to leave, immediately. They will be setting up twenty-four hour surveillance either this afternoon or tomorrow. A patrol found the board we use to help the little ones get over the stream. They also found some footprints. Pierre is waiting for you and will make arrangements when it is safe to return. It is Father Gilbert who moves the flower pot and makes all the arrangements."

"You know, Annette, I'm not surprised. From what you've told me about him he sounds like a holy man. By the way, I found a cardboard box and put a lot of my personal things, like my uniform, airman's jacket, pants and stuff in it. I buried them behind the barn several days ago. I don't think anyone will find any trace of me having been here. I will put my clothes in the dormer and seal it well. Go about your business and work as you would if you lived here alone. They'll get tired of watching. I would lock the doors at night. You'll be safe here as long as I'm not with you."

"What about the attic? Will they find anything there?"

"No, but I took the liberty to move a few of your father's things up there to make it look more like an attic. I have an idea. Turn on the fan facing into the attic and shake the mop in front of it. Do that a few times and some of the dust will lightly cover the items up there. It will look like no one was up there for weeks. I don't think they will look any further."

178

"Good idea. I'll do some cleaning this afternoon." Annette took the letter from her smock and handed it to Paul. "Here is a very important letter that you are to post in Bern. It contains information about the operation and is addressed to people by the name of Schmidt in the United States. Father Gilbert said that if it fell into the wrong hands it would harm us as well as the entire operation. I think it is from the soldier who is secretary to the major. He had three stripes on his arm and speaks French well. I think he is tipping off the Resistance. Guard it carefully. Now say goodbye. I don't think you need to take any clothes with you. You can buy what you need."

Paul and Annette kissed knowing that they would be separated for a while. Annette told Paul that she spoke with the pastor about marrying them.

"Let's think those pleasant thoughts. We will be united soon. Then we will never be separated. I love you, Annette, but I must think about leaving now."

Paul hurried to the house to pick up a few items and the coat Henri had given him. What he didn't take with him he put in the dormer room and closed it securely. He kissed Annette one last time and left for the woods behind the barn.

As he came to the passageway, he had an idea. He backtracked to the woods and broke off a small branch from a bush and as he passed through the passageway he wedged it between the rocks at the narrowest part of the passageway. Unless one was very careful they would dislodge it or at least disturb it passing through the opening. This would allow Paul to know if anyone used the passage while he was gone. It could alert him to the fact that someone knew that this was the way through the mountain. He would consider that critical information.

When Paul got to the woods just before the stream, all was quiet. Yet because it was still light, he was hesitant to cross. It was half past the hour and the time for the usual patrol. He moved parallel to the steam, deep in the woods and worked his way to the wide spot where Annette put the flat rock in the stream. Then he waited. He was glad that he did. A patrol of two soldiers with rifles slung over their shoulders could be heard returning from upstream. They had passed about fifteen minutes before and were completing their task. He was glad that he knew their schedule well enough to avoid their most popular times to patrol.

Paul watched them pass. They stopped near where the stream was narrow and searched the ground looking for fresh footprints. They then moved on. Paul waited ten more minutes. Then he made his way to the wide part of the stream and easily crossed using the rocks as stepping-stones. He climbed directly up the hill and because it was daylight, he had to trust that Pierre was expecting him. He was not disappointed.

Pierre inquired about Annette as he led him to the car. He assured Paul that as long as she stuck to her schedule, she would be safe. Paul agreed although he harbored some doubts and was concerned that the Boche might make it difficult for her.

Pierre drove a short way on a dirt road that was overgrown with trees, and entered a small paved road that was without traffic for several kilometers. Pierre told Paul that they would spend the night in Porrentruy, a small town where he and Marie had an apartment. Paul would stay there with them overnight and they would drive him to Bern in the morning. The plans were that he would stay in Bern in a hotel until it was safe to return to France.

Pierre also told Paul that he had some good news. "Tell me. I could use some good news right now."

"It seems like the Canadians have heard about your situation. The airman who we have in our custody is a Canadian on loan to the RAF, like you. They are now involved with the negotiations and they favor leaving you in France," Pierre explained.

"Let's hope that cooler heads will prevail and this will be resolved soon."

"The British are trying to say that you are a deserter and the Canadians are having none of that. The Canadians are happy to have someone to assist in bringing their flyers across the border. They argued that crossing the border is the most difficult part of the journey and more airmen get caught just as they are about to get out of enemy territory."

"Maybe this will be settled soon. I sure hope so," Paul offered.

"Paul, I think we will hear something this week and with the Canadians involved it should be more to our liking. If I have news I'll get it to you in Bern. Now how about a nice steak, potatoes and some wine?"

CHAPTER 45

Paul spent his first night in Switzerland at Pierre and Marie's small apartment. He had a chance to get to know these two dedicated individuals whom he now felt he could call friends. Most of the meetings with them he had been talking to silhouettes. He now observed that Pierre was a bit taller than he, thin with a dark complexion and black mustache but kind almond eyes. Marie was considerably shorter, probably five feet tall and quite overweight. She had a very pretty face and her voice was sweet and gentle. She spoke French and German fluently, and Paul knew from hearing her with the children just how encouraging and reassuring she could be. She made you like her instantly and that was important to the children since they were forced to trust her immediately.

After a simple dinner of steak and potatoes, some more talk and wine, Paul curled up on the sofa and fell asleep, even though it was only nine o'clock.

The next day Pierre drove Paul to Bern and arrived in the heart of the capital of Switzerland just before noon. Pierre checked him in at the Hotel Restaurant Jardin on Militarstrasse. Reservations had already been made and Pierre told the desk clerk that he would take care of the bill when Paul checked out. He also left a deposit at the desk to cover meals and any other necessities. He gave Paul several hundred Swiss francs and told him that he needed to buy some clothes. Smiling, he and Paul went to lunch in the hotel restaurant.

"Why are you being so nice to me?" Paul inquired.

"You're my golden boy. We started out with five operations when

181

Annette and her father were recruited. Now you and Annette are the only ones left that are working. We lost several people to the firing squad, but the others either fled to another part of France or are temporarily inoperable. I don't want to lose you. Marie and I would be out of business."

"I wouldn't want to take your job away," said Paul.

"The Germans would. They know from their spies in Switzerland that something is going on but they don't know where and who is involved. They are spending a lot of time, money and personnel trying to find out. That's good. But only if they don't find out."

"Your first assignment while in Bern is to buy some clothes. That is a command and not a request. You also need a suitcase or valise to carry those items. And don't forget toiletries like a toothbrush, toothpaste and shaving stuff."

"How long do you think I'll be here?"

"That's difficult to say. But after a while they'll get tired and will have to give up. Perhaps a week, maybe two."

"That's going to seem like forever."

"Look, Paul. Being away from Annette will be difficult but make the most of your time here. Enjoy this beautiful city. You're not going to help her by being miserable. Once she is cleared, our business can resume. When I hear from the British, I'll let you know the results."

After lunch they returned to the lobby. "I have one request," Paul said.

"Tell me. What is it?"

"I would like to call my parents in New York and let them know that I am safe."

"I can arrange that. Do you have the number?"

Paul wrote the number on a piece of paper he got from the desk clerk and handed it to him. Pierre then asked the desk clerk to arrange to place the call, as he knew it could take several hours. The clerk remarked that it was early morning in New York and it might be a good time to make connections before the business day began.

"Paul, don't tell your parents where you are or what you are doing. They want to know that you are well and healthy and not being shot at. Tell them that you will tell them more when you write to them. This clerk is on our side, but it is possible that someone could have tapped the phone line and is listening to your conversation. Just remember that."

Paul returned to his room but had nothing to put away, not even a toothbrush. He stretched out on the bed and was almost asleep when the phone rang. He was pleased that he didn't have to wait long.

"Hello." It was Eleanor's voice.

"Hi, Ellie. It's Paul."

"Paul, where are you? Are you OK? Mom, it's Paul," she said with her hand over the mouthpiece.

"I'm fine, Ellie. It's great to hear your voice."

"Paul, is that you?" his mother asked.

"Yes, Mom. I miss you."

"Where are you?" asked his mother.

"I can't tell you that. I wanted you to know that I am safe and healthy."

"Paul, we were told you were missing in action and only recently were told that you were behind enemy lines but safe. A Canadian officer came to visit us just over a week ago. He asked a lot of questions."

"That's all I can tell you for now. Can you put Dad on? I love you, Mom."

"Paul, I'm so happy that you are alive," said his father. "I was on my way out the door when you called. Harold is at the shop and Edward is at school. Eleanor was getting ready to leave with me for school. Hurry home, Son."

"I will, Dad. I have a lot to tell everyone. I'll write."

"Bye."

"Bye." The line went dead before he was heard to say, "I love you, Dad."

The quiet in the room was disconcerting. One moment he was transported to his parent's home and the war was so far behind him, and the next he was by himself, alone in a foreign land and a strange city. He walked to the window and looked out over the beautiful old city of Bern. It was time to get back to reality. He had some chores that needed to be done and he wanted to visit the city.

The first thing he did in town was to find the post office and mail the letter that was entrusted to him. He looked at the envelope and saw that it was addressed to people by the name of Schmidt and they lived in

Northport on Long Island. He knew where Northport was. He was glad that Pierre had given him some Swiss francs. He made a resolution that he would write a letter home and tell them so much more than he was able to tell them over the phone. He would do that, taking care not to give away all that he was doing.

Looking at all the fine looking and nicely dressed Swiss men convinced Paul that he needed some new clothes. He first decided to purchase some toiletries and new underwear. He spent the afternoon walking around the old city and deciding on the look that he wanted. He saw a manikin in the window of a clothing store that appealed to him. If he shaved his now adequate beard to approximate the manikin, he thought they could be twins. He bought that outfit and another shirt to match as well as a pair of shoes and a jacket. He wore the new outfit and asked the man who waited on him to keep the old clothes until he came back. He went to another store and got a valise. Then he went to a barbershop to have his hair cut and his facial hair trimmed to his specifications.

It was starting to get dark when Paul returned to the hotel with the valise filled with his purchases and his old clothes. He ate a supper of pork chops, string beans and rice at the hotel restaurant, complete with a bottle of Bordeaux. He couldn't finish the wine so the waiter suggested that he take it to his room for a nightcap. Paul appreciated the suggestion and did take the bottle with him when he was finished. In the room he was too tired to enjoy having anything more to drink.

Living in this luxury would have been fun if Annette were with him. He wondered how she was doing and if the Germans had set up their surveillance. He tried to guess where they would set up their observation posts. The woods would be the only spot where they could construct some structure that wouldn't be seen. Otherwise they would be on the road or in the bare fields and clearly visible from the second floor. He drifted off to sleep thinking about Annette.

CHAPTER 46

At noon, the day after Paul left, Annette waited anxiously for Jeanne so she could go home. She was concerned about what she would see, if anything. When Jeanne arrived, Annette gathered her things and pedaled home, alert for any signs of surveillance. She didn't see anything out of the ordinary while she was in town.

As she got near the farmhouse she continued to look ahead, not allowing her head to move like she was searching the area. She didn't want to tip off the Germans that she knew she was being observed. At the house she went about her chores of gathering eggs, shaking out rugs and sweeping the steps. Inside the house she didn't avoid the windows. Eventually, she was able to take a few moments to satisfy her curiosity. She moved the curtains just a bit and searched the woods. She didn't see any motion or signs of surveillance.

Late in the afternoon she looked from the upstairs bedroom window that faced the south. This was the room where her father used to sleep. She noticed a flash, as of a reflection, a good distance from the house. It was to the southwest. She saw it again and made a note of where it came from. The reflection was from the setting sun on something metal. That was her first indication that she was being watched.

While Annette was in her father's room she thought about the binoculars that he owned, but didn't know where he kept them. She started looking in the closet and found them on the top shelf in the corner. She trained them on the spot where she saw the reflection, being careful not to move the curtains. After a moment she was able to see motion. Knowing where to look was half the battle. She continued her chores, made supper, ate and retired with a book to the living room. She had turned out the light in the kitchen and turned on the living room light. After five minutes she returned to the kitchen and trained her binoculars on the spot she thought she saw the reflection. In a moment she saw the light from a match and the red glow of a cigarette. She considered the Germans careless in their surveillance.

An hour later she turned off the downstairs light and went to her bedroom. After turning off her light she waited a few minutes before she searched the woods in the northwest. Not knowing where to look made spotting a light difficult. Eventually she saw the glow of what had to be a cigarette. It was a good distance away but at least she knew she was being watched from two locations. She decided to always remember to return the binoculars to the closet. If the Germans visited and they saw the glasses they would know that she knew about the surveillance.

Annette arrived at the bakery a few minutes before four and didn't notice anything unusual. The road into town was deserted and the streets in town were quiet. She started the ovens, mixed the dough and baked the bread for the day's customers. She stayed a few minutes longer when Jeanne arrived and when the store was empty of customers the two women sat down at the table in the back.

"Jeanne, I'm going to tell you something that must be kept secret. It would be as dangerous for you as it is for me. You can tell Guy."

"It sounds mysterious," Jeanne said with mock sincerity.

"It's a matter of life and death. Is that mysterious enough?"

"Go ahead, Annette. You have my full attention."

"Papa and I were involved with smuggling Jewish children into Switzerland. Before Papa died we took in an RAF airman who had torn muscles in his leg. When Papa died, he helped me do the smuggling since I couldn't take the children across the border and work. It was our intention to get him into Switzerland once his leg was healed. Now we can't get the children over the border without him.

"You are aware that the Boche will execute you if they find out what you did?"

"Yes, and this week they are watching the house day and night," Annette explained.

"Are you certain?"

"I haven't seen them but was told they would be watching the house."

"Thank God you got rid of the airman. They would shoot you on the spot if he was found there."

"The airman is in Switzerland until I am no longer under surveillance. After that the airman will return. I need him to smuggle the children out of the country. I can't do that and work. Besides, they are watching me, not him. They don't even know that he exists."

Jeanne listened and was not aware that her mouth was open and her eyes were big. She was horrified. Finally she said, "How long has this been going on?"

He has been with us since before Papa died…and nothing is going on. I have spoken with Father Gilbert and he will marry us if you and Guy will be witnesses."

"I'll speak with Guy tonight, but I'm sure he will agree. And we can keep a secret, especially one that would get us all killed. Are you sure you're not sleeping with him?"

"For your information, I'm not sleeping with Paul. We both want to and are finding it increasingly difficult to abstain. He wants to stay here after the war, speaks fluent French but with a Canadian accent and will make a handsome Frenchman," Annette said as she began to blush.

Jeanne got up from her chair and put her arms around Annette and kissed her on both cheeks. "I'm so happy for you. I'm most anxious to meet your man. Please be careful, we don't want to lose you both. I'll tell Guy but the answer is 'yes.'"

CHAPTER 47

The rest of the week was a repeat of Tuesday. Annette got up at three, pedaled into town by four, returned home for lunch in the early afternoon, did chores, ate supper and went to bed early. She found the soldiers increasingly careless and five minutes after she turned out the light she would see the glow of a cigarette or the flame of a lighter. She knew they were there but learned not to pay attention to them.

She also noticed that they were watching her when she was in town. If she took a few minutes to visit the grocery, the butcher or pick up some cheese, she knew she was being watched. If she was careful she would usually pick up the observer, very often dressed as a local. She had lived her entire life in this village and was not fooled. She knew every villager.

She was watched when she pedaled home in the early afternoon. She saw several men deep in the fields and knew the people in the fields were pretending to work. Nor were they the men who should be there. Besides, there was no work to be done in these fields in the winter. She also suspected that they observed her in the very early morning on her trip to work. She was unable to see them because of darkness.

On Saturday afternoon the German officer who had visited her on the previous occasion again visited her. He told her his name as he did the first time. This time she memorized his name and was certain she would always remember the name of Hauptmann Horst Schlayer. He said that he would like to check out the barn. She told him that it only had hay in it and some farm implements, but he insisted that it be searched. She nodded for him to do so.

Hauptmann Schlayer ordered the two soldiers who came with him to proceed, and then turned his attention to Annette. He tried not to be so obvious but asked almost the same questions as he did the first time he visited. He hoped to catch her in a lie. He spoke to her in German and she asked him to repeat what he said. He asked to search the house again and she said that she didn't like to have anyone search her house but would allow him to do so if he insisted. He insisted and she walked behind him as he proceeded through the rooms.

In the cellar he again saw the shotgun and asked to look at it. He saw that it was a 20-gauge double-barreled shotgun. He examined one of the shells and observed that they were old and very common. The gun would not have done much damage to anyone and only minimal damage to a fox unless it was at close range.

"May I borrow the gun for several days? I'll return it in a few days if it checks out."

"Again I would rather you didn't but if you must, a few days will be fine," she answered. "I'm not expecting any fox or snakes this weekend."

Annette was calculating that the only reason he borrowed the shotgun was to have an excuse to return. He picked up the shotgun and two shells and carried them up to the kitchen. He knew the two soldiers would still be in the barn. He put the shells in his pocket and left the shotgun by the backdoor.

The officer searched as carefully as before and spoke twice in German, possibly hoping that Annette would respond or do what he was suggesting. Once he asked in German if she had had any visitors. Annette didn't respond but instead opened the closet door. When he got to the attic he asked in French if she had used it since the last visit. She responded that she had stored a few items in the attic that belonged to her father and were no longer being used. He seemed satisfied with a cursory look. She believed that he saw the dust on the floor and concluded that it hadn't been used in some time.

The officer picked up the shotgun on the way out, turned around and said, "Auf weidersehen." Annette said "Au revoir." He turned and left, forgetting to click his heels. That evening Annette observed that the surveillance continued.

189

CHAPTER 48

Paul slept until the sun woke him in the morning. The sun streaming into the room was pleasant and he felt rested and energetic. He shaved and dressed in his new clothes. He liked his new look with a thin mustache and a goatee. He felt that he looked very European and a lot more mature than the young man who arrived in England to fight the Germans not many months before.

After breakfast, he enjoyed the sights of the beautiful old city. The city was surrounded on three sides by a bend in the River Aare. Fairly steep hills rise from the river. The old city has cobblestone streets and quaint old houses. Paul visited the Helvetia Museum on that Wednesday morning. It was warm enough for him to eat a sandwich and drink some espresso at a sidewalk café. He walked through another museum in the afternoon and strolled through a park in the downtown area and late in the afternoon he headed toward his hotel. He was tired and didn't enjoy the steep climb up to the hotel. He was forced to stop halfway to give his leg a rest. Tomorrow he would be a bit less ambitious.

The next day he visited several old but beautiful churches, the Bundeshaus where the laws for the Swiss are made and the Botanical Gardens in the afternoon. He was becoming familiar with the city and found it be the quaintest city he had ever visited. He was reminded of Quebec and was forced to admit that it was even quainter than Quebec.

The following day it rained. Paul walked a short distance to a local bookstore and bought two books for his reading pleasure. Then he sat in the lobby of the hotel and wrote a letter to his family. He realized that there was a lot that he couldn't tell them but all they really wanted to know was that he was alive and healthy. He told them of his parachuting out of the plane and hurting his leg. All he would say about what he was doing was that he was helping the war effort in a way he hadn't expected. He did say that he would help airmen get reunited with their units. When the letter was completed, he sealed it and planned to take it to the post office in the morning. He thought that was wiser than giving it to the clerk at the desk. He completed the morning by reading a good portion of one of his new books. After he finished lunch in the hotel restaurant, he had an afternoon nap in his room. It was a restful day.

The phone rang about three in the afternoon, surprising him. It was Pierre who said he was in the lobby and asked if he could come up. From the look on Pierre's face as he entered the room Paul knew that he had good news.

"This morning," he explained, "I received a visit from my contact. He told me that you are to remain in France. He also told me that you will continue to receive pay as an airman and that a check for back pay would arrive and be deposited to your account here in Bern. I was led to understand that the Canadians insisted that you be promoted and your pay would be based on your new rank of sergeant. I have a letter authorizing you to continue working under my auspices. My contact said that the signatures are genuine."

Paul looked at the letter and couldn't help but smile. He threw his arms around Pierre in a bear hug and thanked him. Pierre explained that he had been quite certain that the British would agree once they realized that their airmen were being held inside France and were not available to fight. That proved to be the biggest bargaining chip. Paul thought that it probably had more to do with who was in charge. The Brits didn't like Frenchmen telling them what to do. They, most likely, didn't like being told that one of their airmen was working in the French underground. Pierre agreed that a power struggle was the more plausible explanation.

"By the way," Pierre began. "Here is the first check for back pay. It came with the letter. The bank is on Nagelgasse, just over the big bridge. It would be wise to deposit it on Monday and ask them to notify you if the check clears. You can give them my name, address and number to notify in case there is any difficulty. That information is on this other slip of paper. Remember that I can access your account but would only do so at your request or to disperse it to your beneficiary upon your death. While you are there Monday, fill out the beneficiary form."

"Can you stay and have supper with me?" Paul inquired.

"No, I'm expected home and I'll be late as it is. Next time."

"Then do me a favor. Keep this letter in your possession. If it were found on me it would mean my death. I'll get it when I need it. Maybe I'll never need it."

Pierre shook Paul's hand and congratulated him again and left after telling Paul to have a nice dinner to celebrate. He promised that he would.

On Saturday, Paul expanded his sightseeing and began to truly enjoy his time in Bern. He planned on going to Mass on Sunday and wanted to confess that he killed a German soldier. He found a Catholic Church and went to confession on Saturday afternoon. The priest was most understanding and encouraged him to continue doing the righteous work of smuggling Jewish children to safety. He told Paul that Jesus said that greater love has no man than to lay down his life for a friend, and Paul was taking the chance that he might have to lay down his life to save an innocent child. He left the confessional feeling more worthy to receive communion the next day.

He went to Mass on Sunday and felt good about being able to do so. Until this day he could not even be seen by anyone while in France, except Annette and her father. Going to town or to church was impossible. He came to the conclusion that having freedom was what made him happy. That coupled with having a woman who loved him and whom he could love in return, completed his requirements for happiness

He appreciated the ancient ritual of the Mass in Bern as much as he would if he were home. The Latin was familiar and the sermon was in French. He looked and felt like he belonged. This was the first time since he was living with his aunt and uncle in Quebec that he was able to worship, and he felt that, at last, he had returned to his faith.

On Monday he deposited the money in his account, filled out the beneficiary card with Annette LaVoie as the beneficiary. He also gave them Pierre's name, address and phone number for contact purposes and told the bank that he would write a note if he wished Pierre to withdraw any money. Then he remembered that he had a letter to his parents to post and was finally free to enjoy the rest of the day, shopping, sightseeing and eating. In the afternoon he realized that he had been away from Annette for an entire week. He missed her and wanted this to be over soon so he could return. He began to realize how much she meant to him and didn't believe that he could live his life if she were not a part of it. He wanted to be with her, always.

CHAPTER 49

Sunday was cold and windy. Annette, nevertheless, went to Mass. She saw Father Gilbert after Mass and all he said to her was the word, "patience." She saw several men who didn't belong to the parish and figured that they were part of those doing the surveillance. She spoke to several friends who expressed sorrow for the death of her father and asked how she was doing. She told her fellow parishioners that she missed him and was finding it difficult to live without her father and her mother.

It was so cold that after she returned home she made a cup of tea and stayed inside almost all day. She knew that those watching the house must be cold but she thought they deserved being miserable. She took some comfort in the fact that so many people were being kept busy watching her. Her calculations told her that with three shifts, a minimum of twelve soldiers had to be involved and probably twice that number.

Monday was a normal day. She received her expected visit from the German officer that afternoon as she was returning from the chicken coop. Hauptmann Schlayer didn't get out of the car but had the shotgun brought to her by the driver. He told her in French that they shot the two shells. She acknowledged his statement with a nod of her head. The driver got in the car and turned the vehicle around and drove off. Annette had the distinct impression that Schlayer was annoyed with her because he was unable to find her guilty of anything and couldn't catch her in a lie. He was not playing a game and Annette knew that this was deadly serious. Her instincts told her that he would continue to make attempts to trap her. He was only giving up for now.

The teams in the woods remained over night. When Tuesday evening came and she turned out the lights to go to bed, she checked the woods in both the northern and southern part of their property. There was no cigarette glow or light from a match or lighter. She stayed at each window for a fairly long time before she was convinced that the surveillance was over.

The next morning Father Gilbert bought a loaf of white bread from Annette. He spoke to several ladies in the store who were parishioners but said nothing to her except to ask for the bread. She accepted his money and acknowledged his smile.

Now she was happy that they were no longer spying on her. It meant that Paul would soon be home.

CHAPTER 50

Paul had a leisurely breakfast on Tuesday morning and decided to visit the Historical Museum. He had done so much walking in the past week that he forgot about his bad leg. While it did tighten up on him, usually when he was climbing the hills back to the hotel, the exercise evidently was good for it and was making it strong. The limp was barely perceptible. He returned to the hotel for lunch. That afternoon he went to the movies.

On Wednesday he walked to a different part of the old city but since it was so cold he decided to make the day a short one. He passed by the bank where his money was being kept and began the steep climb up to the hotel, arriving there for lunch.

Sitting in the lobby of Hotel Restaurant Jardin was Pierre. The smile on his face said everything Paul needed to know. Extending his hand to Paul he said, "Your exile is over, my friend, and you are free to go home. But first, we must have lunch."

After the meal, Paul packed what few items he had while Pierre handled the expenses with the manager. Pierre told Paul that he should feel free to tell him if he or Annette needed anything, especially if the item would raise suspicion if purchased in France and observed by the Germans.

"Pierre, living with Annette is costing her more to keep food on the table. Now that I have some money in the bank I would like to contribute to the household. Would you withdraw money each month from the bank, turn it into French francs and give it to Annette or myself when we meet the first time each month? I'll write a note to the bank authorizing the transaction."

"Of course. How much would you want to withdraw?"

Paul and Pierre discussed what would be a sufficient amount, and Paul wrote out a note giving the necessary permission to Pierre. Then they were free to leave.

They arrived back in Porrentruy and picked up Marie, who wanted to accompany Pierre to the pickup point. They drove down the paved road, and Pierre turned into the woods onto a dirt road to the left where one would least expect a road to be. The entrance was obscured with pine branches that brushed the windshield as the car left the main road. Unless one knew it was there, he would miss the road completely. A short distance down the road Pierre pulled head first into a small opening and then backed the car from there to the end of the road near the shack. It was late afternoon when they arrived at the pickup point and the winter sun was about to set.

Paul expressed concern about the return trip since he didn't have a flashlight. Pierre had one in the glove compartment and gave it to him. "Don't be afraid to ask me for batteries, as it wouldn't be good for Annette to be buying them in town" said Pierre. "That might be considered suspicious."

The last thing Pierre told Paul was that the next smuggling job would be to get the RAF pilot to safety. They shook hands, and Marie hugged Paul and wished him good luck. He started down the hill, his valise in his left hand and the flashlight in his right.

Paul was anxious to get home but not at the cost of carelessness. He moved over the small stream that traversed the hill and listened carefully to the sounds of the forest. Based on past experience, he didn't anticipate a patrol at this time. He moved a bit closer to the border as his eyes became totally accustomed to the darkness of the woods. The patrols had to be finished for the day. He crossed into France over the usual narrow crossing where the stream ran deep and fast. As he climbed toward the mountain he increased his pace and found the usual landmarks with ease. The flashlight wasn't needed.

Approaching the passageway, he remembered that he had wedged a branch in the crevice of the rocks and was most anxious to find out if the branch was disturbed. Using the flashlight, he was pleased to see that the branch was still exactly where he had left it and at the same angle. He considered knowledge of that passageway through the rocks to be the key to the success and safety of their operation.

He entered the woods cautiously, crossed the dirt road, and saw the lights of the farmhouse. As he got closer he saw Annette busy in the kitchen as he hurried toward the back door. Knocking gently on the window, he waited as she dried her hands and rushed to the door. She knew who it was and opened the door and hugged and kissed him without reservation. Then she stepped back, looked at him and commented on his trimmed goatee and mustache and his new clothes. He was thrilled with his homecoming. She sliced a loaf of bread and spread some marmalade on it and poured a glass of wine for him. They were both eager to tell the other of their adventures.

They talked for about an hour and could have kept the conversation going all night. Finally Annette rose, because it was past her time to go to bed. She told Paul that she was overjoyed to have him home.

"If we were married, I would give you a homecoming that you wouldn't forget. But we're not married yet. You'll just have to wait. We'll have a lot of catching up."

"Annette, just knowing that you want me and missed me while I was in Bern is enough for now. We are going to have to get married soon as I believe it is becoming too difficult for both of us to remain this reserved."

"I think we can talk with Father Gilbert and make arrangements."

"Let's. I'm ready to spend my life with you," he said.

"And I with you."

CHAPTER 51

Annette could feel the freedom the following day while at work. No strangers were hanging around the bakery, and no unusual characters were watching her when she visited a fellow storeowner for a brief moment. Nor was anyone in the fields when she pedaled her bicycle home.

That afternoon she and Paul made wedding plans. They had not discussed children and so didn't consider the consequences should Annette get pregnant. They were finally forced to confront what having children would do to their smuggling operation. They sadly came to the conclusion that it would not only shut down their ability to smuggle but would bring suspicion and probably arrest to Annette and Paul. A mother couldn't make babies alone and the Germans believed that Annette was living alone and had no companion. Paul and Annette were reluctant to accept the fact that if she got pregnant they would be forced to flee to Switzerland and leave behind her business and farm. They would no longer be able to move children out of France. They would somehow have to avoid getting pregnant until after the Germans were defeated.

Paul told Annette about his bank account and the fact that she was the beneficiary. He showed her the account number and the password and she told him about her account. They decided that they would easily remember the bank's name and the passwords and would only have to hide the account numbers. Paul suggested that they find a book that had several hundred pages and they would write these account numbers in it.

"How will we remember where we put the numbers and which one is your number and which is mine?"

"You'll see. Your birthday is on the 11th of May. Your number will be on page 115. My birthday is the 21st of March, so my numbers will be on 213. Let's find a good book."

"I know just the book. It is my father's textbook on bread making. It is a thick technical book and no one would think to read it except another baker. That would be a perfect choice."

Annette found the textbook on the shelf in the living room with many other books. They opened the book to page 213 and Paul wrote his account numbers in small print at the bottom of the page and Annette wrote her numbers on page 115. Both felt certain that no one would find the numbers unless they knew where to look and without the passwords and knowledge of which bank the money was in, would render them useless.

"I like the clever way we have recorded our account numbers," said Annette.

"I believe that no one will find them. They're safe."

"Even if they do find them, they won't know what they mean. Tomorrow I'll destroy the old slips of paper that I had been using when Papa was alive."

The couple discussed their plans for after the war. Paul told Annette that one of the first things they would do would be to take a trip to visit his family in America. She was excited about a trip to the States and told him that she was going to start learning English.

Annette thought about all these things and what living with Paul would be like. She wondered if living in confinement for several more years would be acceptable to Paul or to her. She realized that she hadn't adequately considered all the ramifications of getting married.

Paul, too, was having his version of doubts. The doubts, however, were not about Annette. He recognized her character and virtues and believed that he was very fortunate to have found someone whom he could love and who would love him in return. He was most anxious to live with Annette as a married couple but didn't know how long he could live in the house without being able to make a living or doing useful work. He wished he could set up a shop to make furniture so as not to lose the skills he had learned. His biggest fear, when he got to the bottom of his doubts, was that he would get Annette pregnant and he had no means of support to take care of a baby. All of that was in addition to the good work they were doing smuggling children and airmen across the border.

"Paul, there are many things to think about that effect us both. Let's continue to talk and maybe we can resolve the difficulties," Annette begged.

"I wonder," Paul began, "If I'll be able to stay locked up in this house for the next two, three or four years. I'm not able to meet people, take you to church or a vacation or even to work. It may be too much of a strain on both of us. These are things we have to consider."

"We don't have to solve these problems today," Annette said. After a pause she continued, "At least we're thinking about all the problems and difficulties. That's important."

A few minutes later Paul had a thought. "I'm certain there are solutions that we haven't even thought of yet. There are people who are older and wiser than us. I would like to know what Pierre and Marie have to say and Father Gilbert will surely have some advice. Then you may want to talk with Jeanne."

"I would like to speak with Jeanne," she said. "I value her advice. Let's allow all this talk of marriage to rest for a bit and we'll continue to seek advice and see where it takes us. I do know one thing, Paul, and that is that I love you. But is that enough?"

"I love you too, Annette, or I wouldn't have agreed to live with you like this. But living like this isn't easy and both of us are finding it increasingly difficult. Maybe Father Gilbert can visit me here at the house and he and I can have a man-to-man talk. Then we can all talk. Would you try to arrange that?"

"Of course," she said.

The better part of the afternoon was taken up with this discussion of marriage and the consequences to each of them and the cause that they were pursuing. The house seemed to get darker earlier than usual and when they looked outside they saw that the sky was getting overcast and it looked like it might snow. An early snow was not uncommon in the foothills of the Alps. Before they finished supper they noticed that big flakes were falling. In fifteen minutes the world was transformed. The snow made everything so beautiful but it also meant that Annette would have to walk to town rather than take her bicycle. That meant leaving a few minutes earlier. Still the snow gave them a sense of peace and serenity.

CHAPTER 52

It was almost a week before the weather turned sunny and the snow left the ground. Every day Annette looked to see if the flower pot was moved and every day it remained exactly where it was the day before. Then on Thursday, December 11 she saw the flower pot moved to the other side of the door.

She gave Paul the message that he should expect to make a trip across the border that evening. Paul checked the barn at three and found it empty. At four he checked again and found it empty a second time. As he came out of the barn to return to the farmhouse, a man dressed in civilian clothes was walking across the fields toward the barn. He appeared to be of average height and had brown hair tucked beneath a maroon beret. He was bookish looking, not your typical flyboy. Paul waited.

"Are you Paul?" the airman asked in English.

"Yes, and you are?"

"Upton Hadley. I was a spitfire pilot until one of those Messerschmitts got on my tail. At least I was able to get out of Germany."

"Come on into the house. Have you eaten?"

"I'm fine, thanks. At least for several more hours."

Paul was pleased to be able to speak English and was enjoying the visit.

"How did you get away from the Messerschmitt?"

"I found a cloud and banked hard to the left. He must have expected me to go to the right. When I came out of the cloud he was nowhere to be seen, but the plane was smoking badly. Several minutes later I was losing altitude fast and had to jump. I saw the flames from the crash as I floated toward the earth and was extremely lucky that the Resistance got to me before the Jerries did. They hid me for more than a month," Hadley told Paul.

They came to the farmhouse and Paul introduced Upton to Annette.

"If I had known that a pretty young lady was here," Upton said, "I would have insisted that they move me to the border immediately."

Paul had to translate for Annette and she blushed. Paul understood and would have expressed the same sentiments.

Paul and Upton spoke about Canada and Paul found out that Upton came from Toronto. He was a pilot who flew for pleasure on weekends and when he enlisted he was sent immediately to flight school. During the week he was a college professor teaching Medieval History. That was before the war. While they enjoyed the conversation both men knew that they would have to leave and complete the journey. Upton said goodbye to Annette as soon as Paul had his coat and a flashlight. The two men left in fading daylight.

Paul enjoyed Upton's company and appreciated that he didn't have to worry that he might fall or do something childish. This was the first time he escorted an adult over the border. It was also a delight speaking English, something he hadn't done in some time. After they passed through the passageway and around the big rock, Paul stopped for a moment to speak with Hadley.

"We will have to be silent until we get to the shack on the other side. I just want to tell you how nice it is to meet someone from home."

"I appreciate all that you are doing. That passageway through the mountains is well disguised and I hope the Jerries never find it. I'm ready to go."

Paul nodded and smiled knowingly.

Paul used the shallow crossing as Upton easily moved over the rocks in the stream. Of course, the flashlight had to be turned on for a moment and Paul always turned it away from the checkpoint. He was certain it was not visible. The pilot was pleased to be handed over to Pierre and thanked Paul heartily.

"Make sure our superiors know how important it is to have people doing this work. Otherwise you would end up in a POW camp, if they didn't shoot you first. They should also know that it is extremely dangerous. Besides, we are tying up quite a few Krauts who are doing their best to put us out of business."

"I will. I don't know how I would have survived without your organization," he said looking equally at Paul and Pierre. Paul translated for Pierre.

The two airmen said goodbye and Paul started down the hill for an uneventful trip home. Paul knew that Upton Hadley was kept by the Resistance for over a month as a tool in negotiating, but didn't want Hadley to know that. Let him believe that he was kept hidden at some danger to all involved because the weather was not suitable or because it was not safe to move him. It was a shame that he had to be held hostage to the negotiations, but in the long run many flyers would remain out of German prisons and live to fight again. These were Paul's thoughts as he made his way back over the mountain.

Two more children arrived the next day and Paul ferried them without any difficulty. Then four children arrived the following day. Over the weekend it was quiet but continued cold. Three times the following week Paul made the trip, each time crossing the border over the rocks in the shallow section. In all ten children were brought to safety. It was a good week. Then on Saturday, two British airmen disguised as Frenchmen arrived late in the afternoon and continued immediately to the border with Paul as their guide. They sensed that the weather was beginning to change and they wanted to reach safety before they were stranded. The airmen didn't have much time to talk but were grateful for someone to help them travel the final miles to Switzerland.

Sunday, the twenty-first of December, dawned with a foot of snow on the ground. Annette was unable to go to church. It was cold, windy, and the snow blew almost horizontally. Another foot of snow brought any chance of traveling across the border to a halt.

CHAPTER 53

It was late Monday morning, just several days after Christmas, as Paul was puttering around in the kitchen, that he saw a man dressed in an RAF flying jacket walking from the woods toward the barn. He walked like he wanted to be seen, like he was taking a Sunday stroll. Paul was immediately suspicious, as he was not expecting anyone and it was noon. He watched the man for a moment as he walked toward the house. Even though the snow was melting and there were many bare spots he didn't seem to be avoiding the snow. The man continued slowly walking toward the back door.

The airman was tall and blonde and moved like he was someone important. That would hardly be the case of an airman stranded behind enemy lines. A stranded airman would be hesitant to be seen while this man was begging to be noticed. Paul made note of the one bar on his shoulder, a lieutenant.

As the airman approached the back door, Paul recognized the flying jacket insignia as belonging to a squadron based not far from his own squadron. He had seen the insignia when the two squadrons happened to be at the same pub together. Paul was most anxious to speak with this person who was passing himself off as someone who was recently shot down. His first thoughts were that he was an imposter. He opened the door.

"Come on in," Paul said in English. "You don't want to be seen in that jacket."

"Thanks," said the man who appeared to be genuinely surprised. "I was told that you would be able to help me." He had a definite British accent.

"Were you shot down?"

"Yes, on Christmas day. Our plane was hit over Germany and we had to parachute out when we saw that we weren't going to make it back to base."

Paul noticed his formal English, not at all like the speech that he was used to hearing. "Where were you based?" Paul wanted to know.

When he said he was based at Mendenhall Air Base, Paul knew he was a phony. Paul, just to be sure, asked him what he was flying, and he said that he was a gunner in a Wellington. Paul asked him how he liked the four engine bomber and the man said that it was great. At that moment Annette arrived at the back door.

Annette's eyes showed surprise as she stepped inside and she looked from Paul to the stranger for answers.

"Forgive me, this is Annette. I'm Paul. And you are…"

"Lieutenant Charles Foley." He snapped his heels like he was a German officer in front of his superior.

"Annette, get Charles a sandwich," Paul said in French and then repeated the phrase in English. He continued in English, "I'll get a bottle of wine from the cellar. Excuse me a moment."

Annette knew what Paul was about to do and so showed Charles to a chair at the kitchen table while she removed a loaf of bread from the bread box. Paul returned from the cellar with the shotgun and some rope. The airman had his back to him, seated where Annette had pulled out a chair. The airman looked relaxed and his confidence seemed to say that he was certain that he had fooled everyone. Paul handed the ropes to Annette, cocked both barrels of the shotgun and moved to face the flyer. He told the German to remain seated and he might not get hurt. The smug look turned to shock.

Annette tied his hands behind his back and then to the chair. Once tied, Paul asked him who he really was.

The imposter got quiet. Paul told Annette in French to report this to her contact. She left on her bicycle immediately.

"Now, tell me, who are you?"

"Why should I? You tell me how you knew I wasn't English."

"That's easy. I was suspicious from the moment I saw you. I didn't expect you, and you were leaving a trail, as best you could. Also, you would not be wearing those patches if you were based at Mendenhall and you didn't know that the Wellington was a two-engine bomber. You have officer insignia and yet you say you are a gunner. You are wearing German boots and you have some delightful German habits, like snapping to attention and clicking your heels. A few more questions and you probably would have given me a 'Heil Hitler' salute. Now who the hell are you?"

"A German officer," he said. "If you harm me you will bring the wrath of the German Army on your operation. This garrison knows all about you."

"Tell me about Hauptmann Schlayer."

That got a reaction from the soldier. He didn't know what to say. It was obvious that he was surprised by the question. Finally he said, "I don't know a Hauptmann Schlayer."

"That's a lie. Then you are not from this garrison. He's the one who sent you here to find out about our operation. By the way, where did you learn to speak English?"

Happy to change the subject he said that he studied in school and lived in London for several years where his father was a diplomat.

Paul kept him talking for a while, never taking the shotgun away from his face. He rightly surmised that the German was especially concerned about damage to his face. When Paul did lower the shotgun a fraction it was to question him a bit more.

"Why would anyone in the garrison suspect this farmhouse of smuggling people across the border?"

"Hauptmann Schlayer...Well now that I've said it I can't take it back. He knows you are smuggling people across the border. He just doesn't know how."

"And you're going to tell him."

"Well, I guess I can't, since I didn't find out."

Annette returned and asked Paul if the prisoner had given him any trouble. It was obvious the German didn't understand French and so the two felt that they could talk freely. Annette told Paul that someone would be along very soon and would take the imposter off their hands. She suggested that Paul go back over the route through the woods to eliminate any trace of his trail from the road. It was less than ten minutes later that a panel truck pulled up to the farmhouse and two older workers got out. Annette showed them inside and they asked her a few questions. While one was talking, the second man moved behind the officer and stabbed him with a needle in the neck. It took just seconds for the German to collapse.

The two workers untied him, carried the man to the truck and wrapped him in a rug. They then tied a rope around it, closed the rear doors and left.

"They would never have allowed that officer to come here if they suspected that a man was living here," said Paul. "They thought that you wouldn't know the meaning of the insignia and he felt secure wearing German boots. He looked like an English airman and he sounded like one. Therefore he would be taken over the border. Any time he wanted, he could overpower you. I know he's sorry that it didn't work that way."

"You better hurry up and eat and get his trail covered. The snow is melting fast but there may be a few drifts that need to be leveled," the ever practical Annette reminded Paul.

"I'll hurry. You need to stay here. If I return, and you want me to stay away, lower the kitchen shade on the back door. That way I'll know someone is here. Let that be our signal to avoid the house if you have company."

He got his coat and stopped in the shed for a shovel. The snow that the German had come through was almost entirely melted on the property except for one drift near the barn. Paul scattered the snow and the footprints with it. There was another set of prints near the tree line and Paul scattered them also. On the path the snow was melted and no tracks were visible. Paul walked the entire length of the path and only where the German entered from the road near Henri's house were tracks visible. He had to remove and scatter quite a bit of snow before it looked natural. He knew that within an hour the sun would melt enough to cover up his work.

He was glad that he set up this little signal with Annette. He entered the house and told her what he had done and that there would be no trace of the German. Paul also decided to check the driveway to see if the truck had left any tracks. The snow was melting and the truck had made some tracks in the soft dirt. Paul was able to erase them with some brush. It was now time for lunch.

"Paul, will Schlayer be able to trace the German back to us?"

"Probably, but they will have no proof. The Resistance will do what they can to deflect suspicion. In speaking with the German, I don't believe that they are expecting him to return for several days. Next time I see Pierre I'll ask him about what they will be doing. For all Schlayer knows the officer could have defected. I hope they can throw suspicion away from us."

CHAPTER 54

The following Sunday, the first Sunday in the new year of 1942, Father Gilbert spoke to Annette after Mass. "I need to visit your house when you are at work. I'll stop by on Monday morning. Tell him," was all he said.

Annette told Paul to expect a visit from Father Gilbert. On Monday, at nine o'clock, Father Gilbert pedaled into the farmhouse yard on his bicycle. Paul saw him from the kitchen window and met him by the back door.

"Nice to meet you, Father," he said as they shook hands.

"My pleasure. You are doing our countries a great service."

"Thank you, but I have an ulterior motive. I love Annette and want to spend my life with her."

"Yes, I know. We'll talk about that shortly, but first I want to tell you what we found out from the German officer posing as an airman."

"It was obvious from the moment I saw him that he was an imposter."

"Yes, that is because we have a system, and you follow the plan very well."

"We try to keep to a very strict schedule."

"Hauptmann Schlayer sent that officer to find out how Annette was handling the operation. She was to smuggle him into Switzerland so that he would find out all our secrets and contacts. He would return and report to Schlayer, personally."

"That is what we surmised," said Paul.

"The men from the Resistance took care of the German officer and have planted some jewelry on Hauptmann Schlayer to give the indication that he was somehow involved in smuggling."

"You certainly have been busy."

"We are only trying to protect our very successful operation. We hope that this will get rid of Schlayer since he seems determined to implicate Annette and we are giving the Germans a reason to believe that the soldier defected on his own."

"Let's hope the Germans believe it."

"The major was told about the surveillance of the farmhouse and was told that Schlayer did that to find a better way to cross the border. This was all done when Major Decker was on leave in Berlin, and Schlayer was in charge. All Schlayer could say was that he suspected Annette of smuggling children across the border. The outcome of the operation is that Schlayer is now under house arrest and likely to be demoted and moved to another post. Suspicion of Annette is minimal. All the soldiers who spent time surveying the house said that nothing inappropriate had taken place, and their surveillance was unnecessary and a total waste of time."

"Schlayer," Father Gilbert continued, "has been unable to account for the whereabouts of the German officer who had been assigned to him at his request. And what is more incriminating is that he was warned not to do anything behind Major Decker's back. Yet he set up the operation with the English speaking officer without telling his superior officer and put it in motion when Decker was out of the office."

"That sounds to me as if they don't suspect Annette at all. Is that true?" Paul asked.

"Annette goes to work and comes home. She keeps strict hours, goes to church, runs a bakery and is known by all the villagers. What is there to suspect? She barely weighs one hundred ten pounds and could hardly be considered a threat. The major suspects one of his own of illegal activities. He is trying, without much success, to get to the bottom of what has taken place. Besides they still haven't resolved what happened to that young soldier who failed to show up at the checkpoint even though the vehicle he was driving was found nearby."

"One of these days, Father, I'll tell you about that."

"You don't have to tell me. I know enough already," said the priest. "Oh, one last thing. Pierre has been notified and is spreading the rumor that a German soldier has defected. We're not sure who will pick it up but from past results we know it will eventually get back to Major Decker and the German High Command. That should help our cause."

"All this information makes me feel a lot better. Now what about Annette and me getting married?"

"If you get married there will be the chance of Annette getting pregnant. If you don't get married there is the same chance. I'm sorry to be so blunt but that is the situation. And I admire you and Annette for your strength and courage. But we can't afford to lose you two. Your operation has been extremely effective and the only operation in this part of France."

"But, Father, what can we do? Living like brother and sister in the same house is becoming impossible. We want to get married. We will do our best not to have a baby until this war is over. That's the best we can do."

"Paul, I understand. There is a midwife in town that can advise Annette as to her cycle and how to avoid getting pregnant without resorting to contraception. It will not be easy since it means abstinence about half of each month."

"Well that's a lot better than how we are living now. I'm getting cabin fever cooped up in this house without work, and living with a woman I adore and can't touch. I know the importance of saving the lives of those children and an occasional airman but…"

"Paul, I know, this is all so unusual. We are living in difficult times and sometimes we are required to be heroic. I'll tell Annette about the midwife and you two need to talk and decide if you want to live this strange life. I wish there was no occupation and this evil ideology didn't exist. But it does and it is destroying the lives of millions of people. To make things worse, in this little corner of the world, we could all lose our lives if just one person slips or is careless."

"If we decide to get married, can you marry us and keep the documents hidden for a while?" Paul wanted to know.

"Yes, you will be married in the eyes of the church and the state but the paperwork will get conveniently lost for a time."

"Thank you, Father. Annette and I will talk."

They said goodbye and Paul watched the pastor pedal off down the road in his black cassock.

He was anxious to sit down and talk with Annette. He knew what his decision would be but wondered if Annette felt the same way and was willing to make the sacrifices necessary to live half their married lives as if they weren't married. Paul was a bit nervous.

CHAPTER 55

A nnette had visited the midwife one day after work and was surprised at how much she learned about her monthly cycle. Her mother had told her what she needed to do and how to care for herself but she really didn't understand all the intricacies of how the human reproductive organs functioned. After spending an hour with the midwife she felt that she would be able to avoid those times when she was most capable of conceiving. Annette found the midwife most knowledgeable and it was easy to ask intimate questions. The woman told her to come back anytime she needed clarification or had another question.

Annette and Paul were married two weeks later in their own home with Jeanne and Guy as witnesses. Father Gilbert came early and heard the confessions of each of them and brought them the Eucharist. When the witnesses arrived, he performed the ceremony, and they shared a small cake that Annette had made at the bakery. They also had some champagne after the ceremony. Annette was beautiful in her best dress, and Paul looked handsome in the clothes he bought in Switzerland. He looked like a typical Frenchman. They were truly happy.

She and Paul knew that their marriage would be difficult because they would have to look at the calendar frequently and regulate their sex by the time of the month. They also knew they were compatible because they had been living with each other since October, and both were able to give and take and understand the other person's point of view. They were willing to listen and subordinate their wishes to what was best for both. They also had a mutual goal to smuggle as many children and airmen into Switzerland to keep them from falling into the hands of the Germans. They shared the same faith, although Paul was not able to participate in the worship aspect, at present. Further they wanted to remain alive to enjoy each other and the rest of their lives. They both knew that their situation would improve once the occupation was over, whenever that would be.

After everyone went home the newlyweds enjoyed being alone and were able to share their love fully for the first time. Annette told Paul that they had two weeks before her period, and they shouldn't have to worry about getting pregnant during this time. They would enjoy the time without concern so they wouldn't be frustrated when they couldn't make love. They found out that they were both considerate lovers.

They had decided to move into the big bedroom. Annette had fixed it up weeks before and made it bright and cheerful. Paul had few clothes and so it didn't look like a man was living there. He made a small chest from the scrap wood in the shed. It was tucked back in the closet and it allowed him to hide his shoes and clothes. It automatically locked and required pulling out a specific piece of wood to get it to open. For all who viewed it, it looked like the bottom of the closet and one would not suspect that it was a tiny room between the floors of the old farmhouse. Paul was putting his cabinet making skills to good use.

Paul had to adjust his schedule to Annette's work schedule, as his time was not as restricted as was hers. When they didn't plan to make love, Paul usually stayed up late to read or design furniture. He was planning for the day when he would have his own shop. They preferred not to make love by the calendar but they remained affectionate at all times and considered their life together to be preferable to living apart. They also believed that the love they had for each other and what they were doing made the sacrifice worthwhile.

CHAPTER 56

On one sunny winter day several weeks later, Annette and Paul received their first group of five children for the year. The next day they took four across the border. Several days after that they took seven and two days later there were four. Then there was a lull. Annette kept a strict schedule and gave the Germans no cause to be suspicious. With Hauptmann Schlayer no longer in the area, they believed that there was much less reason to fear the occupiers.

The next two months went quickly. When the weather was nice and there was no snow, Paul lead children across the border. When snow was on the ground or the weather was inclement, he spent the time indoors working on designs and plans for his future cabinet shop. By the end of March there were signs that spring was about to burst forth. But winter was not eager to take a rest and had to present one last heavy snowfall.

The first week in April Paul took a walk in the woods to look at the paths near the border. He was concerned that maybe the paths that they had been using were becoming discernable, and he would have to find new trails. Spring was putting new leaves on the trees and all the snow was almost melted. Paul anticipated that the stream might be full.

As he crossed the last of the mountain and was coming down to the valley below he heard the muffled sound of metal hitting wood. Using the big trees for cover he made his way toward the sound. The trees were not so filled out that he couldn't see a soldier driving stakes into the soft earth near the stream. The stakes were off the path about ten feet. They were placed every forty feet or so. A second soldier was threading wire through a hole in the stakes. About fifty feet from them, two other soldiers were nonchalantly standing guard with their eyes looking in the general direction of the woods. Paul watched and remained still.

The thoughts that went through his head were that the Germans still suspected that smuggling was going on. They were placing a wire attached to a small bell to warn them when someone tripped it, especially at night. He would have to get around the wire somehow. It might be impossible to expect children to avoid it when they couldn't see the wire and he wouldn't want to use the flashlight to find it. Paul was glad he happened upon this work. Now he had to find a way to overcome this obstacle.

The next day he again made the trip to the border but this time he took lunch and some water to drink. He didn't see any soldiers, but as he got closer to the stream he could see the wire barely visible among leaves. It was only several inches above the earth and the stakes were driven well into the earth and stained brown so as to blend in with the leaves. They would be difficult to see during the day and invisible at night. He moved deeper into the woods and walked west away from the checkpoint, stopping every forty feet or so to find the stake. It was almost a kilometer before he found the final stake. At this point the terrain was very rocky and was probably considered impassable.

He had two tasks. One was to find a way from the mountain to this point and the other was to find a way from the final stake to where Pierre and Marie would be waiting. He also wanted to know how far it was to the next checkpoint to the south. He sat on a log and ate some of his bread and drank some of the water he brought with him.

Several minutes later, he heard voices in the distance. He was back from the path but needed to hide behind some mountain laurel. Two soldiers stopped when they reached the last stake and one leaned against a tree and lit a cigarette. The other urinated into the stream. They wasted about five minutes before they began the trip back to the checkpoint. When they were out of sight Paul decided to find the way from the last stake to where Pierre and Marie were usually waiting.

Paul searched the banks of the stream for a good place to cross and located a narrow place about one hundred feet beyond the last stake. It was uneven, rocky and narrow. The water rushed over the rocks and would be frightening to small children. Older children would be able to cross at this spot, but it would have to be with the aid of a flashlight. The rocky terrain would make traveling at night extremely difficult, and without a flashlight, there would be many scratched and bruised knees and legs. He was certain that this crossing was far enough away from the checkpoint that any illumination would not be seen. Of that he was certain.

After he crossed the stream he went over large rocks that had to be climbed. A huge stone formation greeted him beyond the rocks. He moved along the base to the east as the formation got smaller and the hill moved higher. He traveled for about ten minutes before he eventually came across the small stream that traversed the hill and was able to see the shack where Pierre would be waiting. The route would be more difficult and would take longer but was safer than trying to avoid the wire. It probably couldn't be used with small children, as the rocks were large. The first task was accomplished. He made his way back to the narrow crossing spot.

Since he had the time, Paul thought it might be wise to travel toward the checkpoint that was to the west. He moved slowly and cautiously but soon began to see why no activity ever came from that checkpoint. The terrain got even more rugged as he moved south. The foliage was heavier, the rocks bigger and sharper and eventually the path was impassible. He could see but could not reach the waterfall that was the principal source for the stream. This was not the way to go, and he understood why no soldiers ever came from the west.

Back at the last stake, he attempted to find a more direct path back toward the farmhouse. He soon found himself entangled in blackberry bushes and had to retreat to find a better way. Where the berries were was noted both so they could be avoided and possibly picked in better times. His other attempts to reach the mountain pass also were unsuccessful, and he was forced to resort to walking parallel to the stream until he reached familiar territory.

Annette had been home for several hours when he arrived. "I worry about you when you are not here when I arrive. I know that nothing is wrong but I still worry."

"I was doing some exploring. I found a way to get older children to Pierre and Marie, but it would probably be too difficult for young ones."

The following day he decided on the path he would take and made mental notes of landmarks to assist him. He returned at dusk and did the same thing, noting where he could safely use a flashlight and where it wouldn't be wise to do so. He also noted a spot where there was a lot of loose slag and stones. He spent some time removing many of the unstable rocks. After he got the worst of them, he felt that it was safer and less dangerous and would cause fewer problems for the children. He didn't want anyone slipping and falling as they traveled over the path. Besides the noise, he didn't want anyone getting hurt. If a child broke a leg, it might be impossible to move the child and that could endanger the operation. It was a busy three days.

CHAPTER 57

The next few weeks were busy with crossings into Switzerland. Paul found that he could handle up to four children easily and five or six if the children were older and there was an older responsible child in the group. If there were more than that, he couldn't lead and supervise. He suggested to Pierre that they not allow small children to cross until a safer route could be used. It seemed that those responsible for organizing each group knew what they were doing, and young children were held back.

Pierre told Paul that he expected the Germans to set up a trip wire like what was done in other places and wondered why they hadn't done it sooner. He was also pleased that Paul had spotted the wire and reminded him that he would have to be extremely vigilant as they were probably not giving up on catching those crossing the border.

"They might start night patrols or set up a lookout spot. That's been done in other locations," Pierre said.

"I'll be cautious and extra careful before attempting to cross."

"I also need to alert you to the fact that we suspect that someone on our side of the border is passing information to the German garrison that an unusual number of Jewish children are arriving in Switzerland."

"What can we do about that?"

"We are setting a trap for the culprit. We have given a different message to each of our three suspects. Depending on which bait the Boche take, we will know who the culprit is. Vie also have our informants," he said, imitating a German SS officer. "We have someone who tells us these things," Pierre began, "but sometimes we find out too late."

"You mean I'll probably find out the easy way or the hard way that there is a night patrol or a night lookout post."

"I wish we could tell you ahead of time. If we hear, we will. Just remain on your guard."

"I'll do what I can to find out if they have patrols at night," Paul answered. "The lives of the children depend on it. By the way, we could use some more flashlight batteries."

Paul returned home and Annette was already in bed. He wanted to talk but knew how important it was for her to get her sleep. He climbed in to bed quietly and snuggled up next to her.

The next day Paul informed her of his plans. "I need to spend some time this evening in the woods. Pierre thinks that the Germans might put a night patrol or a lookout spot along the border."

"Have the Germans taken up the stakes?"

"No. But they aren't doing much good. They were told that many Jewish children are coming into Switzerland and they suspect that the smuggling is taking place in our sector. They want to make sure no one is crossing here."

"Then, please be careful, Paul. I know that you will, but in the dark, you may not be able to see or hear them."

"I promise. I'll be careful."

That evening, before it was dark, Paul returned to his original crossing point. A patrol was expected before it got dark and Paul was surprised that there was no patrol. He moved cautiously looking for a camouflaged stand either on the ground or in the trees. It couldn't be too high because tree leaves would hinder the line of sight. Nothing was visible. He remained in the woods for quite some time even after it got dark but all remained quiet except for the sounds of the night and an occasional owl. After an hour in darkness without a sign of a patrol, Paul decided it was time to go home.

In the morning he was most anxious to find out what the Germans were planning. Something was going on. He could feel it, but didn't know what it was. They had changed their patrol schedule without apparent reason. With a jug of water and a half loaf of bread, he set out for the border. He was fairly close to where he had been the evening before yet couldn't figure out what was different. When he moved closer he noticed that the stakes were still in the ground.

Two nervous days later, about mid morning, as Paul was coming down off the mountain, he heard voices and noise in the valley. Moving down the hill toward the border, and using the trees and bushes for cover, he worked his way closer to the voices.

Through the trees, Paul saw two soldiers working and two soldiers with rifles facing in the general direction of the woods. Paul immediately realized that they were building a blind in the trees, about eight feet above the ground with a crude ladder to reach it. He would sit and wait to see what they would do next. He found some mud to put on his face and hands to make detection more difficult.

After a short while, having finished the blind, two of the soldiers moved east toward the checkpoint. The two with rifles relaxed against a tree, indicating that they expected their compatriots to return. Eventually Paul saw a soldier pushing a wheelbarrow along the path. The wheelbarrow was piled high with lumber, materials and tools.

Paul had to move to keep up with those doing the building. He went deeper into the woods so as not to be seen. He followed them by their noise rather than visually. When they stopped, he moved down the hill closer to the border. Seeing the two guards he waited until they were turned away before moving closer. Hidden behind a rhododendron he could easily see the activity below without fear of being spotted.

He watched the same two soldiers build a blind about eight feet above the ground. Paul recognized that the pieces were precut, allowing the project to proceed quickly. He estimated it to be about five hundred meters west of the recently completed blind. Paul wondered if a third or fourth blind had already been built closer to the checkpoint, possibly the day before

The blind was completed in about an hour, and the soldiers, all four of them, returned to the checkpoint. Paul found a comfortable spot to eat his lunch of bread and then to take a nap. It was after lunch when they returned. This time they came with paint brushes and in a very short time the blinds and ladders were painted brown and green. By two o'clock they returned to the checkpoint.

After a half hour, Paul decided to find out what was actually done. He remained in the woods moving east from the two blinds he watched being built. He spotted two more and dared not go any closer to the checkpoint. He had now seen a total of four blinds and was certain that he had seen them all.

Paul was concerned about the westernmost blind, since that would be the only one he would be near if he needed to cross. He wanted to know how far the soldiers could see from that last blind. Paul went to the base of the tree to observe how far they could see toward the west. He knew that he could see more from the base of the tree than those who were in the blind. As more leaves blossomed and grew thicker with spring growth, vision would be further limited. Paul saw a good-sized rock that he estimated would be the farthest point the soldiers in the blind could see. He walked to that spot and crouched behind the rock. He couldn't see the blind from there and knew that the soldiers could not see him from the blind. There was more danger from sound than sight but Paul calculated that the noise of the stream would mask any incidental noise, especially during the spring rainy season. After continuing west, he came to the location where the last stake had been and beyond that the place to cross. He knew that his planning had paid off but also wanted Pierre to know that this would be a much more difficult operation. He was satisfied with all he learned. He would be able to smuggle children that evening, if needed.

CHAPTER 58

"Expect visitors this evening, Paul," said Annette as she returned from the garden where she was working.

"They have completed blinds," he told her. "I'm certain they will have them staffed throughout the night. This will make it more difficult for us to take the children across the border, especially small children," said Paul.

"I'll go with you to the barn and together we'll decide if any of the children are too small or young to go tonight."

It was with a heightened sense of concern that they went about their chores. Just before they had supper they went to the barn and found two boys and a six-year-old girl. The boys were ten and eleven and would be able to make the journey but the six year old would have to wait. She was just too young and might not understand the need to be absolutely silent. Annette explained to the boys that they would have to be extremely careful as they would never be too far from the German patrol.

Annette brought the girl with her into the house and together they returned with some food for the boys. Paul explained that they would take a new route tonight and it would be difficult. Annette translated to German and they nodded that they understood. They gave Paul the impression that they would enjoy putting one over on the Boche. Paul learned the word, "ruhig" meaning quiet and "schwer" meaning difficult. Paul heard Annette use these words frequently when she was translating. As the sun began to set, the three males left for the woods. The little girl, Rebecca, took Annette's hand and returned to the farmhouse. That's when Annette found out that the child spoke fluent French as well as German. Paul glanced over his shoulder and noted the sight of the little girl walking hand in hand with his wife.

The three took the new path to the westernmost part of the border. It was not yet totally dark. The boys could see the rocks and avoid them or climb over them. Once in the woods they moved quietly around boulders and over logs. They approached the stream at this westernmost spot. Paul couldn't hear any conversation from the blinds, yet knew they were manned. They quietly crossed the stream without the use of the flashlight. The sound of the stream, swollen by spring snow and rain, masked any of the incidental sounds they were making. They headed up to the formation ahead of them. Paul was grateful for a recent rain that made the stream run considerably faster and increased the background noise. Cautiously, to avoid any stray rocks and slag, they moved southeast. When they got to the small stream that traversed the hill, Paul blinked the light twice, using his body to make certain the light would not be seen from below.

Pierre was surprised to see the light from that direction. His eyes were trained to look more to the right but he signaled two blinks in return. Paul turned over the two to Marie and explained to Pierre that there were four blinds along the path and that it would be very difficult to bring any little ones over the rough terrain. Maybe he could suggest that they hold off bringing the very young, at least for awhile. He told Pierre that they had one six-year-old child staying with Annette until he could bring her across.

Marie joined them and after listening to the men for a few minutes, voiced her opinion. "If the Boche construct blinds, we have to consider that they are serious about stopping smuggling in this area. It also means that they are certain that something is happening. We would be wise to wait until they remove the blinds."

"They are using eight soldiers in the blinds and at least two at the checkpoint," Paul explained. "That is only for the night shift. We don't know if they stay all night or if they abandon the blinds after midnight. If they stay in the blinds from eight until eight, they'll be exhausted the next morning."

"We should be finding out soon who is relaying information to the Germans," Pierre began "We've planted three false messages and two have not taken the bait. We think it is the third man who is betraying us. We should know in a few days if he is our mole." "Maybe in a week we will be safe again," said Paul. "Oh, by the way, Marie, we have a six year old girl with us. Annette didn't think she should make this first journey and I agreed. She can stay with us for a few days."

Marie said, "I'm sure she'll like that."

"Paul, be careful," said Pierre. "I'll set it up so that you won't be bringing any others until we give you the all-clear signal. Father Gilbert will buy some white bread from Annette when we have some good news. In the meantime take care of that little one."

Paul made his way down the hill carefully. His curiosity was getting the better of him and he wondered if he could find out if the blind was occupied. He didn't hear any voices on the trip across the border and he began to think that maybe it was unmanned. When he crossed the stream he quietly walked the path the soldiers used until he came to the rock he designated as the farthest point they could see. At night their vision would be even more restricted. He got down on his hands and knees and moved ever so slowly along the path. He didn't hear a word. The splashing of the stream was welcome.

He crept closer and between the leaves of the gently moving branches, saw the glow of a cigarette. He only saw one and heard no voices and was about to conclude that only one person was on duty. Then he heard a voice and a response and a soldier tossed the burning cigarette into the stream and started to climb down from the blind. The soldier walked along the path toward Paul, causing Paul to panic.

The German stopped less than ten feet from Paul who stopped breathing as he stared at the soldier's back on the other side of the rock. He realized that he would have to breathe. He did so very gently. When the soldier was finished urinating, he returned to the blind. Paul waited for him to take several steps up the ladder before he moved away, knowing that they wouldn't be able to hear him with the noise the soldier was making in addition to the gurgling stream.

When Paul reached home, all was quiet. Annette was asleep and Rebecca was asleep in the room that was formerly Annette's. Paul went downstairs and took out his drawings of designs for furniture. He had already designed one kitchen set, complete with table and chairs and matching cabinets, made out of oak. It could also be made out of cherry or hickory, but he liked the oak best. He poured himself a glass of wine as he considered all that had happened that evening. Near midnight he eased into bed next to Annette.

The next few weeks Paul had a chance to play 'daddy.' Rebecca took to him, and he enjoyed the fact that she spoke fluent French. She liked gathering the eggs and even enjoyed weeding the garden. Paul kept an eye out for any cars that might pass on the road and used the house to shield them from unwanted attention. When they were in the open, Paul was careful to observe the road. They also played in the barn and Rebecca liked to hide and wanted Paul to find her. They became friends, and she was his constant companion during the morning hours. Both of them were pleased when Annette came home. Paul and Annette knew that they were becoming attached to Rebecca. They also knew that she liked them. It couldn't be helped. Those were happy weeks.

Rebecca told Paul that her father and mother ran a grocery store but they went to Switzerland to make arrangements to go to America or Canada when the Germans invaded and they couldn't return to get Rebecca. She said that she was looking forward to seeing her parents again.

Both Paul and Annette were able to observe each other around a child. They liked the way the other treated the child. Both were forming a bond with Rebecca that would carry over to other children they had to deal with and eventually would convince them both that they wanted to be parents. Rebecca had no idea what she was starting.

CHAPTER 59

Rebecca was with them several weeks before Father Gilbert bought a loaf of white bread from Annette. Several customers were in the store and so no words were spoken. When she got home she told Paul, and he wondered what the signal meant. Did it mean that the Germans were abandoning the blinds or that the spy in Switzerland was caught, or both? Since no one was going to be smuggled that evening Paul thought it might be wise to check the border and see if the blinds were still in service.

Paul took the path that led to the westernmost crossing and walked slowly toward the rock that was his marker. From the rock he could not see the blind. He moved closer, checking the woods as he did so. The blind was still there, but he heard no sound coming from it. He stayed on the path and moved ever so quietly until he could visually see that the blind was empty. Cautiously he moved along the path looking for the next blind. It too, was abandoned. As he walked east along the path he was unable to find any blinds that were manned. For now he was happy that the blinds were no longer being used and he began to suspect that operations could resume.

The following day Annette reported that the flower pot was moved. In the afternoon there were six children, three boys and three girls. Rebecca knew several of the girls. That would make Annette and Paul's job a bit easier saying goodbye. At least it would be easier for Rebecca. Annette said goodbye to Rebecca and tears filled her eyes in spite of her resolution to not cry. The little girl showed her thanks by hugging her as hard as she could and saying, "Merci, Merci."

They left when it was still dusk. Paul led the group to the line of trees just over the mountain. By pantomime he told them to sit and be quiet and he would return in a few minutes. He was certain that they understood.

He moved toward the path and the original crossing spot where the stream was narrow and didn't see or hear anything. By now it was almost completely dark, and Paul felt it was safe to complete the journey. The group moved silently to the crossing place and five of them crossed without difficulty. Paul carried one child over the stream and then returned and picked up Rebecca. She remained in his arms as he carried her up the hill, hugging his neck all the while. He blinked his flashlight and met Pierre and Marie moments later. Rebecca was reluctant to leave, but Marie gently pried her fingers from around Paul's neck. Tears were in Paul's eyes.

When he finished wiping his eyes, Paul was brought up to date on all that had happened. "We found out who the spy was among our people, and he has been eliminated," Pierre began. "The Germans don't appear to want to continue using all their resources trying to prevent any smuggling. We believe that they want to underestimate how extensive it is. They have no idea that so many children have been saved. We think that the Major may even be sympathetic to our cause and may not want to harm Jewish children. We actually don't know."

"Has he stopped all patrols in the area?" Paul asked.

"We can't say that but I think that night patrols are out There may even be fewer during the daytime. You still need to be cautious."

"We will. This is a delightful turn of events. By the way, I could use a pair of pants, a pair of size ten boots and several shirts. Can that be arranged?"

"I'll bring them next time."

"Oh! I could use some stationery. A notebook would be great."

"No trouble. What's that for, if you don't mind me asking?"

"I design furniture and would like to keep all my designs and ideas in one place. I could use a compass, a few drawing pencils and a ruler, if your budget can afford it."

"Paul, I'm glad you asked me for those items. They would definitely cause suspicion if Annette were to buy them in town. I'd be glad to get them for you."

"Thanks. See you next time. Take good care of Rebecca. She's special." With that Paul retraced his steps down the hill.

The next several weeks were productive. Paul found out that daylight patrols were carried out every other hour. They started at six in the morning and went until six at night, with German precision. That made Paul's job much easier. He was taking six or seven across the border at a time and he could do it while it was still light. He would leave the children at the point where the woods and the mountains met, and he would watch and wait until the patrol was returning to the checkpoint. Then he would get the children and bring them across the border, in broad daylight. He felt that his task was so much easier, and because they could see where they were going, it was also easier to avoid leaving a trail. In addition, Paul led them a different way each time so as not to wear down any one spot.

One afternoon, after arriving home, Annette told Paul that he would be taking a group of children from a Jewish school across the border that afternoon.

"What do you mean by a group and how did you find out?" Paul inquired.

"Father Gilbert stopped by to tell me that there would be twenty children from Chalons-sur-Saone that needed to get to safety as quickly as possible. They are all older children, at least fourteen or older. Pierre will have several cars to transport them to Bern," she explained. "And he also told me that the major who is in charge of the post will be transferred and a new major will take his place. He said that the change would not be to our satisfaction. Hauptmann Reuter, who took Schlayer's place, will also be leaving."

"You know, Annette. I almost believed that the major knew what we were doing, and in so far as he was able, he was helping us."

"Can you be certain?"

"No. But I have the distinct impression that he wanted his soldiers to be punctual and predictable. It was like he was saying that we shouldn't cause him any trouble and he wouldn't cause any for us. This was a nice assignment for them compared to the eastern front."

"You might be right. Just when Schlayer was on to us, he was transferred. I only hope that this transfer will benefit us," said Annette.

"Tonight I'll take all the students the westernmost way so they don't leave a trail," he said. "Since they are older they can handle the rough terrain and the rocks will keep them from leaving footprints. It will be fine."

The group of students arrived just a few minutes before five o'clock. Since there were so many, the people transporting them saw to it that they were fed. Paul left immediately and arrived at the base of the mountain about five-thirty. He checked to make sure there were no soldiers in the area and then led all twenty to the rough terrain that led over the stream. They climbed over the rocks and boulders and up the hill to the stone formation. Paul saw that they still had plenty of energy and so continued east across the small stream to Pierre and Marie.

There was no need to use a flashlight, as there was still a lot of daylight. Pierre, Marie and another couple were there to help them. Pierre said that two more cars would come down the road as soon as the two cars departed. Paul stayed with the ten young people while they waited several minutes for the last two cars. He was at the stream at six and thought that he would see just how prompt the soldiers would be. He estimated that it was about fifteen minutes to the checkpoint from his place of crossing since he didn't return by the most southern route. He found a good spot to hide in a thick clump of bushes and waited. At six-fifteen the two-man patrol came by in a very nonchalant walk. He was pleased that they were sticking to their schedule.

CHAPTER 60

The new major immediately imposed a curfew from ten at night until six the next morning on the entire village. This was a mixed blessing for Annette. It meant that she couldn't start making bread until about six-fifteen and she decided to not open until ten since she would only have day-old bread if she opened before then. Her hours were shortened from ten until six but the amount of business remained the same.

He also posted a decree in the town square that all Jews had to wear a yellow Star of David on their clothing. No stars were seen on anyone in town. Several days later Father Gilbert bought a loaf of dark bread.

A polite Hauptmann August Richter visited Annette at the bakery. He spoke a broken sort of French. He knew all the words but his accent was atrocious. He introduced himself and explained that he was visiting all the businesses in town and wanted to know whom they employed.

"Why are no villagers wearing stars on their clothes as they were ordered?"

"I am not aware of any Jews living in Faymont. I've lived here all my life."

"I don't believe you," he said in a threatening tone of voice. "If you don't cooperate you might be forced to choose which life you will save."

He turned around abruptly and stopped at the door. "Next time I want the truth." He opened the door, then left, slamming it behind him.

Paul observed several changes at the border. Patrols were now sporadic and at varied times. The soldiers walked faster and were expected to be more alert. Occasionally a third soldier, possibly a corporal or sergeant, would accompany the two soldiers, walking behind them. They also walked a bit farther, approximately to where Paul considered his westernmost crossing.

One afternoon a German car came to Annette's home and Hauptmann Richter and two soldiers approached the farmhouse. Paul was in the hills looking for a better way to cross the mountain and reach the border. Unsuccessful in his searching he was returning from the woods when he saw the vehicle in the driveway. He knew exactly who was visiting. He sat down on a log in the woods, to wait and watch.

Hauptmann Richter was using his polite personality when he knocked on the farmhouse door. Annette opened it but didn't invite him in. He explained that he wanted to know all the villagers and so was visiting each and every home. She still refused to invite him in. He was forced to ask if he could come in. She told him that she'd rather not have visitors, as the house wasn't totally presentable. He insisted that this meeting would be better inside.

In the kitchen she seated herself at the kitchen table and asked him to do the same. He refused to sit, so she got up and stood. He began questioning her in very extensive French, but with his terrible accent.

"You are the same women I met in the bakery. Are you not?" he began.

"Yes," she responded.

"And you live on this farm?"

"Yes."

"For how long?"

"All my life."

"Who lives with you?"

"My father did until he died last year and my mother the year before that."

"So you live alone?

"Yes."

Annette answered his questions but was not trying to make it easy for him. She wanted him to know that she was cooperating under duress. He asked about her hours at the bakery and who worked the farm. She told him that the curfew hours made it especially difficult for her. She was not able to get to the bakery early and for that reason she had to open the shop later. She asked him to change that restriction if it was possible. He said he would talk with the major.

"And Henri Arsenault plows the fields and raises the crops?"

"Yes."

"You do this out of the goodness of your heart?"

"No, he pays me for the use of the land and a percentage of what he sells. It allows me to survive since the bakery brings in so little money. That had been the arrangement between Henri and my father and I see no reason to change it."

"And have you frequently traveled to Switzerland?" he asked, attempting to surprise her.

"When I was a child my uncle drove my parents and myself to Bern. That was the only time I was in Switzerland," she lied since every time she took children across the border she was technically in that country.

"And you speak German."

"No, I only speak French and have learned a few words in German."

"Well, Fraulein, I enjoyed the visit."

He abruptly turned and went to the door. Annette didn't respond but watched him as he left. She was very pleased to be alone and was not unhappy with her end of the conversation. He hadn't insisted on searching the house but she knew that if he did, he would not find anything. Paul kept everything he wasn't using either in the chest in the closet or in the dormer room. She felt that he didn't find out anything that was important and she hoped that he would consider her harmless.

Paul returned to the farmhouse after the vehicle left.

CHAPTER 61

Annette arrived home one afternoon, an hour later than usual. Paul could tell that something was wrong just by her demeanor. Paul had fixed lunch and Annette entered the house and immediately sat down at the table. No kiss, no greeting, no words. She buried her face in her hands.

"Annette, what's the matter?"

"Something terrible."

"Please tell me. We can handle whatever it is."

"The Germans shot the sacristan from the church. Monsieur Moreau was standing in the square. The Germans ordered everyone in town to go to the square. The major asked why he wasn't wearing a star like all Jews were ordered to wear. Monsieur Moreau said that he wasn't a Jew. The major took out his pistol and asked him again and got the same answer. The major shot our sacristan in the head and ordered that his body remain in the square for the next twenty-four hours."

When Annette paused, Paul expressed his sympathy. "I'm sorry, Annette. Now we know what kind of a murdering bastard we are dealing with. We will have to be much more careful as this man will kill anyone upon suspicion of wrongdoing."

"Monsieur Moreau was a good man. Next to Father Gilbert he was the keeper of our church, bell ringer, sacristan, handyman and altar server. They killed a good man...for nothing."

Paul tried to comfort his wife but what she saw had been devastating to her. The occupation was brought home to her vividly, and she was surprised at how distraught she had become over the incident.

"Paul, it will take me a while to get over what I witnessed. I have nothing but hate for that major, and I don't like myself for feeling this way. Give me a while to recover and get rid of this terrible hatred I'm feeling. I don't ever remember a time when Monsieur Moreau was not involved in our church. He will be missed."

"I understand. It will take time."

Annette closed her shop two days later and attended the Funeral Mass for Monsieur Moreau. Father Gilbert gave the eulogy and had nothing but kind words for the man who faithfully served him and the church for so long. No Germans attended Mass, giving Father Gilbert the opportunity to urge resistance to what those who unlawfully occupied their land were doing. He urged them to remember that this man was surely enjoying his rewards in heaven.

As the weeks went by without being able to smuggle children into Switzerland, Paul and Annette were both getting nervous. There was increased traffic on the road past the house, but then the vehicles would turn around and come back a few minutes later. They surely knew that the road was barely passable and their only reason to use it was as a pretext to stop and observe the farmhouse. The increased traffic had to be a form of surveillance and harassment. In town, the Germans were pressuring villagers to tell them who were Jews. Since there were none, the pressure was wasted. But Major Oberdorf persisted in wasting his time.

The worry that at any moment a German patrol might knock on their door was a serious cause for concern. Paul had to be extra vigilant not to leave any article of clothing anyplace but in his closet or in the dormer. When he used a cup or a glass, he put it away. He was becoming as meticulous in his housekeeping as Annette.

During the summer, patrols constantly went by the house. He saw them drive slowly past and sometimes search the woods along the border. Using the binoculars he would observe them and wondered just how serious they were. It appeared as if they were simply going through the motions.

The frequent patrols going past the farmhouse caused Paul to be on the lookout for any vehicles. Often a cloud of dust in the distance would tip him off, or possibly the sound of their truck motor. There was usually a convenient place to hide, behind the house or in the shed or barn. Paul and

Annette knew they would be fine as long as the soldiers weren't coming to search their house or property. When Paul went outside for any occasion he first made sure the road was clear from every direction.

One evening before Annette left the kitchen for bed, Paul asked, "Annette, do you think there is another way across the border?"

"If there is, I am not aware of it. We have always known of the passageway to the top of the mountain but never went any farther than the stream. That is until we started smuggling the children for the Resistance."

"I would like to find another way that would make the crossings safer. Since I have nothing to do these days, I might do some exploring."

"Be careful. There are a lot of drop-offs and it wouldn't be too difficult to get lost."

"Do you have any suggestions as to where I might start?"

"When you get through the passageway, go west until you see the break in the trees that allows you to see Henri's farm and the town in the distance. I always thought that maybe that would be worthwhile exploring. Go slowly and watch for drop-offs," Annette cautioned.

It was September now and the days were getting shorter and the leaves were just starting to fall. Paul had been in France almost a year, yet it seemed like forever. He went through the passageway, and it never ceased to amaze him how invisible that way through the rocks appeared. He climbed up the pass and circled around the big rock as he had always done. Instead of going forward he stayed to the right going west along the ridge, yet far enough away from the edge. As he climbed he could see that the drop-off was now extremely dangerous but the way along the ridge was flat and passable.

Paul stopped several times to orient himself for his return trip. He made note of several landmarks, especially when he had to change direction. At the top of the ridge he could see Henri's house through the break in the trees and noted again how precipitous the drop-off was.

Every attempt up to this point to reach the border was met by a rock formation or a drop-off that would prevent further passage. There was no passage for a normal healthy adult and certainly not a child. His efforts didn't look promising. Returning to the ridge he continued moving west. The mountains in this section were much more rugged. That first day he returned home discouraged.

The next day began early. Paul was determined to continue searching. He had to be certain that there was no other way to get into Switzerland or risk taking his chances through the valley. He understood just how treacherous the passage was. Just one mistake and he and Annette could be killed and children sent to Dachau. The stakes were high. These thoughts filled Paul's mind as he continued his search.

Late in the afternoon, on the fifth try that day at finding an opening in the rock, he found a narrow crease in a formation. It was hidden behind a cedar. He tried it and except for having to turn his shoulders to get through the tight fit, it allowed him to advance forward. Rocks rose up on both sides and his path zigzagged through and around formations. The passage, nevertheless, continued to the south. Most of the time the passage could only accommodate one person and in two places an adult would have to duck to avoid hitting an overhanging rock. But to his surprise and great pleasure he was able to move forward. Paul was praying that this path would bring him to the border. Since it was getting late and he was concerned about getting lost and possibly causing Annette to become worried, he started back toward the farmhouse. He moved a rock and placed it on the path as an indicator of where to turn the following day.

He discussed the possible discovery with Annette and they celebrated the potential success with a glass of wine just before bedtime. Paul had trouble getting to sleep contemplating the possibility that he had found a second more secure route to Switzerland.

Shortly after the sun rose, Paul was anxious to get started. He ate breakfast, put an apple, a hunk of cheese and some bread in his pocket and started what he hoped would be a successful exploration. He moved cautiously, observing anything that would cause children to get hurt. He found the rock that was his marker and soon found the cedar and the narrow crease in the formation. He returned to where he had traveled the previous day.

The terrain remained rocky but not impassible and Paul was getting a bit worried that he might get lost in the woods on his return trip. He got a bough of pine and he left a trail of small pine branches to mark his way home. He made sure he could see each piece from the one he was dropping. The green of the pine was in sharp contrast to the rocks and red and yellow leaves along the path. He was forced to break off several boughs in order to have enough branches to mark his way.

A fallen pine tree, which was bare of all foliage, blocked his way. He had to decide whether to crawl under or climb over the trunk. He took the upper choice. It was a minor obstacle for now but Paul knew that he could make it go away with a saw and some elbow grease. He continued on. There were some rocks along the way that Paul knew should be moved if they were to travel by night. None were so big that couldn't be moved by a fulcrum and stout pole.

He estimated that he was probably near the border but at this height there was no stream. Eventually he heard water in the distance. He assumed it was the waterfall. He was unable to get close enough to the drop-off to confirm his suspicion. Nevertheless he was certain that this was the waterfall that eventually became the stream that was the border between the two countries. It helped him determine where he was. His next task would be to find the shack in the woods on the Swiss side where he would meet Pierre and Marie.

Almost imperceptibly he noticed that he was climbing and then was walking on level ground. The trees were thicker and the ground was not as rocky. He was also traveling downhill. He came to a gnarled oak tree and decided it was time to make a ninety-degree turn to the east. In a few minutes he came to a dirt road, which he correctly assumed was the road that led to the pick-up point. He had overshot the shack by several hundred feet. He walked along the dirt road for a few minutes and arrived at the familiar old shack.

Paul was excited to have found a second route to the pickup point. He was also tired and was tempted to travel the short way home like he usually did. Yet his instinct told him he needed to learn how to get back the way he had come. So after a few minutes rest he started through the woods directly west.

He was concerned that he might overshoot the path he had taken finding the pickup point. His eyes searched the trees for signs of the pine branches that he left to mark the way. When he saw a small pine branch hanging from a tree he was relieved. He turned right and picked up the trail marked with his markers. He made a note of several trees that he would have to find on his next trip so as not to have to travel farther than necessary. He also partially broke the bough of a pine tree so that it hung down and would hit him when he passed by on the following trip. He would use that tree as his turning point. He estimated that he saved ten minutes or more by using this more direct route on his return.

Following his pine branches back toward the path through the rocks, he soon came to the pine tree that had fallen over the path. He passed through the very narrow slit in the rock formation and came to the flat spot overlooking Henri's farm. It had taken him twenty minutes to get through the woods and another twenty minutes to reach the ridge that overlooked Henri's house. Because of the drop-off he moved some rocks to block the path, and to alert him that he was almost to the end of the path. The drop-off was twenty feet ahead of him. He moved seven good-sized rocks to divert anyone from going forward. If he had to make the trip in the dark the rocks would cause him to stumble and he would know that he had reached the end of that trail. It took another twenty minutes to reach home. He estimated that the journey home under good conditions was about an hour. The trip to the shack would take a bit longer because the children would have to go slower.

Annette was surprised when Paul told her of his success. "Paul, I can't believe that you found a second way to the pickup location."

"It's a bit longer but much safer. We'll be able to take the children in the daytime."

"Will it be difficult for them?"

"No. Just longer. The patrols won't be able to reach us."

Paul explained that this route would be difficult to use after dark. "The flashlight would have to be used almost the entire time and there were many obstacles that could hurt a child. Let's keep that route for daytime use."

"That sounds fine. It would be much better if we could travel during the daylight hours, especially in the winter. Paul, your efforts have really paid off."

"Patrols would still hit a rock formation below the falls that would make them turn back as they have all these months. This passage will be a lot safer, even if it is difficult and longer."

"Being safer is what's really important," said Annette.

Paul told her about the downed pine tree and she suggested that he leave it as it was. She suggested that just as long as the children could crawl under it or climb over it, it shouldn't be disturbed. She encouraged him to keep the path as natural as possible, just in case it was somehow located by a German patrol. He promised to show her the new path as soon as they could arrange a day off. She would have to know this new route if Paul was unable to take the children for any reason.

"How will you notify Father Gilbert that we are in business again?" Paul inquired.

"I guess it's time for me to go to confession," she said with a smile.

"Are you telling me you were a naughty girl?" Paul said teasingly.

"Yes. I've had some evil thoughts regarding the major."

"I'm certain you will be forgiven," Paul suggested.

"I'll get the word to our pastor."

CHAPTER 62

October and November were very busy months. Paul could shepherd the children to Pierre and Marie and make his way home in less than two hours. He requested that the children be delivered to the barn during daylight hours so they could travel while it was still light. They were no longer forced to wait until dusk to move the children. Keeping them in the barn or house made both Annette and Paul nervous, not knowing when or if the Germans would make a surprise visit.

Paul didn't clear the tree that blocked the path but that didn't bother the children. They went over or under and most thought it was fun. He moved a few rocks but left the path as natural as possible. Absolute silence for most of the trip was not now a requirement.

Annette was ecstatic with the new route. She recognized that it was safer for all involved and worried less that a patrol might suddenly surprise Paul and his charges. She didn't have to concern herself about the children leaving footprints or broken branches on the bushes. And she knew that if a child fell and cried, his or her cries wouldn't alert a patrol. It was now a much safer operation.

In addition to the children, Paul led eight adults and five airmen into Switzerland during October and November of 1941. It took almost an hour longer to complete the operation but was so much safer. Then the snow came and the operation had to be postponed.

Annette found her days frantic with two hours less time to do her morning work. Jeanne and her daughter, Michelle, remained available and were dependable. One or the other arrived so that Annette could go home after lunch. She liked working shorter hours but had to work extremely hard when she was there. Yet she was happy because everything was going smoothly, and she was in love.

Paul had received a notebook and some drafting tools from Pierre and had almost filled his book with creative ideas for his furniture. He was designing a desk with all sorts of cubbyholes and hidden compartments that he knew would be desired by some busy, rich executives. He would have to remember to tell Pierre that he needed another notebook.

On December 7 while Paul and Annette were listening to the BBC they heard the news that the Japanese had bombed Pearl Harbor in Hawaii. They wondered if this would be the event that would cause the United States to join this war. Several days later they had their answer. The United States declared war on the Japanese and the Germans and their allies. Paul assured Annette that this would be good for those fighting the Germans. He also used the expression, "It's about time." Neither he nor Annette believed that the war would end soon.

Just before Christmas, Father Gilbert came in to the bakery. He bought a loaf of white bread. The store was empty and so he spoke openly to Annette. He said that he wanted to ask Paul to bring three airmen into Switzerland but was afraid that they would leave tracks in the snow. The snow remained on the ground since the second week in December. He also said that they couldn't remain where they were and asked if it would be possible for Paul to get them to safety this evening.

"Father, isn't it supposed to snow this evening?" asked Annette.

"Yes, but not until after sundown. Even then it isn't certain. The weather can be so unpredictable. The snow should arrive before ten o'clock. I can have the airmen delivered at dusk, not before. By the morning their tracks will be covered but would be seen if anyone checks the path at dusk. Will that be all right?"

"If you can arrange for the airmen to be picked up right after it gets dark, he'll be able to return before the snow. Then a good snow will cover all their footprints. Paul will get them there. Don't worry. We'll just have to take a chance that the tracks from Henri's woods to the farmhouse are not seen. I believe that it will snow later this evening and all the tracks will be covered."

"I'll make sure they're dropped off shortly after it gets dark. Paul can meet them in the woods with a flashlight," he suggested.

"I'll tell Paul. I'm sure that it will be all right."

"Thanks Annette. These men will be forever in your debt."

"We're glad to be helping defeat the Boche. Goodbye, Father."

"Goodbye, Annette. God bless you and Paul."

Paul was agreeable, as Annette knew he would be. She knew that Paul liked to be busy and was happiest when he was helping to keep people out of the hands of the Germans. He believed that this was what God wanted him to do and was his protector just as long as they did their part in being diligent. He prayed that snow would come soon enough to cover their tracks. At sundown he left the farmhouse and made his way to the wood and path that led to Henri's farm. It was cold and Paul had to keep moving in place to keep himself warm. A quarter of an hour after he left the house three airmen approached along the path. Paul flashed his flashlight.

"We're glad to see you. I'm Captain Norris and this is Sergeant Jones and Corporal Abington."

Paul took off his gloves and shook their hands. "I'm Paul Fortier, RAF."

"What are you doing smuggling us across the border?"

"It seems the job fell to me by default. Anyway, I'm your guide. Let's get going. This will take about an hour and it is always more difficult in the dark."

"Lead the way," said Captain Norris.

"Stay in single file."

After they passed through the passageway and were on the path that overlooked Henri's house, Paul heard one of the men say that he was probably AWOL. Another added that he might even be a deserter.

When they got to the spot overlooking Henri's farm, Paul told them to take a rest. He told them that there would be no more talking from that spot to the final destination. While the airmen were resting Paul overheard one last remark and felt that something needed to be said.

"Helping you get across the border," he began, "is my assignment. If it weren't for a dozen people who have risked their lives, you would be forced to spend the rest of the war in a POW camp. This is my assignment and what I'm paid to do. This route is a risk for everyone, since, if it doesn't snow, your tracks can be traced and this passage will be shut down. If that happens many will be executed in the days ahead and this passageway across the border would be closed to hundreds of others."

Captain Norris started to interrupt Paul. "We were just wondering about your status…"

"All because three airmen were considered important enough to be smuggled across the border and out of France," Paul concluded with an edge in his voice. "You should be grateful that there are people fighting the Germans by being part of the Resistance. My status is not your concern. I told you that this is what the RAF wants me to do. Now shut up and follow me," he said as he started walking.

Paul was angry for some time and the walking was good for him. He enjoyed watching them struggle through the very narrow passage. At the last minute he shined the flashlight on the rocks that jutted out and would have harmed the airmen if unseen. They kept their mouths shut and followed as they were told. As they were approaching the shack and after Paul flashed the signal, he noticed some snowflakes starting to fall. When they were told it was acceptable to talk, the Captain told Paul that he was sorry for the unfortunate and stupid comments. He didn't realize just how dangerous the work was. Paul told him to get back to England and drop some bombs on German factories. The three men shook Paul's hand, and Marie led them to the car.

"Paul, I'm glad it's snowing and I hope you can get back home before it's too deep. Any snow after that will cover all the tracks," said Pierre.

"See that the airmen get home safely," Paul said.

The trip home was peaceful though difficult. He didn't hesitate to use the flashlight. It did Paul a lot of good to be exercising and eventually his anger subsided. He didn't realize how upset he actually became when those soldiers even insinuated that he might be a deserter or went AWOL. Those comments touched a nerve. He was now glad that he pursued authorization from the Brits and wasn't considered a deserter.

The path was slippery and looked different in the snow. Some of the landmarks were covered up and he was forced to go a lot slower. He couldn't afford to miss the trail. Going downhill was also extremely dangerous and

Paul had to use care as he made his way toward the passageway. Finally he reached the big rock where he rested for a moment. The heavy flakes were beautiful and Paul was enjoying them. He still had to complete the climb down to the passageway and to the woods on the edge of their property. Paul could see that his footsteps were already starting to fill up with snow. In an hour all trace of his journey would be erased. He stood for a moment on the edge of the woods and thought about how lucky he was.

CHAPTER 63

The day in late December could not have been more beautiful. There was a chill in the air and a light wind. Paul had been outside doing some work in the shed with one eye on the road. When he finished his chore, he returned to the house for a cup of tea. He was still drinking his tea when Paul heard the roar of several trucks. He barely had time to look out and see two trucks filled with soldiers pull into the yard, led by Hauptmann Richter being driven in a staff car. Paul quickly put his cup and saucer in the closet, still filled with tea, locked the back door and moved upstairs to his attic room. A moment later he heard the pounding on the locked door. He pulled his attic dormer door closed and locked it from the inside. From his attic retreat he could peek through the curtains and see the soldiers moving toward the rear of the property. They spread out into the woods, now devoid of leaves. Several were ordered to search the barn, which they did with bayonets fastened to their rifles.

Hauptmann Richter was sitting on the fender of the staff car watching the operation when Annette pedaled up on her bicycle.

"What's going on?" she asked.

"We heard that people are being smuggled into Switzerland," he replied, "And I'm going to put an end to it."

She watched for a few minutes then nonchalantly wished the officer good luck. She used her key to enter the farmhouse.

Richter knocked on the door five minutes later and asked permission to search the house. Annette said she would permit it but only if she could accompany him. He asked his aide to come with them. They searched the cellar, the living room and kitchen and then the bedrooms. Richter told his aide to look in the closets and under the bed. At the attic door Annette told Richter that it was the door to the attic, before he asked. He sent his aide up the stairs and he climbed to where he could see the entire attic. He asked about the presence of the cot as did his predecessor and got the same response. The aide walked around and looked out the front dormer window and was then ordered to come down. Satisfied that the house was empty, Hauptmann Richter returned with his aide to his vehicle.

An hour later she heard Richter blow a whistle and soldiers came out of the woods and filed toward the trucks. When they were all aboard and counted, they left as noisily as they came. Hauptmann Richter didn't say a word to Annette.

Moments later Paul came down from his hiding place and he and Annette made tea and sat at the kitchen table. Paul said he watched the operation from the window and didn't believe the soldiers even came near the passageway. All routes appeared to result in dead ends. Annette commented that the soldiers didn't realize that they would have to go to the end of the opening before they could see that it continued. She hoped it would always remain hidden.

CHAPTER 64

The American entry into the war brought many more planes dropping bombs on German cities. That meant that more airmen were parachuting behind enemy lines and the Resistance was rescuing more. They needed to be smuggled to safety. The days were busy since Paul could now move his charges by daylight. He found the task satisfying and fulfilling. He moved a dozen flyers during the summer of 1942 and several hundred children. There were no incidents with the German patrols. The new route made detection almost impossible.

The Germans increased their slaughter of Jews during 1942. More camps were built; more Jews were rounded up and sent to these camps to work or to be gassed and cremated. The hearts of many Frenchmen went out to these people who were being taken away from their families, their homes, their country and all that they possessed. Many lost everything, including their lives. It was difficult to imagine that it was happening, but few doubted that it was.

Over the holidays of 1942, Annette and Paul discussed the past year and both agreed that it was the most successful year so far, at least as far as transporting children and airmen across the border was concerned. They could take comfort in that they had done some good and were still in business.

Each night they listened to the BBC and knew that American bombers had joined the RAF in nightly raids on key German cities. Paul repeated to Annette some of what he heard. Annette asked. "Paul, do you miss flying and shooting down German planes?"

"I joined the Canadian Air Force to defeat Germany. If this smuggling operation is helping to defeat the Germans, then I'm satisfied. Besides, there are some nice bonuses," he said as he kissed her on the cheek.

They followed the Allied advances in North Africa and heard rumors of the mass executions of Jews. Their work took on greater importance when they heard these reports of atrocities. When the broadcast was over, the radio was hidden in the small storage space in the closet that Paul had built for his clothes.

The young couple had a map of Europe they took out almost every night to chart the advance of the Allies through Africa. They could tell that the Germans were being beaten back and for that they were grateful. They prayed that the occupation would be over soon but knew that it was still at least a year away.

Germany's successes in 1943, if you can call them that, were in defeating the defenseless Jews in the ghettos of Poland and in putting millions into concentration camps for eventual extermination. The only other bright spot for the Germans was the success of their submarines against Allied shipping in the North Atlantic. They received stunning defeats, however, in North Africa and Sicily.

By the new year of 1944, it was difficult to disguise how poorly the war was going for Germany. The Allies had pushed into Italy and landed in Normandy. Anyone who knew anything about geography could tell that Germany was being pushed back on every front.

The need for more German soldiers was so great that the number at the garrison at Faymont was cut back by half. That created a problem with securing the border. Fewer soldiers were assigned to each patrol.

Now, with fewer soldiers in the garrison, Paul and Annette felt that they were in much less danger. They had experienced so much that they knew how and when to be cautious. They had a pastor with access to what the Germans were doing, and they would be alerted if their operation was involved.

Since the start of 1944, allied aircraft were meeting much less resistance and were bombing German cities nightly. The number of allied aircraft increased monthly while the number of planes that were being flown by the Luftwaffe decreased, either because they had been shot down or there was little or no gasoline. With all those bombers in the air, the Germans increased antiaircraft shelling, making for more airmen parachuting into France, if they were lucky. Paul and Annette noticed the increase in airmen that they helped across the border.

The American armies continued advancing north through Italy and the Allied forces were moving across France, after having established a beachhead at Normandy. The liberation of France had begun.

Annette and Paul continued to listen intently each evening to the news. They religiously followed the Allied advance on their maps. Paul would most often be home by dinner as he was able to do his job almost entirely during the daylight hours. If he were late, Annette would show him on the map where the Allied troops had advanced.

The war was not all victories for the Allies. The Germans captured Minsk from the Russians. They used their technology to develop rockets, which they dropped on London. They also wiped out the French town of Oradore-sur-Gland. An attempt to assassinate Hitler failed.

CHAPTER 65

One incident in early September 1944 almost cost Paul and Annette their lives. Paul took a group of children across the border and was on his way back to the farmhouse near suppertime. He gave a cursory look as he was about to emerge from the woods. He had taken several steps from the woods when he spotted a car parked in the shade under a tree. He dropped to the ground and didn't move. Fortunately he was still in shadow. Slowly he lifted his head to see if he was spotted. He believed that he was unobserved as he crawled back into the woods. Paul berated himself for his carelessness. The green car was barely visible but Paul understood its purpose. It was a German staff car and as Paul's eyes adjusted he could see a soldier using binoculars pointed toward the farmhouse. If they had been focused on the woods he most likely would have been spotted.

Paul scanned the area back toward town and saw another car near Henri's property. This car was farther away and Paul couldn't tell if they were also using binoculars to observe. He would just have to presume that they were. Paul could see Annette moving about in the kitchen through the back door. There was nothing to do but wait. He did so with fear that they would come and take Annette for interrogation.

An hour later the cars were still there and Paul was getting hungry. His tardiness put Annette on alert. She began to suspect that there was a reason why Paul was late, as he was always so predictable. She slipped out of the kitchen, went upstairs and got her father's binoculars. Without turning on a light she moved the curtains in the bedroom just enough to observe the car under the tree to the southeast. Looking out the other window she saw the other vehicle near Henri's farm. She returned to the kitchen and lowered the shade on the back door, a signal she and Paul agreed upon but had never used. Paul saw her lower the shade and was pleased that she knew she was being observed. It wasn't until it was totally dark that the cars moved slowly back toward town, never turning on their headlights. Paul continued to wait until he was certain it was safe.

The following week the Germans left their garrison north of town and abandoned the checkpoints into Switzerland. The Americans arrived several days later. While the war would not be over until May of the following year, it was over for the villagers of Faymont.

EPILOGUE

Paul and Annette went on a brief honeymoon in Bern while Jeanne and her daughter Michelle operated the bakery. While on their honeymoon they were able to make plans for the future. Paul would immediately report to his squadron in England to help finish the war. Annette told Paul that she didn't want to spend the rest of her life in the bakery. Her secret desire was to be an interior decorator. She told Paul that she had no reason to stay in France except to see her Uncle Andre, whom she could visit. She believed that there were more opportunities for her and Paul in America or Canada.

And so it happened. Paul completed his service as a gunner and Annette sold her bakery to Jeanne and Guy Cartier. The brother of Henri Arsenault made an acceptable offer to buy the house, farm and furniture after the young couple left, which they did in August, 1945.

Two years later the young couple was sitting by the fireplace, listening to music in their new home on Long Island, not far from Paul's parent's home. They were reminiscing about their role in the war. Since returning home they found the German soldier who was really an American, by searching for Schmidt in the Suffolk County phone directory. They became good friends. Annette and Paul learned how important his information was for the Resistance.

Annette's English became quite good. She had taken a class in Interior Decorating at a local college. Paul was doing well making designer furniture and had both a store and factory. Business was good and Paul was able to get several small decorating jobs for Annette. She found that having a French accent was an asset.

"Both heard a song on the radio that triggered a response from Paul.

"Annette, do you remember Rebecca?"

"How could we ever forget her? I was just thinking about her."

"I wonder what happened to her and where she is living."

"That is something we will never know."

"Yet the children will always remember their trip to freedom."

"I'm sure they will."

In the spring of 1948 Annette gave birth to a baby boy and two years later a girl was delivered. They were named Paul Jacques and Jeanne Marie.

There were nights when the two would sit by the fireplace and talk about their life together in France and the excitement of smuggling children into Switzerland and avoiding capture by the Germans. They were proud that they did their part and lived to tell about it. Their thoughts always included Rebecca.

LaVergne, TN USA
06 August 2010

192312LV00004B/9/P